Ann Granger has lived in cities in various parts of the world, since for many years she worked for the Foreign Office and received postings to British embassies as far apart as Munich and Lusaka. She is married, with two sons, and she and her husband, who also worked for the Foreign Office, are now permanently based near Oxford. Ann is currently working on a new Mitchell and Markby mystery and the second book in the Fran Varady series.

Asking For Trouble

Ann Granger

HEADLINE

First published in 1997
by HEADLINE BOOK PUBLISHING

First published in paperback in 1997
by HEADLINE BOOK PUBLISHING

10 9 8 7 6 5 4 3 2 1

ISBN 0 7472 5575 X

Printed and bound in Great Britain by
Caledonian International Book Manufacturing Ltd, Glasgow

HEADLINE BOOK PUBLISHING
A division of Hodder Headline PLC
338 Euston Road
London NW1 3BH

Asking For Trouble

Chapter One

The man from the council housing department came on Monday morning. He served us with summonses, one each.

'According to our procedure!' he informed us in a voice pitched nervously high. He wasn't very old, curly-haired, his round cherubic face doing its best to express authority but losing out to an expression of incipient panic.

I can't believe he was seriously scared of us. Granted we outnumbered him but we weren't strangers. He, and various of his colleagues, had been before. In the past we'd locked them out, so that they had to shout up at the windows to communicate with us. But that day we'd let him in. It was decision day. We knew it and he knew that we did. There was no longer any point in those spirited exchanges hurled between pavement and windowsill. It was a curiously muted ending to a long-running dispute.

All the same he watched us anxiously, just in case we tore up the individual summonses in a last protest. Squib took his from its envelope and turned it over as if he expected to see something written on the back. Terry pushed hers into the pocket of her knitted coat. Nev looked for a moment as if he were going to refuse to accept his, but took it eventually. I took mine and said, 'Thanks for nothing!'

The official cleared his throat. 'I shall be attending the court tomorrow, together with the council's solicitor, to apply for an order for immediate possession. We anticipate it will be granted. We're prepared to give you until Friday to enable you to find alternative accommodation. But the matter is now in the hands of the court and its bailiffs. So it's no use arguing with me! Argue it out with the court tomorrow, if you want. But it won't do any good.'

He was still defensive, though no one bothered to answer him. We'd always known we'd lose. Even so, the reality of knowing we were out induced a physical sickness in the stomach. I turned away and stared at the window until I could control my face.

It was one of those slate-coloured mornings, threatening to tip rain at any moment, though it would probably hold off until evening. Dense cloud cover kept the traffic fumes and other odours trapped at street-level. You could even smell the charred meat and burnt onions from the Wild West hamburger bar which was two streets away.

I hadn't been feeling very cheerful that morning, even before our visitor came, because I'd lost my job the previous Friday. The manager had found out that my address was 'irregular' and that was that. Irregular meant I was currently living in a squat.

Although technically our occupation was illegal, no one had prevented us moving into an empty – and to all intents ownerless – house, and now we'd been there long enough for our presence to have acquired an air of permanency. Moreover, we had a purpose. We called ourselves the

Jubilee Street Creative Artists' Commune, though none of our work would have attracted a subsidy from the Arts Council or the National Lottery. But in between conforming to the norm or plummeting to the depths, whatever our individual destinies might be, we planned stupendous careers from the anonymity of Jubilee Street. In every way we possibly could, in fact, we deceived ourselves. Dreams beat reality any day.

By the way, I have to leave Squib out of the great careers scenario. Squib lived strictly from day to day and hadn't formed even the ghost of a plan that anyone had ever heard of.

Nev had plans. They came in the form of a twenty-page synopsis for his novel, which was likely to rival *War and Peace* in length. Every day he tapped away relentlessly on an old W H Smith manual machine. I've sometimes wondered if he ever finished it.

Squib was a pavement artist. He could copy anything. Some people would say that wasn't truly creative because it wasn't original, but they hadn't seen what Squib could do with a box of chalks and a few clean slabs. Old masters, which had been reduced by familiarity and brown varnish to the status of museum pieces, emerged breathing new life from Squib's fingers. They spoke so eloquently to passers-by that several were visibly disconcerted by the vibrancy of the chalked faces at their feet. In an episode which Squib regarded as deeply embarrassing, a passing art critic became so enthusiastic that he talked of presenting Squib to the world, together – presumably – with some purpose-acquired slabs to work on. The idea of being taken up by the establishment had so terrified Squib that he'd simply melted away with his tin of chalks and taken to improving the pavements of the provinces until he thought it safe to return to London.

As for me, I still clung to my early ambition to be an actress. Life had somewhat got in the way. I'd dropped out of a college course in the Dramatic Arts. Since then, apart from some Street Theatre, the role of star of stage and screen had eluded me. I still hoped to make it some day. Short term, keeping the wolf from the door was enough to occupy me. That, and maintaining an eye on the other two.

We three had moved into the house first. Soon afterwards we'd been joined by Declan, a small wiry fellow with straggling shoulder-length hair and features like a good-natured elf. Both his arms had been heavily tattooed: a fearsome snake on one; a sacred heart on the other. He recalled having the sacred heart done, but claimed to have no recollection of the snake being tattooed. He'd woken up one morning with a monumental hangover and there it was, crawling up his arm. 'I thought I had the DTs,' he observed. Sometimes he'd stretch out his arm and study the snake thoughtfully. I think it worried him.

Declan had arrived as a rock musician without a group, owing to his former group's lead guitarist having been accidentally electrocuted whilst rehearsing in a church hall.

'The poor sod's hair stood on end,' Declan would relate with mournful wonder. 'God rest his soul, it was bloody funny to see. Until we realised he was dead, you know. That sobered us up. We all stood round trying to remember how to do resuscitation while we waited for an ambulance. Though we could see he was a goner. On top of which, the amp was just about fried and we hadn't got the dosh to buy another. Just then, would you believe it? A wee man came running in, mouthing off at us because we'd fused all the lights in the place. It pissed us off that much, him no showing any respect for the dead like it, that the drummer and I, we picked him up, kicking and yelling like a banshee, and dropped him out of the window. It wasn't a long drop. He bounced. But we got done for assault, all the same.'

Declan played bass and a bass-player needs a group.

A little later Lucy and her two children had come along. Lucy wasn't an artist of any sort. She'd run away from a violent husband and had been staying at a battered women's refuge a few streets away. I'd got talking to her one day while I was serving in Patels' corner greengrocer's shop. She was buying carrots for the children to gnaw. Raw carrots are full of vitamin C, don't contain the sort of acids which drill holes in tooth enamel, and are cheaper than most fruit.

She was trying to get herself somewhere permanent to live and a job. The refuge was full and she felt she couldn't stay there much longer. The palm of her left hand was badly scarred where her husband had forced it down on a glowing red hotplate during a row about his dinner being late. The scars were unsightly and had impaired the hand's flexibility. She was conscious of it and always told anyone who asked that she'd done it herself, by accident. She'd told me the truth one evening after she'd come to live at the house. I'd expressed amazement that she'd stayed with him so long and put up with so much abuse.

'It's not easy walking out with two kids,' she'd said.

But she had walked out when he started hitting the

children, as well as her. She said he had a drink problem. In my view he had a head problem. But it had underlined for me, if I'd been in any doubt, how precious my independence was.

As for the house, that stood all by itself at the end of a row of redbrick terraced others. It was older than the terrace, we thought early Victorian, and once it must have stood here in a big garden. All that was left of the garden was a patch of jungle at the back and a litter-strewn strip between the front of the house and the pavement. There were holes indicating posts for railings but those too had gone. The house had dirty white stucco facing, dropping off in patches, a pillared front entrance, sash windows which stuck and a water-logged basement. When it was new it must have been graceful and welcoming. Now it was like the dishevelled old baglady who lived down the street, out of tune with the world around, kept together by grime and makeshift repairs. All the same, we'd been prepared to take it on and make something of it.

Unfortunately, we weren't allowed to. Within weeks, we were informed by the council, which legally owned it, that the house was scheduled to come down as part of redevelopment plans for the area, and there was nothing we could do about it. We'd asked the council, when we'd moved in, to give us a regular tenancy, a request which they'd ignored. Now a stream of communications couched in official mandarin fluttered through the letterbox, and the council cut off the electricity, just in case we still hadn't got the message. They hadn't turned off the water but perhaps they hadn't needed to, since they were calling in the bailiffs.

Nev suggested we try to get the house listed as of

architectural interest. We wrote to English Heritage and the National Trust. They thanked us for our letter but the house wasn't interesting enough and they didn't want it.

One by one, the people moved out of the terraced houses, leaving empty, boarded-up shells. We hung on like legionnaires in a desert fort. It became a battle of wills between us and the rampaging Rif warriors as represented by a string of council officials.

The uncertainty caused a shake-out of residents. The council, hoist with its own petard, rehoused Lucy and her children, one of whom was asthmatic. Declan, too, had left, to go no one knew where, though he spoke vaguely of having heard of a group needing a bass guitarist. There'd been a couple of mean-looking blokes at the door asking for him about a week before that, so we reckoned he was in some kind of trouble. But who wasn't? We never asked people personal questions.

Terry, however, had arrived, a small damp figure with dark blond hair, parted centrally and falling to either side of her pinched little face, like spaniel's ears. Her appearance coincided with the electricity being cut off, so that for me, from the start, she symbolised the deterioration in our situation. It was uncharitable of me to think that way, but, as things turned out, dead right.

On that Monday morning, until the moment we were handed our final notices to quit, I hadn't thought things could get worse. The manager of the mail-order packing department where I'd been working had the usual idea of squatters, and he hadn't been able to get rid of me fast enough. There had been nothing wrong with my work – despite the fact that it was boring and badly paid. I'd never turned up late or skived off early. I never broke anything, or packed the wrong item by mistake, or sent off something totally inappropriate to a customer for a joke. But he claimed I hadn't been 'completely frank' about my circumstances and 'the company had a policy'.

I wouldn't have taken that job if I could have got any other. I was earning hardly more than I would have got on the dole and the conditions we'd worked in were like something out of Dickens. But it was better than no job. Now I was unemployed, technically homeless and soon to be literally so, and thoroughly fed up.

Our silence seemed to rattle the man from the council, who added, 'Look here, you've really got to get out by Friday. The bailiffs will put you out by force if necessary. The police will be on standby and it won't be any good climbing up on the rooftop or putting your feet into bags of cement or anything like that.'

We all just looked at him. A remark like that really wasn't worth answering. Even Squib wouldn't have done something like that.

Nev said, 'Anyone who got up on this roof would fall straight through it! You've got to be joking.'

I was feeling a little sorry for our visitor so I asked him if he wanted a cup of tea. We'd only just brewed up. Nev had lit a fire in the hearth with a load of kindling he'd got from chopping up an old wooden garden seat out the back and we had the kettle going, hanging from a hook screwed into the arch of the grate.

Declan fixed that up when he was living here. It was at the time the electricity had been cut off. He said his granny in Ireland had cooked for a family of thirteen all her life, just using a pot hanging from a hook. Declan was full of stories like that. You couldn't believe half of them.

But the other half, which sounded just as mad, you could believe so you never knew which were true and which weren't.

We didn't do all our cooking in the hearth. We had a stove fed by Calor gas bottles. But that cost money to run and so, whenever we could, we used the open fire.

He refused the tea but he didn't look so nervous. Instead he looked pompous and I stopped feeling sorry for him. 'We've written several times explaining what would happen. You've had several stays of execution. We've done everything we could to be reasonable. All these houses are due to come down. The others are already empty. The squatters in those saw sense and moved out. Only you lot stay on. We've explained all this till we're blue in the face. You must have had the letters.'

'I know all that,' I said, trying to sound ultra-polite and reasonable. 'We understand the council's argument, but we've got our point of view, too. We're homeless. Or we will be if you put us out of here. Will the council house us?'

'We can't,' he said wearily. 'We haven't got anywhere. Mrs Ho and her children had priority. Of the remaining four of you, Miss Varady, you're the only one who could argue you have any real link with the borough at all, and that's pretty tenuous! All we can do is put you on the list. We're not responsible for the other three. You and they will have to try the private sector.'

'No private landlord would take us on. And we couldn't afford the sort of rent he'd charge if he would! Look, we keep the place clean,' I went on. 'We don't hold wild parties or do anything you wouldn't do yourself. We don't let other people doss here. We're really very good tenants.

Or we would be if you'd let us pay rent and put us on a regular footing. That's all we ask. What's wrong with it?'

'The house is due to come down within the next six months. In the meantime, it's unsafe, not up to habitable standard. The electricity has been cut off.' He didn't look cross or unpleasant, just rather tired. 'We explained all that in our letters, too. You did read them, didn't you?'

Squib spoiled things then, by saying, 'Yeah, we used 'em to make spills to light the fire. Saved on matches.'

The housing official went red in the face and read us the riot act again, and then he drove off. Only just in time. While he'd been inside the house, talking to us, I'd been able to see, through the window, a couple of kids hanging round his shiny new Fiesta, and in another few minutes they'd have been inside it. The last he would have seen of it would have been the exhaust fumes and a squeal of skidding tyres.

We held a council of war after our visitor had left. We knew we had to go, of course. We just didn't know where. It was the end of summer and none of us fancied being out on the street just as the cold weather was about to start. Anyway, it was a lot less dangerous living in a squat, even one with an unsafe roof and dry rot in the staircase, like this one. As the man had said, we didn't qualify for any help.

Terry sat on the bare staircase, twisting a strand of hair round her finger and waiting for someone else to suggest something, so that she could criticise it. She was the world's greatest whinger, evaded housework and always jibbed at parting with her share of the house-keeping money. Looking at her I just wished she'd disappear and Declan come back. At least Declan was good at fixing things and good company as well.

It's dangerous to wish. Sometimes your wish is granted and then you're stuck with it.

She had noticed my scowls and immediately made herself look small and helpless. It was something she was very good at and which had led us to adopt her in the first place. I was the actress in our company, but that girl had missed her vocation, believe me. She peered through the curtains of hair and said pathetically, 'I haven't got anywhere else to go.'

'None of us has!' I snapped.

We all got up and trailed back into the main room. The three of them sat around looking at me, just like hopeful puppies. Each one of them was nursing a mug of tea. We each had our own mugs and no one ever drank from someone else's. It was a house rule.

Nev asked, 'What do we do, Fran?' in a trusting sort of way which made it all so much worse.

It was always down to me in the end. The trouble was, I was really out of ideas. I had to say something. They expected it. So I said, 'If we could get an old van, we could go on the road.'

'I'd rather doss in a doorway,' Squib said straight away. 'I've tried that New-Age stuff. Digging holes in mud before you can crap and having to listen to folk music all night long. Forget it.'

'He's got a point. It's all right in summer,' Nev added. 'But wintertime, it's no joke.'

'The police keep moving you on, anyway,' Terry tossed in her usual handful of objections. 'And it's really awful in a tent when it rains. They always leak. You'd do just anything to get somewhere dry, anywhere. I know, I've tried it.'

'I like it here,' said Nev wistfully. 'In this house.'

Squib took off his woolly hat and looked into it. Perhaps he thought he'd find an idea in there. He didn't, so he smoothed a hand over his shaven head and put the hat back again carefully.

'I don't,' said Terry. 'It's got rats.'

'Everywhere's got rats,' said Squib. 'Rats is all right. I've had some really nice pet rats. I had a white one. I carried it inside my coat. It never bit me, not once. I sold it to a bloke in a pub. He give me a fiver for it. Mind you, he was pissed at the time. I reckon that rat bit him, after he got it home. It bit other people. It never bit me. Animals like me.'

That was true. Terry mumbled it was because Squib smelled like barnyard and the animals just accepted he was one of them. The pouty, discontented look on her face grew worse. She had wrapped herself in an old knitted coat she always wore and was sulking. The coat was grubby and matted, but I'd seen the label in it once, and it was a very expensive one. I'd remarked on it and Terry had promptly said she'd got the coat from Oxfam. I hadn't believed her then and it set me wondering again now. She might have stolen it. She was inclined to be light-fingered although she wasn't stupid enough ever to touch anything of mine or Nev's. We probably didn't have anything she wanted. Only a complete nutter would have touched anything of Squib's. The dog would have had him in a flash. Even if the dog hadn't been there on guard, Squib's belongings wouldn't invite investigation.

As I said, we never asked people about themselves. If they were desperate enough to want to share a condemned house riddled with dry-rot, illegally and without electricity, then they needed a place to stay, not questions. Only, sooner or later, most people told you something about themselves. Not Terry. She'd never said a word. But whatever her background, there'd been money around there. You could tell. It made me wonder about the coat even more.

We talked about our problem all morning but we didn't get anywhere. It ended with an argument, not about what we should do, but about Squib's dog.

Terry said it had fleas. It was always scratching. You could say anything you liked about Squib, but not about his dog. It was a funny-looking dog with one ear turned over and one pointing up. Its legs were crooked. Squib had found it on a pile of rubbish when it was a puppy. He thought someone had chucked it out because it was the runt of a litter. Anyhow, he'd looked after it and it grew up all right except for the crooked legs. It was a nice dog. It was friendly to everyone except when guarding Squib's gear. We all liked it, except Terry. But she didn't like anything.

So when she insulted his dog, Squib told her a few home truths. They were well into a squabble when I lost my temper. I always tried to keep my temper in the house because once one person starts yelling, everyone starts. But we were already arguing and, somehow, Terry's moaning was the last straw. Her criticism of the house itself had hurt. We'd taken her in, given her a home there, and all she could do was to let us know it wasn't up to her accustomed standard.

I yelled, 'You're a real pain in the bum!' Only I didn't say 'bum'. 'Nobody asked you to move in with us. We let you stay here and I don't think there's been one day when

13

you haven't whinged from morning till night! We've all got problems! You're no worse off than the rest of us.' Remembering the coat label, I added, 'I know your type. When you've had enough, you'll just push off back wherever you came from!'

She turned absolutely white. She pushed back the spaniel's ears and hissed, 'Shut it, Fran! You don't know anything about me! You fancy pushing us around, that's all! Do this, do that! You give the orders and we all jump, right? Well, wrong! I don't! And that's what you don't like. You always act like some kind of Mother Superior! This is a commune, we've got equal rights, OK? Equal say? Just because Nev's a nervous wreck and Squib's got no brains, they let you do the thinking and talking for them and you think you can do the same for me! You can't, you don't and you'd better remember it!'

There was a viciousness in her voice that I hadn't heard before, but it wasn't that which shook me. It was the accusation itself. I hadn't thought of myself as overbearing, pushing anyone around. I didn't like the picture much and it made me defensive.

'I don't order anyone around! I'm just trying to be helpful! If you tried, it would be something! Even Squib tries!'

Squib looked surprised at getting a compliment. It must have been a first for him. He said, 'Thanks, Fran!'

Nev said nervously, 'Look, we've got to stick together. We mustn't all fall out now.'

'You, Squib and I were together – she came along later and she can go any time!' I shouted. I was still mad at her and madder because she'd rattled me. I'm not proud of any of this. I shouldn't have turned on her like that. She was right when she said I knew nothing about her.

Looking back, I don't remember exactly how Terry got to be with us. I think Lucy introduced her. I'd once wondered if Terry had stayed originally because she fancied Declan who was still with us at that time. I think perhaps he'd fancied her just a little. But it didn't stop him leaving. He was better off without her, if you ask me. But then, I never liked her, not from the beginning. It's no use pretending. But I would never have wanted what happened. None of us would have wanted it.

All that was on Monday morning. We didn't have a lot of time to waste, so on Monday afternoon, Nev and I made a long trek up Camden way, to see a squat he'd heard about. Just to see if there'd be room for us there. Only, when we got there, it was all boarded up and empty so their council had been and cleared everyone out. Pity, it was a classier area than the one we'd been living in. We went to Camden Lock and messed about. We saw a few people we knew and asked around.

Squib had gone up West with the dog. He'd taken along his chalks and a picture postcard of El Greco's *Assumption of the Virgin* and the idea was to find a patch of pavement. He couldn't afford to waste time, not with the weather threatening to break up again.

Terry hadn't said what she was doing and we hadn't asked her. None of us expected her to be doing anything useful, like finding us another place to live.

I suppose I oughtn't to talk about the dead like that. You're not supposed to. You're supposed to say nice things about dead people or they come back and haunt you. I know that's right because Terry haunted me. It was probably because of all the sour things I'd said about her over the time she'd been with us, quite apart from what I said after – well, after it happened.

Going back to Monday. Nev and I got back from Camden quite late. Some people had invited us to stay and eat with them. They were vegetarian, like Nev, so it was all beans but it was quite nice, very spicy and hot, but I knew I'd suffer later.

When we got back, the place was very quiet. It was dark because the electricity was disconnected. We used candles. Only, apart from the emptiness and the usual dry-rot smell, there was something else. It was a sort of impression, a different, foreign one. I knew, just knew, that someone had been there who wasn't one of us. A stranger. A real stranger, someone totally outside our circle and not from the council. There was a very faint perfume as well, a type of cologne. I worked in a cut-price chemist's shop one time. I know colognes. I know good ones from cheap ones. This was a good one, the sort that sells well at Christmas.

The scent of it there in the hall made me cross. I thought perhaps Terry had been shop-lifting again and I was always telling her off about that. It was possible she'd had more money than she let on, and had gone out and bought it for herself. Those colognes, frankly, smell better on a woman than a man, just my opinion. She always kept quiet if she had any money. She'd spend it on junk or on glossy magazines, the sort which tell you how to transform your semi-detached into something you'd be happy to invite a *Hello!* camera team into. And that at a time when we were putting buckets under the leak in the roof and were living on bread and marge.

I mentioned the cologne smell to Nev but he said he couldn't make it out, not with the smell of the dry rot as well. The other thing, the impression of someone, an outsider, having been there, I kept to myself. It wasn't something easily explained. Lucy had been into the paranormal and she'd have told me I was a natural psychic. I don't believe in that sort of thing. Or I don't think I do. If I had to explain what I felt at that moment, looking back with hindsight, I think I scented danger. If I'd been a cavewoman, it'd have been a woolly mammoth outside the cave. Only this wasn't outside, it was inside, with us.

We went into the main room and got the fire going again because it was getting very chilly. Neither of us said anything, but we were both thinking that it was going to be a whole lot colder next week, when chances were we'd be sleeping rough until we found some new place to stay. After a while Squib came back with the dog and a four-pack of lager. He'd also brought a packet of sausages which he roasted over the fire using a metal shovel as a frying pan.

They smelled delicious. The fat spat up and fell in the flames so they roared up, red and yellow. It was very cosy and we felt happy. When they were done, crispy and dark brown, Squib offered them all round. Say what you like about Squib, he always shared. Nev refused the sausages because he didn't eat meat and I refused them because the beans we'd eaten earlier lay on my stomach. Besides, I knew Squib probably hadn't eaten that day.

Squib cut up half the sausages for the dog and put them up on the mantelshelf to cool off. Then he asked, 'D'you think Terry will want any when she gets in?'

I said, 'Why bother about her? She never bothers about

us.' That shows how I was feeling just then, because even if I didn't like her, she was one of us and I wouldn't normally have left her out.

But she didn't come back that night, or we thought she hadn't. We didn't see her.

The next morning she still wasn't around and Squib suggested she might have done a runner, like Declan.

'She's found somewhere else to live,' he said. 'She's ditched us and moved in with some others. After the council came, you can't blame her. There's probably no point in hanging around here.'

Knowing that he was right, that our days here were numbered, didn't make us feel any better. But it was still a relief to think we'd seen the back of Terry. She was one fewer to worry about.

Nev suggested we ought to check her room and see if her things had gone. If it was empty, fine. We could forget her.

We trooped upstairs, all three of us, and the dog. The dog was good at getting up and down the staircase even with its crooked legs.

But outside Terry's room the dog began to act strangely. Its pointy ear flattened out to match its other ear and it crouched down and began to make a weird whining in its throat.

Squib knelt down and stroked its head and asked it what was wrong. But it just lay down and looked miserable.

Nev said, 'Perhaps it's eaten something it shouldn't.'

That worried Squib who'd heard of squatters' dogs being poisoned. He was sitting on the floor outside the door, trying to get the dog to open its mouth so he could see if its tongue was stained, when Nev and I opened the door to Terry's room.

She was there, after all. She must have stayed behind indoors the previous day, when we'd gone out. She'd been there when we came back and there all night. There when Squib cooked his sausages downstairs and there when I got up in the night because of the beans.

Hanging there from the ceiling light.

I remember the scene very clearly, almost as if my mind took a snapshot of it which I can take out and mentally consult. The room, like the rest of the house, must have been beautiful once. Pale sun was shining through the tall, thin windows, one of which still had half a broken brass rod across the top of it. The sun just clipped the rod and made it gleam like gold. The corners of the high ceiling were festooned with ancient cobwebs and dead spiders. Running all around was a plaster frieze in Greek 'egg and dart' pattern. In the very middle of the ceiling a sculpted plaster round, caked with dust, displayed intertwined oakleaves and acorns. It was easy to imagine an ornate light, a chandelier perhaps, hanging from it in days gone by.

There was nothing hanging from it now but Terry. There was a length of something round her neck which turned out later to be the dog's lead. Squib hardly ever used it because the dog was very well behaved and always kept to heel. It had been lying around the house and now it was round Terry's throat.

Even given the shock of the moment, or perhaps because of it, the shutter in my mind snapped her in the same detail. She – rather, that thing which had been Terry

– wore tattered jeans. The front zip fastening was undone and they gaped open over her bare stomach. A considerable gap had opened up between the gaping waist of the jeans and the bottom of a badly shrunk and faded tee-shirt. I could see her lower rib cage protruding over the convex stomach muscles, pulled taut. Her feet were bare, mottled mauve. She had the makings of a first-class bunion on her left big-toe joint, but it wasn't ever going to trouble her now.

Like the room, she'd been pretty once, and, like it, she wasn't now. Overnight the weight of her body had elongated her neck to resemble a giraffe-necked African tribeswoman whose head is supported on a stack of metal coils. The doglead had cut into her throat horridly, causing her face to puff and turn black with congested blood. Her mouth was open and her swollen tongue protruded as if, even in death, she was dishing out one last insult to us. Her eyeballs were popping out at us, netted over with crimson veins.

Nev gasped, 'Gawd! She's topped herself!'

I had no reason, then, to suppose he wasn't right. There was a rickety old chair nearby, lying on its side, not far from Terry's dangling bare toes. I imagined her climbing on to it, fixing the noose, jumping off.

You don't die quickly that way. The old-time hangmen knew how to knot a rope to break the neck. This way, she'd simply strangled, slowly. Her flailing feet had kicked over the chair. Perhaps, in a moment's realisation of how it was going to be, she changed her mind, and sought out the chair's support again, intending to release the pressure on her neck, disentangle herself from the noose and climb down, bruised but wiser.

She wouldn't have been the first to change her mind, nor the first to discover it wasn't that easy. You didn't fool around with death. It liked to be taken seriously. So, whether, in the end, she'd intended it or not, there she was.

And there we were, with a dead body for company, and an awful lot of trouble in store.

Chapter Two

I couldn't have guessed all that lay ahead following our horrifying discovery. But I was aware that we'd receive much unwelcome attention from the authorities. The other two weren't thinking ahead, too busy coping, or not, with the sight of that hanging shape. Nev rushed out and could be heard being sick in the loo. It turned out that he'd never seen a dead body before. I had, but it didn't make it any easier looking at her.

Squib left the dog and came into the room. He'd stood his ground, but he had an even chalkier complexion than usual. He always had a pinched look about him and now must have resembled that white rat he'd once kept as a pet.

'We'd better get out of here!' he said. He was sweating. I could smell the odour, rising up from him as from a hunted animal. 'Come on, we're wasting time! Let's get our gear together and go!'

'Don't be daft,' I told him. 'The council knows all about us, our names, everything. They'll find us.'

'Why'd she do it?' he asked. 'Was she worried about us being chucked out? Here—' His eyes gleamed. 'That's what we tell that wally from the council! We tell him, he drove her to it!'

'Shut up, Squib!' I told him. I needed to think. No one else was likely to do any constructive thinking. It would be down to me, as usual. Squib in a blind panic wanting to run and Nev throwing up, that was likely to be the sum total of their contribution. Looking after Nev and Squib was sometimes like looking after a pair of infants. You had to do all the thinking for them and be worrying every five minutes where they were and what they were doing.

Nev came back, still looking ill but trying to pull himself together. 'Oughtn't we to – take her down?' His voice couldn't rise above a whisper and it cracked on the last word. 'We oughtn't to leave her hanging there. It's obscene.'

It was obscene. He was right. But we couldn't touch her. We mustn't touch anything. I explained the point forcibly to them both.

Squib looked relieved. He wasn't keen to touch her. Nev, however, reacted with a cry of dismay.

'We can't leave her hanging there!' His voice sounded like something produced by computer. The sounds were all there, making up the words, but it wasn't human.

He made a sudden lurch towards her and before I could stop him, he grabbed her legs. I don't know what he thought he was going to do. Lift her down unaided, maybe. But as almost as soon as he touched her, he staggered back with a strangled scream.

'She's stiff . . . '

The body, set in motion by his clumsy attempt, began to rotate on the doglead like a grotesque mobile hanging from the ceiling. I took a look up at the light fixture. It wasn't going to hold much longer. It was astonishing it'd held out so long. Any moment now, especially with the movement, the body was likely to come crashing down without our help. If it did, we'd be in even more trouble.

But the stiffness, if Nev was right, had set me thinking. I wasn't clear on the finer point of rigor, but had an idea it took around twelve hours to come on and then lasted around another twelve before it passed off gradually, depending on circumstances. If she was good and stiff, she'd died yesterday afternoon. We had to fetch the police at once or we'd have to explain the delay.

Nev wasn't in any state to object further and nodded listlessly.

'I say we oughta make a run for it!' Squib objected, unconvinced. He didn't like the law. It wasn't too keen on him. The dog sat up and lifted its muzzle to let out a howl as if it agreed with him.

'Hear that?' Squib pointed at the dog. 'She didn't like him, Terry didn't. She was always saying he'd got fleas. He hasn't. But he's crying for her, see? Animals are better than humans, that's what I think. Animals have got decency.'

'Decency', I told him sharply, 'means we fetch the police.'

We might have argued about it for ages, but it got settled for us. There was a shout from downstairs.

We stared at one another, all panicking. I ran downstairs and would you believe it? There was the man from the council again. This time he had a colleague with him, a sweaty, tubby charmer with a malevolent scowl.

'We came to check you're preparing to move out,' the

first one said, 'and to make sure you mean to attend today's hearing.'

I'd forgotten the hearing. It hardly seemed to matter now. They were the last people we needed there and I wondered frantically how to get rid of them. 'We can't!' I blurted. 'I mean, we'll see you there. We're getting ready to leave, so you can't come in, not just now.'

He came nearer to where I stood, halfway down the uncarpeted stair, and frowned up at me. 'It's Fran, isn't it? You're in charge here, aren't you? You always seem to speak for the others.'

That, I recalled ruefully, was what Terry had accused me of.

The reason I always spoke for the others was because, left to themselves, they always said the wrong thing. I was thinking wildly now, trying to think of the right thing to say, to find some way of explaining.

'Something's happened. One of our friends has – has had an accident. I've got to fetch help.'

'What kind of accident?' It was the fat one speaking now. He moved forward, looking nasty.

'Fran?' The younger one looked at me, worried. 'Do you need an ambulance?'

It crossed my mind that he wasn't such a bad sort. But I hadn't time for character analysis.

The other one snapped, 'Drugs, you bet! One of 'em's oh-dee'd! They would choose this bloody morning to do it! How long's he – she – been unconscious?'

'We're not druggies!' I shouted. 'None of us is!'

That was absolutely true. It was another house rule. No drugs. Terry sometimes had cannabis. But that was it.

Fatso was sniffing the air now. 'I'm not so sure!'

'The smell's the dry rot!' I snapped at him.

There was a creak on the stair behind me and I heard the dog growl. Squib's voice soothed it. Then he spoke.

'You can't go upstairs,' he said. 'One of our mates is dead.'

That put the cat amongst the pigeons. The first council official was up the stairs like a greyhound, racing past me and Squib and pushing Nev aside on the landing. The dog began to bark and wanted to jump up at him but Squib held it by its collar.

'Where?' the official was yelling. 'Are you sure?'

'She topped herself!' Squib yelled back at him. 'It was you coming yesterday to tell us we'd gotta quit that did it! She got depressed!'

The fat man was plodding heavily up the stairs. He squeezed past me giving me a dirty look. He had BO, the sort his best friend hadn't told him about. The stair creaked. I hoped the dry rot would give way under his weight but it didn't. Probably just as well. We'd have had two corpses.

Nev mumbled, 'She's in there! We didn't touch her!'

The two men had opened the door to Terry's room. There was silence and then the fat man began swearing.

We heard him say, 'The press will get hold of this!'

The thinner one told him to shut up. Then they began whispering together. Eventually the first one came out of the room and spoke to us all.

'We'll fetch the police. You lot stay here. Don't let anyone in. Don't talk to anyone!' He paused. 'My colleague, Mr Wilson, will stay with you.'

Fatty plodded across the landing, glowering. He looked

an awful lot less confident than when he'd arrived. Squib's dog, not liking the look of him, growled again.

He moved back. 'What sort of dog is that? Is it a pit bull?'

'Does it look like a pit bull?' I asked. 'It's about half the size, to start with.'

'He's got a bit of Staffordshire in him, I reckon,' said Squib with pride. 'Once he gets his teeth into something, he don't let go.'

'For Gawd's sake,' said Wilson to his council colleague, 'Hurry up and get back here with the cops!'

We waited for the police, all of us sitting in the living room, Wilson included. He sat by the door like a heavy, with his arms folded over his beer belly, in case any of us tried to rush him. When he wasn't watching us, he was watching the dog.

Squib huddled in the far corner with his arms round it, whispering into its pointy ear. It kept turning its head and looking up at him. Once or twice it licked his face. No way was anyone going to be able to claim it was dangerous. I hoped.

Nev was managing well. He sat by the hearth, only a nervous twisting of his hands betraying stress. From time to time he glanced at me for reassurance and I smiled back. It took some doing on my part. I didn't feel like smiling. My head was in a whirl and I knew I had to sort it out before the police got there.

To begin with, they'd ask us about Terry and there wasn't very much we could tell them. We could suggest they ask Lucy. That was about it. I tried hard to remember all the things she'd said, every word since she'd arrived. But I hadn't liked her and I hadn't talked to her unless I'd had to, so there you were. All opportunities missed.

She'd been very well spoken, an upper-class sort of voice. She reminded me of the girls at the private day school I attended until they politely requested my dad to take me away. Of course, she used to use all kinds of words she'd picked up out there in the streets, trying to sound like just anyone else around the area. But it hadn't worked. She still sounded different. There was that woolly jacket with the expensive label. She'd had that with her when she came. She was wearing it the night she arrived with Lucy. I know she didn't get that jacket from Oxfam. She'd brought that with her from home, wherever home was.

As for her friends, I didn't even know if she had any, or where she went during the day. The police would ask if either Nev or Squib had been her boyfriend. Neither had. Nev was generally considered to be with me, but the arrangement was a platonic one. I acted, if anything, as Nev's minder. He didn't cope well on his own. Squib had his dog for company. He didn't really need people.

Declan was the one Terry had been keen on. But we didn't know where Declan had gone and anyway, he'd had troubles of his own. I didn't want to put the police on to Declan. I'd liked him.

So, to come back to the most important question, why? Why should she kill herself? I couldn't accept it, even though I'd seen the evidence. She hadn't appeared depressed or worried, more than any of us were worried about the eviction. Despite Squib's theory, I didn't believe she'd worried enough about that to take such extreme action. Generally, she'd just been her normal, grousing self. Alarm bells were starting to ring at the back of my brain and I didn't like the sound of what they were trying to tell me.

I remembered how she'd been dressed when we found her, just in the unzipped jeans and crumpled shirt. I couldn't understand why the jeans weren't zipped up. If she'd been walking around like that before she died, the jeans would've ended up round her ankles. So, had she pulled them on in a hurry and, with suicide in mind, not bothered with the zip? Or, an idea, as grotesque as it was unwelcome popped into my head, had someone else dressed her unconscious body, panicking, fumbling with the zip and giving up? I remembered the aroma of cologne in the house when Nev and I returned from Camden and my feeling that some outsider had been there in our absence.

I put that unpleasant thought on hold and concentrated on another. The rigor. Accepting that she had died yesterday afternoon, the police would want to know where we'd all been, when was the last time we'd seen her and if she'd appeared distressed in any way. They were unlikely, in the circumstances, to accept anyone's plea of total ignorance and absence from the scene, without some confirmation. We were not the sort of people whose word they took. So what we were looking for here were alibis, not to put too fine a point on it.

Nev and I, with luck, could prove that for part of the time we were eating Mexican bean stew with his friends. As for Squib, a pavement artist must have hundreds of witnesses to his activities. But all of them would have been hurrying by, glancing at a hunched figure rubbing industriously at a square of paving with chalks. Some would have taken a closer look at the picture, but few would have troubled to look closely at the artist.

I must have shifted in my chair because I met Wilson's beady gaze fixed on me. He had tensed as I moved and probably thought I was planning to leap through a pane of glass and run off down the street like they do in movies. If so, he watched too much television.

Nev said, 'I need a glass of water,' and stood up.

Wilson ordered, 'You just stay where you are, sunshine!'

'He's been sick!' I snapped. 'You stay there, Nev. I'll go and get you the water.' I marched over to Wilson and stood over him. 'You don't have any right to prevent me!' I told him. 'And don't forget, your mate was here yesterday and our friend died right afterwards!'

'You've got a big mouth!' he said.

'And you've got a fat gut!' I told him.

'All right,' he snarled. 'You won't be so lippy when the police get here. Go and get him his glass of water. Where's the kitchen?'

'It's the next room. If I leave the door open, you'll be able to see me in there from just outside this room, OK?'

He grunted and moved out into the hall where he could see both the living-room door and the kitchen door. I went into the kitchen and turned on the tap. I had a drink of water myself while I was there, even though I could feel Wilson's eyes boring into my back. Then I took Nev's glass back with me.

He said, 'Thanks, Fran!' and sipped at it. After a moment, he whispered, 'Stick with me, won't you, Fran? I don't think I can manage to face the police alone!'

I smiled again. But he was going to have to manage somehow because they'd interview us separately for sure.

Honestly, I'd never seen so many coppers in my life, not all in one house. They brought all sorts of equipment, lights and cameras and I don't know what else. It would have been interesting to watch if we hadn't been at the centre of it all.

A Detective Sergeant Parry arrived. He had crewcut ginger hair and bright blue eyes too close together. His eyebrows were almost non-existent and possibly by way of compensation he was trying, not very successfully, to grow a moustache. It sprouted unevenly along his upper lip with varying thickness and hue as if it were infected with mange. His manner was sarcastic. Whatever he told him, he obviously didn't believe any of it.

'All right, what happened?' He'd produced a notebook and was thumbing wearily through it.

We told him we didn't know.

'Don't give me that. And don't waste everyone's time, mine, yours, the inspector's. Do you know how much an investigation like this costs the taxpayer? No, don't suppose you do. You lot don't pay any taxes. Just scroungers, live off the social. Come on, let's have the whole story.'

What can you say to someone like that? We said nothing.

'What is this?' He scowled at us. 'Someone told you you've got a right to silence? Got something to hide?'

'No,' I said patiently. 'We already told you that we just don't know what happened.'

He sighed. 'Look, it was a game, right? It went wrong.

It was a stupid bet or something. You were pissed out of your skulls at the time. Or high as kites. Which? Both? There will be a post mortem. We'll find out what you were using. It'll be much easier if you tell me now. Stand you in good stead before the court.'

'What court?'

'Coroner's court. What other? Sounds to me as if bad conscience is troubling you.'

I'd meant to keep cool but at that, I couldn't. 'I thought you were supposed to make tactful and sympathetic inquiries when this sort of thing happens – not try and invent something you can stick on us?'

'Sassy little madam, aren't you?' He pointed his Biro at me. 'But you're talking yourself into a lot of trouble, lady. Don't cheek me! I'm writing it all down here.' He tapped the pad. 'Every word.'

I told him, 'That moustache looks like something the cat brought up. Go on, write that down. You're supposed to write it all down, not just pick out the bits which suit you.'

He put his notepad and Biro away. 'All right, have it your own way. We'll go down to the station and interview you all there. It'll be recorded on tape. You can make all the smart remarks you want, darling. But when the tape's played back they won't sound so clever.'

I asked, 'Are we being arrested? What's the crime?'

He looked mock-shocked. 'Of course not, dear! The very idea!'

I knew we could refuse but, on the other hand, we were hardly flavour of the month and it might be best not to make things worse. So we went.

* * *

33

They took our fingerprints. I'd never been involved in a suicide enquiry, but this didn't seem justified to me. I asked why. 'For elimination. Once we don't need them any longer, they'll be destroyed,' I was told.

I asked, 'Elimination from what?' But I didn't get any answer.

They split us all up so that we couldn't confer. I don't know where Nev and Squib went. Nev looked awful as he went out, grey-faced, sweating and looking as guilty as hell. I hoped the police realised he wasn't well.

I sat for ages in a bare little room, watched by a bored copper who kept scraping his finger round inside his ear and inspecting the tip of it to see what he'd found there. I wished they'd offer me a cup of tea, but they didn't. Eventually, Parry came again and said Inspector Morgan would like to talk to me.

Before we left the house, the younger, nicer, council official had come back and I'd found out his name was Euan. So now I began to wonder if they were all Welsh and if they were, what they were all doing in this part of London. Were they all plotting some sort of revenge for the death of Llewellyn?

Inspector Morgan turned out to be a woman. I suppose they thought that was clever of them, all girls together stuff, and I'd confide in her. But I did get that cup of tea at long last.

She was quite young which surprised me. I'd always imagined inspectors would be old fellows with grey hair and bad teeth. Or, if they were women, built like brick barns. Morgan was smartly dressed though her hair was a bit dowdy. If she looked like anything, she looked like a schoolteacher. She had something of the same manner, bossy but wary at the same time.

'Miss Varady?' she asked, although she knew I was. 'I don't think I've come across that surname before.'

'It's Hungarian,' I told her. 'But before you start checking on me, I'm British by birth.'

My father came from Hungary with his parents in the fifties when they had the revolution. He was five years old at the time.

'I see,' she said. 'Well now, Francesca—'

I interrupted her to ask, 'What's your first name?'

She looked surprised so I went on, 'Because if you're going to call me by my first name, I ought to be able to call you by yours. Otherwise, I call you Inspector, and you call me Miss Varady.'

The copper by the door hid a grin.

She took that quite well. 'Fair enough,' she said. 'Just when we're on our own, then, my name's Janice. So, Francesca—' She underlined it faintly. 'Just carry on telling me about yourself, and the squat, and your friends – and Theresa Monkton.'

'We called her Terry.' There really wasn't more I could say than that. We hadn't known her very long. I had nothing but my own guesswork for the things I'd deduced about her, so I couldn't mention any of them. She hadn't talked about herself. Lucy might know something. I told Inspector Janice all this.

'What about her other friends?' she asked.

'I don't know. She didn't say. No one ever came to the house.'

'Had there been any disputes between you, any of you, at the house?'

35

There'd been plenty, Terry being so lazy and grumbling all the time. But I thought quickly before I answered. I didn't like the drift of the question. What did they think had happened?

I said, 'Nothing much, just the usual squabbles about whose turn it was for the washing-up. She kept herself to herself. We always tried to respect one another's privacy. Even people like us have the right to a private life, you know! It's not easy, when you're all living together. You have to be careful not to ask questions and we didn't.'

'Which of the men was her boyfriend?'

'Neither! People come and go in squats! It just happened that we were two women and two men!' For good measure, I added, 'I don't have to stay here and be grilled by you, you know.'

'You volunteered to come to the station, Francesca.'

Not that I remembered. I said so.

'We know it's been a shock,' she said soothingly. 'But we need to know the circumstances. We're grateful for your cooperation. Now, let's get through it as quickly and painlessly as possible, shall we? Tell me the last time you saw her.'

'Alive? Yesterday around lunchtime. Next time I saw her, she was dead.'

'Hanging from the ceiling?'

'Of course, hanging from the ceiling! Where else?' Morgan was waiting. 'Nev wanted to take her down because she looked so hideous, hanging there. But I told him, we mustn't touch her. We had to tell your lot. But the council men turned up first.'

'But you were going to notify the police?'

'Yes!' I said fiercely. 'Believe it or not, we were!'

'Oh, I believe you, Francesca. Why shouldn't I?'

'Because we're squatters. Don't tell me the law's impartial. Tell your sergeant. He doesn't know it.'

Janice's eyes were pale grey and now they looked like bits of steel. For a few minutes she forgot she was being nice to me and this was a cosy girls' chat. 'You've a complaint against Sergeant Parry?'

Not if I knew what was good for me, I didn't.

'Lovely feller,' I said. 'Every woman's dream.'

She was studying me. 'We'll be getting a complete post mortem report. But there are already one or two things which puzzle us. You're absolutely certain that when you left the house yesterday, you all left together?'

'I told you, yes! Nev and I went over to see if we could get a place to live up Camden way. Squib went somewhere else. Up West, probably. He was looking for a clear piece of pavement to make a picture. He's a pavement artist.'

'Yes, we're checking on that. Why do you call him Squib? I understand his name is Henry.'

'He doesn't look like a Henry. I didn't give him the name Squib. He's always had it as far as I know. No one calls him anything else.'

If she'd known Squib she could have worked out for herself that he had a low-wattage brain and someone somewhere made a joke about his being damp.

I added, 'But he's all right. He likes animals and they like him.' I leaned forward. 'I know what he looks like and I know what you're thinking, but Squib is all right! You can trust him!'

'And Nevil Porter? What about him?'

I fixed her with a look and said very quietly because I wanted her to listen and take it in: 'Don't bully Nev. It would be easy for you to do that. He couldn't resist. He'd tell you anything you wanted him to say whether it was the truth or not. He's been ill, had a breakdown. He's very intelligent but he can't cope. That's why he packed in his studies. Get a doctor to talk to him. And you can check all this. He hasn't done anything and if you got him to confess to anything, his medical history would mean you couldn't take it into court. So leave him alone.'

She gave a thin smile. 'We already know some of this. We've had a call from his family's solicitor.'

That was quick. They hadn't wasted much time. But I guessed what had happened. Once they'd got Nev on his own, he'd panicked and asked for that solicitor. 'Did Nev ask for a lawyer?'

'Yes.' Then she asked silkily, 'We appreciate that he's very nervous and it appears he has a medical history of breakdown. But all the same, why should he need a solicitor? Wouldn't a family friend do? Or one of the doctors who treated him? If he hasn't done anything, he only needs to answer a few routine questions.'

I was angry because I'd just tried to explain all that and it was as if I hadn't spoken. But I knew I mustn't lose my temper. I met her eye and said firmly, and nice and clearly, just the way they'd taught us to speak up at that school, 'Surely he's entitled to have his solicitor?'

She blinked. 'Yes.'

'So what's the problem?'

I'd hit the ball back into her court. She didn't like it, but there wasn't much she could do but give me a frozen smile. The corners of her mouth turned up, but her lips stayed clamped together. It was more like rictus than a smile and reminded me of Terry.

I thought about Nev again. He must have been really afraid he'd go to pieces when he asked for the family lawyer. He would have known that the first thing that legal eagle would do, would be pick up the telephone and inform Nev's parents he was in trouble. Next thing, they'd be down here from the wilds of darkest Cheshire before you could say knife.

Still, I was relieved to know Nev had someone looking after his interests. But it had made the police even more suspicious. Neither Squib nor I had anyone to look after our interests. But we were probably luckier than Nev. I'd met Nev's father once and he would be the last person I'd want around if I had problems. He's one of those who are always ready to tell you what you ought to do, even if any idiot can see you're in no state to do it. When Nev had his breakdown, his father just stood over him telling him to pull himself together! What use is that?

'Why, when you came home and, according to what you told Sergeant Parry and me, you cooked sausages, didn't someone go upstairs and ask Theresa if she wanted to join you? Didn't you usually eat together?'

I don't know why she had to repeat the same set of questions so many times in as many ways. Either she was slow to get the picture, or she thought that, eventually, I'd start contradicting myself.

I repeated for the *n*th time, 'I told you, Nev and I had already eaten and Nev's vegetarian. You can check everything I've said. I don't know what Terry did after we left her Monday midday. We didn't go up to her room when we got in because we thought she was out of the house and

39

would be back later. I also told you she didn't confide in us. She just went off and did her own thing.'

'So why did you go up to her room this morning? Had something happened to make you suspicious?'

'No! We just thought she'd gone for good – and we were checking.'

But she had gone for good, poor Terry. I wished I'd phrased it differently. All the same, trust her to make trouble for everyone else, even in dying.

The image kept coming back to me, although I tried to keep it away. It was as if that hanging body was there in the room with us, the purplish-black face which hadn't looked like Terry at all, her delicate features bloated and discoloured and her swollen tongue protruding at us in a grotesque, childish gesture of defiance.

It seemed Morgan could read my mind. 'When you found her, Francesca, did you notice the bruises?'

The alarm bells were jangling ever louder. Every visible bit of Terry's skin had been mottled mauve and grey when I saw her, but since then, a doctor must have had a closer look. They couldn't have done a post mortem yet, only a preliminary check, establishing death. But someone, unless Janice was even more devious than I had already credited, had noticed bruises.

'You mean, as if she'd fallen?' I, too, could be devious.

'Uh-huh. More as if someone had hit her.'

'Someone had roughed her up recently?' This was very bad news.

'Well, we don't know, do we, Francesca.' She gave me that rictus smile. 'Or at least, I don't. There appear, on cursory examination, to be bruises on her thighs and upper arms and a serious contusion on the side of her head resulting from a blow hard enough to knock her cold. Also a graze on the right hip.'

Getting worse.

'So I'll ask again, were there ever any fights in that house?'

'I'll tell you again, no! We may have had a few spats. No punches were thrown – ever!'

'These spats? Were they ever – emotional in origin?'

I sighed. 'Whom would we have been fighting over? Nev? Squib? You've got to be joking. We had house rules and it kept the peace, more or less.'

But I was thinking of something else. Janice was, too.

'How about the way she was dressed, when you found her. Did it strike you as unusual?'

I admitted it bothered me a little.

'It bothers me, too,' she said. 'Jeans and a shirt. No underwear of any kind. Did she usually go around without any knickers on?'

'How should I know?' I snapped. 'She never wore a bra. She didn't have much to put in one. The graze on the hip. Was the skin broken?'

'Definitely and a couple of wood splinters lodged in it. Forensics will find the origin of those. Did she ever bring men back to the house?' The last question was slipped in like a knife beneath my guard. I knew what she was getting at, but I thought she was wrong.

'She didn't bring back anyone, male or female. If she was on the game, she was operating well away in another part of town. I never saw any sign of it.'

Janice abandoned that line of questioning and the tone of it, becoming conciliatory again. 'I'd like, if I may, to ask you about the dogleash. The dog belongs to the one you call Squib, is that right?'

'Yes. The leash just lies round the house. The dog's very well trained and it isn't often he put it on a leash.'

'So anyone could have got hold of the leash? Is that what you're saying? We can expect to find all your finger-prints on it?'

The question hit me with an unpleasant jolt to the solar plexus. So this was why they'd been in such a hurry to take our fingerprints, before we could object. The sick feeling below my chest intensified.

I didn't want to say anything else to make her more suspicious of me. But I'd been told by someone who reckoned he knew that there still wasn't any really reliable way of taking clear fingerprints off rough surfaces. Not clear enough to stand up in court, anyway. To be used as evidence, so the person who told me said, there had to be sixteen points of similarity between a print taken at a scene of crime and one taken off a suspect. And that's an awful lot. That dogleash was a scuffed-up bit of old leather. They'd be lucky to get sixteen points of similarity off that.

She was still giving me that steely look. I countered it with one of my own.

'I don't think I should answer any more of these questions without a lawyer.'

'My goodness,' she said. 'First Porter, now you. What's your reason for wanting a legal adviser, Francesca?'

'Simple. You indicated you only wanted to ask about the circumstances leading to our finding Terry's body. You did say there were a few things puzzling you. But this line of questioning seems to me far more than is necessary for a suicide. I'm not daft. You think you've got yourselves a case of murder.'

Chapter Three

When they realised I really wasn't going to answer any more questions, the interview came to an abrupt end – for the time being. They weren't keen to see any more of us legally represented, even by the most incompetent of lawyers, at that stage. They didn't know for sure they had a murder case. For that they'd await the final report of the post mortem. Janice thanked me icily for all my help and murmured that they might need to talk to me again. What was my address?

I pointed out they knew. She said, still smiling, she understood we were about to be evicted within the next few days. I told her it was still the only address I had, and suggested she ask the council what it meant to do about us. I was asked to wait outside.

Eventually someone came to tell me they'd been in touch with the council and understood it meant to rehouse me – though not Squib or Nev. All this was news to me. The police must have put pressure on and succeeded where all else had failed. But it made me uneasy, as it turned out, rightly so.

They also brought me a transcript of everything I'd told

them. I signed after I'd read it a dozen times because I wanted to be sure what I was putting my name to. Then I asked, 'Can I go now?'

They weren't happy about it but they let us all go. We trailed back to Jubilee Street to find a gallant specimen of the Old Bill was guarding the entrance to our house. He wouldn't let us in. We told him all our gear was in there and, as far as we were concerned, it was still our home. He told us we'd have to wait till someone told him officially he could let us inside. After some argument, he let us know that the forensic team was busy in there, and nothing had to be disturbed.

'What are they looking for?' Squib asked, as we walked away. 'They got the body. They took photos of the place.'

I didn't want to worry Nev, so I just said that the police were like that, pernickety.

Squib made what, to his mind, was a joke. 'They think we strung her up, do they?'

He cackled away happily and I didn't tell him that he'd hit the nail right on the head. That's exactly what their nasty little minds were thinking.

Shut out of the house, we were at a loose end, if that's not an inappropriate expression in the circumstances. Nev and Squib went down the pub and I went to the corner shop to talk to Ganesh.

I'd walked along the stretch of pavement going to and from the house or the shop at the corner I don't know how many times. I knew every crack. I knew all the places rain collected and where edges stuck up and could trip you. I could walk down the street in the pitch dark and not put a foot in a puddle or fall flat on my face. Quite often, I had walked down it in pitch dark because the street lighting was inreliable. The council never came around and fixed our pavement or resurfaced our road.

The reason they gave was that the area was due for redevelopment. It was as part of the redevelopment that our row of houses was scheduled to come down. I don't know what they intended putting up in their place. Smart flats, probably, for young executives.

If you kept going when you got to the end of the street, you got to the river. Looking across, you could see on the far side the luxury flats built in the docklands for Yuppies, before Yuppies became an endangered species, like snow leopards. Looking down the narrow defile between crumbling brick terraces towards those shining towers always made me feel like Judy Garland gazing at the Emerald City. Because of that, and the way the sun sparkled on all the glass of the high-rise office blocks, I called it 'the Crystal City'.

'Sounds like a football team,' Ganesh said.

'That's Crystal Palace. I'll call it what I like.'

Sometimes of a summer evening, Gan and I walked down there and sat on a crumbling wall above the mudflats, looking across and making up stories about the people who lived there. Once, we actually went across there and walked round, but we felt like little green men just dropped in from Mars. It was so clean, so prosperous. The people looked so fit and healthy, well dressed and trim. They had a purposeful air as if they were all going somewhere and knew where it was. We couldn't wait to get back again.

Now the developers were starting, at a much slower rate, on our side of the river. Our houses sprawled around the edge of the cleared building sites like a shanty town or squatter camp in the Third World, clinging to the skirts of a big city. Most of the people round here had no more chance of making it across the great divide to the affluent part of the area than they could sprout wings and fly.

It was the older ones who were bewildered. Old men who'd worked all their lives down at the docks before the work disappeared and the wharves became tourist sights. Old women who'd lived here all through the Blitz and who still scrubbed their front doorsteps. People like Ganesh's parents, who'd come here thinking that it would be upward and onward in a new country and who had worked hard to achieve success, but who had found themselves trapped now in this urban wilderness, a far cry from anything they'd ever imagined.

I think Mr Patel was hoping the development would bring quality housing nearer, as it had done across the river, because no one round here had very much money at the moment. If people started moving in who had more dosh, they might spend some of it in his shop. He had all kinds of plans, speciality Indian foods and so on. I didn't like to suggest the council might decide to bulldoze his shop as well. Everyone needs a dream.

Right opposite the shop, on the other corner of the street, was a disused chapel and burial ground. We called it 'the graveyard'. The building was locked up, the glass in its mock-Gothic windows broken, weeds growing from cracks in the masonry. It had originally been a congregational chapel. It had changed hands and religious viewpoint several times since then. The last people to use it as a place of worship had been the Church of the Beauteous Day.

The Church of the Beauteous Day had been really

something. When they turned up of a Sunday morning, whole families dressed in their best, it was like Mardi Gras. And they knew how to worship with songs and cymbals, all right. To say nothing of trombones, choirs and hand-clapping. When they weren't making music they were listening to the preacher, the Reverend Eli, and shouting joyously 'Hallelujah!' and 'Yes, Lord!' For one day a week, they brought light and life and faith to our street. But the premises weren't suitable for all their social events and they moved out, led away by the Reverend Eli, a tiny man with crinkled grey hair. Away he took all those smiling ladies in the floral hats, smart young men, little boys with bowties and little girls with snowy socks, like Moses leading the children of Abraham into the desert. I don't know whither he led them. Some said to Hackney. I was sorry. I missed them, especially the Reverend Eli, who, when he saw me, would sing out, 'You ready to repent, child?' and beam a gold-toothed smile.

Though the chapel was abandoned, the burial ground was still in use, by the living. A crazy old baglady named Mad Edna had her home there among the headstones with a tribe of feral cats for company. People taking a short cut through the graveyard were alarmed when Mad Edna sprang out from behind a tomb, like Magwitch the convict in *Great Expectations*, and began a conversation with them. She always treated them graciously, as if they'd come to call on her. She told me she'd been a débutante once, long ago, and I believed her. The council was having trouble over demolishing the chapel because of the graves alongside it, so Edna was safe for the time being.

A load of fruit and veg had been delivered to the shop during the afternoon. It was stacked on the pavement and

Ganesh was moving it, putting some on display outside the shop, and carrying the rest down the side alley to the yard at the back.

He was wearing grubby jeans and an old Fair Isle sweater, because it was a mucky job, and his long black hair was tied back with a piece of ribbon. He ties his hair back when he's working because it's more convenient and because his father insists on it. If Mr Patel had his way, Ganesh would be working round the shop wearing a suit and with his hair trimmed short back and sides, or so Ganesh reckons.

Parents have ambitions for their children, I suppose. My dad had ambitions for me. Sometimes I hope that I'll still manage to fulfil some of them, someday, and he'll know, in heaven. I'd like to please him, even at this late date. Make up for all the disappointment.

Ganesh looked up as I came along the pavement. His expression had been worried but it cleared. 'Fran! Thank God you're all right! What's going on? I've been worried sick about you! Someone said a person had died in your house!'

'Someone did,' I told him. 'Terry.'

We both looked down the street towards the house. Besides the police, quite a few sightseers had gathered. There was a van parked, just down from the police vehicles, which hadn't been there earlier. My heart sank, if possible, further. If it had been any one of the other of us, there wouldn't have been half the fuss. Nev, with his history of breakdown, would have been written off as suicide. Squib hanging from the light fitting would have been written off as one fewer problem for society. They might have said the same about me. But Terry – there was something about Terry. She was going to be trouble. The police sensed it, just as I'd always sensed it. They knew they were not going to be able to write her off, just like that. They were doing it all by the book to head off any criticism at a later date.

Ganesh didn't like the sight of all the activity down the street either. He dusted his hands and wiped them on his sweater, and by mutual accord, we set off down the alley.

The yard was full of stuff. Empty crates, full crates, packing cases, dismembered cardboard boxes baled up for the refuse people to take, and everywhere scraps of squashed fruit and withered leaves.

Ganesh picked out a couple of apples and handed me one. I was surprised to find I was hungry. We sat down side by side and between bites at the apple, I told him as much as I could. It wasn't much. Inspector Janice had given strict instructions that I wasn't to talk to anyone about anything. But Ganesh wasn't just anyone. Anyway, if he'd already heard someone had been found dead in the house, he knew nearly as much as I did.

However, I'd had some theatrical training, so I made a good story of it and finished up on a highpoint by suggesting the police thought it was murder.

Cheap theatricals didn't impress Ganesh who looked sceptical. 'Gossip around the place says she hanged herself.'

Word travelled fast. 'They think someone helped her.'

'Who?' That was Ganesh for you, always the awkward question.

'Us, probably. We didn't.' Something had occurred to me and it made things worse. 'Gan, if it's true, if someone killed her, she let him into the house.'

We had fixed up a proper lock on the front door. Or

rather, Declan had. We locked it when we went out to stop anyone else taking over our squat, quite apart from the council getting in and repossessing us. When we were at home, we locked ourselves in as a matter of principle. Apart from the council, there were plenty of people out there who might like to make trouble for us, the developers for a start. We even blocked up the letterbox after dark to prevent anyone pushing lighted rags through it. That had happened elsewhere.

If one of us was alone in the house, we took extra care. Entrance was strictly by the front door. Terry would have locked it and not opened it for anyone she didn't know and trust. The downstairs windows didn't open easily. The wooden frames had swollen with damp and warped with age. The old sash cords didn't work. Just to push the window open an inch took two people and more effort than it was worth.

'When the police realise that, it's going to make it look worse for us,' I concluded. 'Like an inside job.'

'She knew people outside,' he said, 'people she'd have let in. Let the police go and hassle them.'

'That's the point, Gan. I can't name a single one. We knew nothing at all about her, where she went, what she did when she left the house. She was always suspicious, secretive.'

Ganesh said unkindly that Terry had always struck him as a headcase.

At this point, his father came out to see why Ganesh had stopped working. Mr Patel has a sort of sixth sense which tells him where and when anyone he's employing isn't working one hundred per cent. I've worked in the shop on a Saturday and I know.

When he saw me, he looked relieved. 'Ah! There you are, Francesca! We have all been extremely worried about you, my dear. What on earth is going on?'

'She's just telling me about it, Dad!' Ganesh said patiently.

'Terry's dead, Mr Patel,' I told him.

'That other girl? This is very bad. How has she died?'

His brow furrowed into deep worry lines as I told him. Unwarily I let slip that the police thought the death might be suspicious. As that, he erupted, jabbing a forefinger at me in accusation and looking as if he was going to have a fit.

'Murder! Murder, are you saying, Francesca? In this street? So near to my shop? In this place where you are living?' He rounded on Ganesh. 'Have I not told you so?'

Ganesh snapped back at him in Gujarati and, the next thing, they were at it hammer and tongs with me unable to understand a word.

But I didn't need a translator. I could guess what it was all about. After a while Mr Patel turned and stamped off back into the shop.

Ganesh, breathing heavily, said, 'Sorry about that.'

'Never mind. I understand.'

'Look, they do like you!' He thrust out his jaw pugnaciously. 'Don't get Dad wrong. I know he flew off the handle then, but that's because murder on the doorstep isn't what he expected to hear about. It wasn't anything to do with you!'

'Leave it, Gan!' I said sharply.

The muscles around his mouth and jawline tightened and he got up and began to stack some empty crates, throwing them around with unnecessary force. After a few minutes, when he'd got the anger out of his system, he sat down again and asked in a reasonably normal voice, 'Yesterday afternoon, that's when the police think she died?'

'They haven't said, but we were all out of the house between one-thirty and around seven when Nev and I got home. Squib came in later. The body was stiff. I'd guess some time during the afternoon.'

He was looking thoughtful. 'Look, it's probably nothing, but yesterday afternoon, I noticed this guy . . . '

Irritatingly, he fell silent.

'Go on, then! Where?' I prompted in frustration.

'Hanging around in the street. By the post box on the other side about half way down. I'd never seen him before. I took a good look at him because, well, if a stranger starts hanging around casing places, you do, don't you?'

'If he was thinking of breaking in anywhere round here, he was being a bit optimistic!' I said. 'No one round here's got anything worth pinching.'

'He didn't look that type. He was a big chap, six-footer, well built, pretty fit. He'd have been aged about, oh, early thirties, and he was well dressed. Casual clothes, I mean, but nothing he'd got down the market. Quality gear. Sort of huntin', shootin' and fishin' things. Tweed jacket.'

I thought about this. 'What time was this?'

'I couldn't swear to it. Early on, around three or just before. At least, that's when I saw him. I don't know exactly what time he arrived. I was in the shop. I came out and there he was. I fooled around outside to watch him, then went inside and tried to keep an eye on him through the window. Then I was distracted and when I looked again, he'd gone.'

'Did he have a car?'

'If he did, he hadn't parked in this street. But he was definitely looking at the houses and it could have been yours.'

I thought about this for a while. That there'd been no car parked in the street didn't surprise me because no one who had a decent car and any sense would park it around here. He might have been an estate agent or a property developer or any of the people connected with the proposed redevelopment. It was more than likely that's who he was. I suggested this to Ganesh.

'I thought of that. He wasn't making any notes or taking any photos. He looked shifty, as if he didn't want to be seen.'

'Then he probably *was* a property developer!' I got up. 'Show me exactly where you saw him.'

We went back into the street and Ganesh pointed out the spot. The pillarbox is about twenty feet from our house, on the other side of the street. The stranger could well have been watching our place. I know it was a squat but I still called it 'ours'.

'I think he realised I'd spotted him,' Ganesh went on. 'Because he stooped and made out he was reading the collection times on the box. He wasn't any great actor, I can tell you! Think I ought to tell the police?'

'Perhaps you should.' I was more worried by the news than I wanted to let on.

Just then a car turned into the street and pulled up sharp by us. I recognised it as Euan's Fiesta. He got out and came over to us, glancing worriedly down the street towards the activity outside the house.

'There you are, Fran!'

'Suddenly everyone's looking for me,' I murmured.

'You forgot about the court, didn't you?' He gave a wry grimace. 'So did I – nearly! We got our order for immediate possession. But I don't suppose that now you want to stay in that house? Not now this has happened.'

'Yes, there's been a murder!' Ganesh broke in angrily before I could speak. 'And still you lot come harassing her, wanting to throw her out on to the street!'

Euan had reddened angrily but he wasn't going to argue with Ganesh who was a by-stander and not, in Euan's view, involved. He turned his back on him and went on to me, 'But cheer up, Fran. I've got some good news for you. We've got you temporary accommodation.'

So I'd been told correctly at the police station. But I still asked suspiciously, 'What sort of accommodation?'

'A flat. Only for six months, mind!'

'Oh, great!' Ganesh burst out. 'So this is what it takes for you lot to offer her somewhere decent to live? A violent death?'

'It's not marvellous,' Euan warned me, still ignoring Ganesh. 'But it's somewhere. Come over to my office and I'll give you the key.'

He drove off and I said goodbye to Ganesh. As I was walking off, however, I heard someone calling my name. I turned round, and saw Mr Patel hurrying after me.

'Francesca!' He came up panting. 'I wanted to say to you that I am truly very sorry about shouting like that and the carry-on.'

'It's OK, Mr Patel,' I told him.

'No, no!' he said excitedly. 'It is not OK! It is terrible, terrible! Such a crime! But you are all right, my dear. That is good. You are not hurt.'

'I'm not hurt,' I assured him.

He waved his hands. 'You see, it is very difficult for us, for my wife and myself. You are obviously of good family and an educated young woman. An education is a fine thing. But you should not be living like that, in that place. You see what happens in such places?'

I told him I appreciated his concern but he shouldn't worry about me. He looked at me in a lost way as if he couldn't think of anything more to say, much as he wanted to say something, a worried man with a balding head and a Biro stuck behind one ear, trying to make sense of something beyond him. Then he gave up and went back to the shop.

I knew what he wanted to say. He couldn't understand how someone like me, who was neither deranged nor a criminal, could end up living on her own or with a group of other loners in a condemned house. It puzzled him that I hadn't any family or anyone to care for me. It seemed all wrong to him and it presented a threat. Most of all, he was worried about the effect I had on Ganesh.

I could have told him that I wasn't the cause of the problems he had with Ganesh.

About six months ago Ganesh's sister, Usha, had married a chap named Jay who was in accountancy and had prospects. Ganesh had been mooching about scowling ever since. He felt he was being left behind here. 'One more year!' he'd told me privately, 'One more year and I'm out!'

But he hadn't told his people that yet. They knew though. They were putting pressure on him. He hadn't said so to me, but I guessed what their answer to the problem would be. It would be a pretty sixteen-year-old with beautiful manners and a dowry. They thought I'd be the obstacle. They were wrong.

I started wondering and worrying about Euan's promised flat.

Chapter Four

Euan was right. The best you could say about that flat was that it was somewhere. It was on the fifth floor of one of a pair of condemned tower blocks. The building was already half empty and pretty well all vandalised. The lift didn't work. The staircase was graffiti-covered. There was a hole in the corridor ceiling outside my door with funny stuff hanging out of it which looked to me like asbestos lining. So he was also right to say it wasn't marvellous.

My heart sank when I saw it, but I knew I couldn't stay in the house where Terry had died. This would have to be it for a few weeks, anyway. Euan had come with me and I told him thanks.

Naturally I offered the hospitality of my new roof to Nev and Squib. Nev accepted gratefully. Squib, a natural loner, looked uneasy. Living with others had already shown itself too likely to attract attention. We went to Jubilee Street in another attempt to collect our belongings. Either the council or the police had boarded up the house and we had to break in at the back. We put everything portable into black plastic rubbish sacks and took them over to the shop so that Ganesh could ferry them in the van to my new abode. He wasn't able to do it straight away, so while we waited for him to be free, Squib and Nev went to the pub and I went for a last walk round the neighbourhood I'd got to know so well, or what the developers had left of it. Not that I was going far, but even a block or two is moving away.

I was walking through the graveyard when Edna jumped out from behind a headstone, doing her Magwitch impersonation.

'Where are you going in such a hurry, dear?' she asked.

'Nowhere,' I told her. 'I'm not in a hurry.' Even the thought of not being waylaid by Mad Edna any more made me feel sad. I sat on a tomb. She sat down beside me and began rummaging in her grubby coat. She had an excited air about her, like a child who has learned a new trick and is going to try it out.

Eventually she produced a gold-coloured Benson and Hedges cigarette packet, very clean and not crushed. She held it tenderly in her mittened hands and touched it with a yellowed nail sticking through the chopped-off ends of the glove-fingers. She stroked it reverently a few times, then opened it with infinite care and very hospitably offered me a cigarette.

I declined but she continued to push the gold box at me, peering up into my face to make sure I'd noticed how beautiful it was, if only card. If it had been real gold, she wouldn't have been happier and she wanted me to share her pleasure in it.

I said, 'It's nice, Edna!' but still refused a cigarette.

She looked disappointed but took one herself.

She'd got matches, too. One of those little booklets you get for free in bars and restaurants. Watching her struggle to light it, I offered help, struck the paper match for her and lit her smoke.

Before handing the booklet back, I read the name on it. It came courtesy of a wine bar in Winchester. She didn't like me studying it, or even holding it, and snatched it away, tucking it and the precious gold-coloured packet away in some best-not-to-think-about place. The mittens didn't hide how rheumatism had swollen her knuckle joints. She oughtn't to have been living rough in a grave-yard. But I knew anyone'd have a dreadful job moving her out. She liked it there. She smelled a bit high, though, and I moved along the tomb as far as I could.

Two of the feral cats lounged nearby in the long grass watching us through half-closed eyes. Another was curled up asleep on a grave. Wherever Edna sat, a cat or two was generally nearby. She was part of their extended tribe.

As she was puffing happily on her cigarette, I told her I was being moved into a temporary flat.

'Why don't you get yourself a little place in Chelsea?' she asked. 'Chelsea is interesting. Wonderful parties. Although some people think living there rather fast.' She gave a rasping cough. She wasn't used to this amount of fresh tobacco.

Mentally she was back in her débutante days again, whenever they'd been. I had no idea how old she was. She always appeared incredibly ancient.

I told her I depended on the council and had to stay in the borough. She mumbled at that and began ferreting among several plastic carrier bags she always had with her. Smoke curled up into her eye and made her squint. Knowing that Edna normally collected her smokes from bins and gutters, I wondered about the gold packet and asked, 'Splashing out, Edna? Buying the ciggies in a proper packet now?'

'He dropped it,' she muttered. 'He didn't see. I saw, though. He didn't see me. He walked through here.' She waved the cigarette at the path through the long grass and tipsy headstones.

'Who was he?' I wasn't really interested, just making conversation with her. She seemed reasonably sane today.

'Smart young fellow,' she said. 'Stranger. Well set-up. He'd left his car over there . . . ' This time she pointed behind us to an open patch behind the buildings in the road beyond, accessible through a gap, which the Church of the Beauteous Day had cleared so that the Reverend Eli could park his purple transit van there.

'I don't like strangers. They keep coming these days and telling me I can't live here any more. Where should I live? What about the cats? I've told them, I've got to look after the cats. So when he came through, I hid and watched him. He was up to no good.'

The hairs prickled on the back of my neck. 'How do you know, Edna?'

'He looked it. Dodging about from headstone to headstone, didn't want to be seen. So busy hiding himself away, he didn't spot me. I was over there.' She waved at a jumble of overgrown bushes.

It didn't surprise me the stranger hadn't spotted her. In her dirty coat and with her amorphous outline, she blended perfectly into her surroundings. I'd often passed by her myself, and jumped out of my skin when she'd greeted me. She had a trick, like the cats, of sitting perfectly still and watching. I'd seen her sitting on the grass, quite surrounded by them, just blinking her eyes at them as they blinked back. I'd sometimes speculated whether they were the spirits of the dead buried in this place. That Edna could communicate with them didn't surprise me in the least.

'When was this you saw the man, Edna?'

She looked vague. Days were all the same to her. 'Must've been yesterday,' she said uncertainly.

I asked her if it had been morning or afternoon but she couldn't remember. She wasn't, however, completely out of touch. Unexpectedly, she asked, 'Is that right the girlie hanged herself, dear?' She peered at me with a flicker of interest in her rheumy old eyes.

'That's right, Edna.'

She puffed on the cigarette, staring ahead. It was impossible to say what she made of it. She didn't seem surprised or frightened. Even her curiosity, now I'd confirmed the rumour, was cured.

It was hopeless. She may have seen the same fellow Ganesh saw. We'd never be able to establish it for sure.

She came to life and leaned towards me confidentially. 'Got something to show you!'

My spirits rose briefly. What else had she found? I should have known better.

She took me to a corner of the graveyard and proudly showed me some new kittens, mewing blindly but safely inside a ramshackle stone tomb. The tomb's inscription commemorated Josiah and Hepzibah Wilkins who'd died within a week of one another of the influenza in 1819, leaving seventeen children. There had been enough money to build them a decent monument so I suppose there'd been money to take care of the seventeen children. Perhaps the older ones had looked after the younger ones.

The fact remained that if anyone asked questions of Edna, they'd get nothing sensible in reply. She might or might not be a vital witness. Her only concern was for the cats and what would happen to her and to them, if the developers succeeded in levelling the surrounding monuments.

I gave Edna all the loose change in my pocket and she squirrelled it away in another hiding place in her grubby old coat.

'Call again!' she invited, as I walked away.

We were allowed to remove our furniture, such as it was, from the house. We ferried it over to the new flat in several lots, using the Patels' van. Between us we manoeuvred it up the filthy staircase and staggered with it along open windswept balconies lined with unwelcoming doors. Some flats were abandoned and boarded up. Others, though still inhabited, were nearly as well barricaded, like medieval castles. It didn't promise a spirit of neighbourliness.

The flat itself had been cleared and swept out, but still looked as if a major riot had taken place in it. The walls were pitted and scarred; parts of the skirting had been ripped out. There was something very odd about the kitchen sink unit which was at an angle. Anything placed on the draining board simply slid down into the basin.

Squib, looking more than usually perplexed, wandered around rattling loose fittings and opening cupboards. Eventually he said, sounding pleased, 'Got it!'

We waited apprehensively, expecting him to turn round, holding some furry creature he'd found lurking in the corner.

Instead, empty-handed but triumphant, he declared, 'Worked it out. It's the wrong place. The council gave you the wrong key, Fran.'

I told him I wished that could be true. Sadly, I thought it wasn't. This, despite all appearances, was home sweet home.

He shook his head. 'Can't be. Look, they condemned our house and it was better than this. They got it wrong, Fran.'

He took some persuading and, finally accepting my argument, became offended and muttered, 'Well, I'm not staying here.'

I found that hurtful, considering I'd generously offered him the shelter of my roof. For Squib, of all people, to object ... But he said he'd been offered a place in a hostel and he'd try it out. The police had told him he had to stay there so they could find him again. But if the hostel made a fuss about the dog, he'd leave.

I suggested that if the hostel wouldn't take the dog, Mad Edna might look after it for a while. The dog would probably like being in the churchyard and Edna, in her crazy way, could be relied upon for something like that.

But Squib wouldn't even think about being parted from the dog, even temporarily. Besides, he thought the cats were quite capable of ganging up on a dog. He'd seen them do it.

I leaned over the balcony to watch him walk across the wasteland between the condemned blocks, his rucksack on his back and the dog trotting nicely by his heels.

Euan, whom I liked more and more, had promised to try and rustle up some extra furniture. He had a friend in the Salvation Army. At least the hot water was working.

It was ages since I'd lived in a place with hot water. While Nev dragged our existing furniture around trying to make the place look habitable, I spent an hour cleaning out the bathroom before I got in the tub and lay there in the steaming water, just looking up at the cracks in the ceiling and another hole in the plaster where the lavatory cistern was coming away.

As it turned out, Nev only stayed twenty-four hours before his parents descended on the place. I wasn't surprised to see them. I don't think Nev was, either. He'd had the air of a condemned man about him since walking in the door.

His father stood in the middle of the sitting room, heels together, bolt upright, hands clasped behind his back as if he were reviewing the troops. His mother looked at me just as my old headmistress did when I was being carpeted for something.

I've mentioned my school before. My mother ran off and left my dad and me when I was seven, so I was brought up by Dad and my Hungarian Grandma Varady. I think my father felt he owed it to me somehow to give me every opportunity he could because my mum had left. I always told people she was dead, because we didn't know where she was and for me, it was as if she was dead. So they scraped and saved, Dad and Grandma Varady, and paid for me to go to this school for young ladies.

I was in and out of trouble from the first day I went there and by the time I got to be fifteen they told my father it really wasn't worth keeping me on there. They meant they wanted me to go.

They wrote a final report on me. It read, 'Francesca is extremely bright but lacks application. She has consistently failed to take advantage of the opportunities offered by this school.'

I have never been so ashamed of anything in my life as I was the day I watched my father read that report. He and Grandma Varady had gone without virtually every luxury to keep me at that school and I'd let them both down completely. I was sorry, but it was too late. I loved them both and wouldn't have hurt them for the world, but I had hurt them.

If they'd been angry, shouted and stamped up and down, it would have helped, but they didn't say anything. Dad even said, 'Never mind, *édesem*,' and hugged me because he was afraid the report might have hurt *my* feelings. Grandma Varady had to be forcibly restrained from marching round to the school and socking the head-mistress. She came of a long line of Austro-Hungarian hussars. We had faded sepia portraits of some of them, waxed moustaches, tight jackets with frogging, tighter pants and shiny boots. She firmly believed that the answer to every problem was a cavalry charge.

I went away and shut myself in my room and howled. Afterwards I made a resolve that never again would I ever act as plain stupid as that. But I suppose I have.

Anyhow, the upshot of the visit from the Porters was that they frogmarched poor Nev away with them, back to that luxury gaol they called home. The way they talked to him, he might just as well have been four, not twenty-four. Even worse, they told him their very good friend, some high-powered head-doctor, had a whole set of bright new ideas for treating Nev's nervous breakdown.

As he left he said, 'I'll be in touch, Fran. I've left you my books.'

I said, 'Thanks!' but I knew I'd seen the last of him. So I just added, 'Good luck!' He might just as well have left me the books in his will. It was that final.

His mother gave me a really nasty look. His father didn't look at me at all during the whole time he was there. He was pretending I wasn't there. Anything he couldn't handle, he pretended didn't exist – like poor Nev's illness.

I knew that, for better or worse, my life had changed for ever. Probably for worse.

Chapter Five

I was on my own. I hadn't lived completely on my own for quite some while. It was a strange feeling, rattling around that depressing flat. But, although I might be alone, I certainly wasn't forgotten, not by the police at any rate. Janice Morgan was presumably busy on more important matters and I was left to the tender mercies of Sergeant Parry. His expression of sceptical disbelief at whatever I said and his ginger moustache began to haunt my dreams.

'You're getting paranoid,' said Ganesh, heaving a sack of potatoes around, preparatory to slitting it open and emptying it into a bin.

'How can you say that?' I'd been having my usual moan but still felt I'd every right to sound incredulous. 'Parry's on my neck from morning till night. Always the same questions, dished up in different ways. What do the police think I know?'

'How about Nev and Squib, are they chasing them in the same way?'

'That's what I came to tell you this morning. I tried to phone Nev last night and his father told me Nev is in a private clinic. They've got him hidden away where the police can't question him. As for Squib, I went over to the hostel yesterday. It's run by some kind of religious group. They smile all the time and their skins look as if they've been sitting in the bath too long.'

'Hey!' interrupted Ganesh disapprovingly. 'They're doing their best, right!'

'All right. Anyhow, Squib wasn't there. They said he'd be back this evening and, if I wanted, I could leave a note pinned on a corkboard they've got in the entrance. So I did, though I don't suppose Squib will even look at the corkboard and I can't count on anyone telling him I was there. They call him Henry,' I added. 'Just like the police do.'

'It's his name.' Ganesh can be very irritating. 'You can't expect them to call him Squib.'

I wasn't going to argue about that. I had other things on my mind. 'Let's face it, Gan, I'm the only one the Bill can really get at, and I'm the one getting the treatment. They can't seem to get it into their thick heads that it's wasting everyone's time and getting none of us anywhere. It's certainly not going to find out exactly what happened to Terry, if we ever do that.'

Ganesh grunted and tipped out the spuds. They rolled and bounced down into the bin with a strong smell of earth.

Grumbling to Ganesh worked off some of the frustration but I couldn't pretend the continual police questioning wasn't worrying me. They were starting to wear me down, which was the name of the game as far as they were concerned, I suppose. I was beginning to get confused in my own mind. They'd managed to convince me I hadn't told them everything or that I'd forgotten something of great importance. I'd started racking my brains in the still of the night.

'Quiet today,' I offered Ganesh. The shop had been empty but as I spoke a woman came in with a grubby child in tow and started picking over the vegetables.

Ganesh glared at her. 'Who's doing any business with half the houses emptied around here? You want those beans or don't you, love?'

She moved away from the beans and stared mistrustfully at the newly decanted spuds. 'I want potatoes but those are covered in mud.'

'They grow in the ground,' Ganesh told her. 'What do you expect?'

'I expect them cleaner than that. Mud weighs, mud does. It's heavy. I'm not paying for mud.'

Ganesh sighed and pushed the top potatoes around. 'These are cleaner.'

'I'll pick 'em out, thanks!' she said crossly, shoving him aside. She began to pick out one potato at a time, peering at each for signs of mud or damage.

'I ask you,' said Ganesh to me. 'Who wants to be a greengrocer?'

'Beats being a police suspect,' I told him. 'Leave you to it, Gan. See you later.'

There was a car parked opposite the shop, outside the graveyard. Someone, a woman, was attempting to talk to Edna. Our resident baglady was huddled in a heap among her plastic bags and I could tell she was pretending to be deaf. When I appeared the woman lost interest in Edna, who scurried away among the tombs. The newcomer called out to me, 'Francesca!' It was Inspector Janice.

'Glad to see you,' she added as I joined her.

'What is it now?' I asked grumpily. I really had had enough.

'Nice to know you're pleased to see me, too,' she retorted.

'Don't take it personally,' I told her. 'But I'm not. I'm out of a job, living in a set left over from an old Hammer movie, and every time I turn round, there's a copper wanting to ask me questions.'

'No questions,' she assured me. 'I was going to suggest we take a drive.'

It was an unmarked car and she was in plainclothes. Janice liked her clothes very plain. She was wearing a sort of blazer today, with broad navy stripes. It made her look as if she'd been leaning against newly painted railings. However she dressed, and had she been riding a tricycle, no one around here would have had any doubt who or what she was.

'Give me a reason,' I suggested.

'I'm trying', she said, 'to get you off the hook. That's what you want, isn't it?'

'Go on.' I had justification in feeling suspicion. Greeks bearing gifts, and all the rest of it. The way they worked, Parry had been sent to wear me down and now I was at rock bottom, Janice was moving in for the kill.

I winced as the last word crossed my mind. But Janice was smiling, conciliatory today in voice and manner. Softening me up.

'You told us you were out of the house for the whole of Monday afternoon and early evening. You were in Camden with Porter, so you say. I'd like to believe it and we've done our best to check it out. But so far, anywhere we've asked, everyone has denied knowing either you or

Nevil or seeing anyone like you on that day.' She waited.

I sighed. 'They would. They don't want to be involved. You can't blame them.'

She hunched her shoulders. 'I thought we could drive around there. You might see someone. Look, I'm in my own time. I don't have to bother with this!'

I got in the car.

'Theresa Monkton's family has been in touch,' she said casually, as we drove off.

That startled me. 'You found them?'

'They found us.' She explained that apparently the family had been trying to find Terry for some time. She'd left home before but this time they'd feared something had happened to her. They'd kept a sharp watch on the news reports concerning any unidentified young women. The best they were hoping for was an amnesia victim. The worst – the worst of their fears had come true. I felt sorry for them.

We drew a blank around Camden High Street. We called at the house where we'd had the Mexican bean stew, but the people Nev knew had left, or so the others there said. I thought they were lying. They just didn't want to get involved, just like all the others Janice had already asked. I wasn't surprised but, what with one thing and another, my life at the moment was akin to trying to paddle a canoe with a tennis racket.

It was a nicer day weather-wise than it'd been for a while. Pale sunshine inspired shops to put out racks of clothes on the pavements. But Camden was having one of its grotty days, nonetheless, its gutters choked with litter. There were a couple of stalls with fruit and veg in side alleys, adding to the debris with dropped leaves and squashed fruit. They made me think of Ganesh and I wished I hadn't bothered him with my troubles. He had enough of his own. There were plenty of people about but no one and nothing of any help to me.

'We're wasting our time,' I said, exasperated. 'I can't prove we were here. But it's the truth.'

We carried on looking without much joy. Then, just as we were giving up, I did see a couple I recognised, a man and a girl. The man was called Lew, I knew that, but I couldn't remember the girl's name. I leapt out of Janice's car and raced after them, yelling, 'Lew!'

They very nearly took off, but I managed to grab his arm. His girlfriend misinterpreted my enthusiasm at seeing him and took a swing at me. It took a fraught few minutes trying to explain. She was quite a bit taller than me and several pounds heavier, and neither Lew nor anyone else seemed inclined to intervene, although a few gathered to watch and cheer us on. Eventually, I managed to make them both understand that I wanted some help from them, not to break up their one-to-one relationship. As our fight broke up, the onlookers drifted away. One or two left small coins on the pavement, perhaps under the impression we'd been taking part in some Street Theatre.

During all the time I was in active danger of getting seriously done over by an enraged Amazon in fishnet tights and combat boots, Janice had been hanging about in the background, not making any effort to come to my rescue, much as all the other gawpers. When she saw things had calmed down, she joined us. Grudgingly they told her they'd seen me and Nev on the Monday afternoon at Camden Lock and we'd had a coffee together. I could see neither of them liked being asked to give me an alibi. But at least they didn't issue flat denials and perhaps their reluctance made Janice more inclined to believe them.

I told them thanks and that I was sorry I'd had to ask them. They weren't very gracious about it, but at least supplied names and an address before the Amazon hauled her man away like a hunting trophy. It wasn't my fault but I knew they didn't see it that way, and if I knew what was good for me, I'd stay away from that part of town. I'd had my last free meal of beans.

'Well, it helps, Francesca,' Janice said encouragingly.

'Not much,' I told her.

'No, not much,' she agreed. She was honest, at least. But I still didn't trust her.

Since she was feeling generous towards me, I asked her about the post mortem. 'Is this or isn't this a murder inquiry? If not, why do I need an alibi? If it is murder, I should be told so, outright. I don't have to cooperate if I don't know what's going on.'

She didn't answer at once. She pulled over behind a stall selling curtain material, and twisted in her seat to face me.

'It's not that easy to answer your question, Fran. It wouldn't be the first case where foul play has been suspected and then, after exhaustive and costly inquiries, it's been decided the injuries were accidental or self-inflicted. People do harm themselves in a multitude of ways. I wouldn't like to guess how often an investigation's taken time, money and manpower, everyone's got frustrated and tired, and still we've ended up closing the file. No one likes that. On the other hand, murder has been made to look like suicide before. The killer's found it easier to try and fake a suicide than to fake an accident. In this case, we've an apparent suicide, but with so many inconsistencies about it that we have to be suspicious. Sergeant Parry, who was one of the first officers to see the body—'

I interrupted bitterly, 'I know what Parry thinks! He thinks we had something to do with it!'

'No,' she contradicted me. 'You don't know what Sergeant Parry thinks. Despite anything he may have said to you, he's not leaping to any conclusions about this, nor am I. Parry is a very experienced officer. I, for one, respect his opinion. So, if we haven't a suicide, what do we have?'

Janice glowered through the windscreen at the billowing net curtaining strung along the trader's stall ahead. 'The worst is trying to explain all this to the family. Suicide appals most relatives. They want to believe it's an accident. Even murder is more acceptable to them. They can't be responsible for the accident or the murder – but the suicide leaves them with a personal burden of guilt. If I went to Theresa's family today and said, sorry, folks, the murder theory was a mare's nest. It was suicide, after all. You know, they'd be more upset than if I went to them and named a killer?'

'But yourself,' I persisted. 'You think that, out there somewhere, is a killer?'

'Personally and off the record, yes, I think so. But hunches, mine or Parry's, aren't enough, even when there's circumstantial evidence to back them up. Eventually it has to be proved to the satisfaction of a jury. That's not easy. Juries nowadays mistrust forensic evidence. They shouldn't but they do. A couple of cases of verdicts declared unsafe which get wide media coverage, and there you are! Unsupported confessions are no longer acceptable. The boundaries of reasonable doubt get hazier every day. I think someone attacked her, that she was either naked or was stripped partially naked in the process, there was some struggle which took place on the floor and the splinters of wood entered her skin. She then received a blow to the head which rendered her either unconscious or semi-conscious. The attacker finished the job, making it look like a suicide. There's evidence to support all that. But as yet, *I* don't know why and *I* don't know who.'

'I don't know who, either!' I hadn't missed the stressed pronoun.

'You see why I keep asking about a fight,' Janice said. 'If the bruises were come by in an earlier incident, some significant physical evidence drops out of things.'

'No fight,' I said.

She smiled. 'I'm glad you didn't invent one. It wouldn't have helped – either of us. I think someone killed her, Francesca. But I need to be sure. I can't afford a mistake.'

I must have looked surprised because she flushed. 'You have to understand, there are – certain tensions among police officers as amongst people working together in any job. I have – there are certain people who resented my promotion. They'd like to see me fall flat on my face. Clash of personalities, call it. An office of any kind is a claustrophobic place. You get that.'

She'd said more than she'd intended and looked away, embarrassed.

I was thinking of the blow to Terry's head. She would have to have been disabled in some way or she'd have put up a fight. Perhaps she did put up a fight and that's when he hit her. I must have sat there thinking for long enough to make Janice curious.

'Remembering something, Francesca?'

'Nothing that matters.'

'Why don't you let me decide that?'

I was in no mood to be patronised and said so.

'Sorry,' she said. 'I didn't mean it to come out like that. But if there's anything, tell me. You want the killer found, don't you?'

'Of course I do,' I said. 'He chose to string her up from the light fitting and leave her there to strangle to death.'

'People get sexual kicks all ways. Maybe he sat there and watched because that's the sort of thing he likes. There are a lot of very sick people around, Francesca, and a lot of them act and look normal – most of the time.'

'You don't have to tell me! Do you think I haven't come across enough weirdos?' I couldn't help sounding exasperated. 'This wasn't a sex game gone wrong. This was someone who wanted her dead. Someone who hated her enough to do what he did, quite deliberately and for no other reason than to kill.'

'So,' she was watching me carefully with her pale grey gaze. 'Any ideas who? If you're so sure, you must have some theory.'

'I don't have a theory,' I told her. 'But I do know there was someone else in the house that afternoon while we were away. The place reeked of one of those male colognes when Nev and I got home. Ganesh saw a stranger earlier, acting odd. He told one of your boys in blue about it.'

'He told Sergeant Parry. We haven't been able to find anyone else who saw the man he described. He's a friend of yours, Mr Patel, isn't he?'

'Yes. Sometimes I lend a hand in the shop on a Saturday. But he didn't make up seeing someone just to help me out.'

'I didn't say that. Why should he have felt it necessary to do that?'

They like doing that, the police. They like asking you the sort of questions which, however you answer them, you sound guilty. They have suspicious minds. Even when they try to be fair, as I suppose Janice was, it comes out sounding like a caution. They can't help it. It's the mentality they have or the way they train them at police college. I could have told her that Edna had also seen a stranger, well dressed, and too intent on sneaking through the churchyard to notice her or that he'd dropped his cigarettes. But what use was Edna as a witness? Even if I could get her to talk to Janice? From what I'd seen earlier, Janice herself hadn't been having much luck with Edna. I wondered suddenly why she'd been trying.

'For about the hundredth time,' I said, 'I didn't have anything to do with her death and I don't know who killed her or why.'

'Neither do I, Francesca,' she said cheerfully. 'But by the time I've finished, I shall!'

'Bully for you!' I muttered.

The stallholder, squat, grubby little fellow, had had enough of us sitting there chatting. He came storming up and mouthed through Janice's window.

'Listen, darling, this undercover obbo or what? I'm selling a few yards of nylon net, not bleedin' heroin!'

'Got a stallholder's licence?' Janice asked.

'Do me a favour, doll!' he pleaded. 'Haven't you coppers got anything else to do but harass honest businessmen?'

'Get a licence!' Janice told him.

I could see something was bothering her as we drove off.

After a moment she asked, sounding bemused, 'Francesca, tell me honestly, do I look like a policewoman?'

'To some people, perhaps,' I told her diplomatically.

She seemed puzzled.

When I got back to the flat, Ganesh was waiting for me, sitting on the landing. A net of oranges lay on the top stair by him.

He greeted me with, 'I came to see how you were getting along in this place.'

His voice and manner were more sympathetic than when we'd last spoken at his shop, and put me vaguely in mind of someone visiting a friend in hospital. Dealing with a person who is ill and one who's having trouble must be similar. The oranges, presumably, equated with taking flowers to the patient. I've always thought that it was nicer to take fruit to the sick than flowers. Fruit doesn't make you think of funerals.

'Don't ask!' I said as I opened the flat door to let us in. 'I've been trawling Camden with Inspector Janice, trying to find an alibi.'

'And did you?' Ganesh dropped the string of fruit on the table and gave me a sharp look.

I told him what had happened. 'It's something,' I finished.

He shrugged and looked disapprovingly round the flat. 'I'll make us a cup of tea,' he said and went out into the kitchen whence I could hear him rattling crockery.

Whilst it's always nice to have a lover, sex can get in the way and sometimes what's needed is just a friend. That's what Ganesh is, a friend.

A friend is someone you can tell your troubles to, argue

with, not see for weeks and then meet again and take up where you left off, all without getting tied up and wrung out emotionally. Problems, I think, are what constitute the basis of the friendship between Gan and me. He has his problems and I have mine. I don't entirely understand his, nor he mine, but it doesn't matter. I listen to him and he listens to me. It doesn't solve anything but it certainly helps.

Of course, I'd be fooling myself if I told you the familiar man/woman chemistry played no part at all. Sometimes I see Ganesh looking at me with half a question in his eyes, and I dare say he catches me looking at him in the same way from time to time. But that's as far as it's ever got. Things between us work well as they are and you know what they say, if a thing's not broke, don't fix it. Sometimes I think it's a pity, though.

Right now I felt absolutely whacked. I really didn't want to talk to anyone, even Ganesh, but I needed all the support I could get.

As we sat in the kitchen drinking the tea he said, 'I've tried asking around too, Fran, customers, mostly. But it's hard to get anyone to talk about it now. It was a nine-day wonder. Now all they do is moan about our prices. If they ever knew anything they've forgotten it.'

'My impression exactly,' I said gloomily. 'But thanks for trying, anyway.'

'Dad says, he still needs someone in the shop on a Friday and Saturday, if you want to earn some extra money.'

I told him I didn't think his father really wanted me around the place. I was a bird of ill-omen, filling Gan's head with ideas of independence and a free lifestyle, consorting with suspicious types, at odds with the police.

'They like you,' Ganesh said obstinately. 'You personally. The other – it's a clash of cultures. They don't
understand but they still like you.'

'They think I'll lead you astray,' I said unwisely.

He got angry then. 'For God's sake, Fran! Do you think
I want to spend my entire life flogging spuds and bananas
to old women with string bags? Listen!'

He leaned across the table. 'I've been thinking. We
both need to get out of where we are. There is a way. If
I've learnt something from the shop it's the basics of
running a business. You and I together, we could run any
kind of business we liked! We can go to the bank, get
them to put together a small business package for us! Get
one of those Start-Up grants! I've been keeping my eye
open, looking for a suitable place. And if we needed help
with the accounts, to start off, Jay would do that for us, no
charge, family.'

It was the most hare-brained idea I'd heard in a long
time and coming from Ganesh, whom I saw as sensible, it
was unbelievable. He didn't honestly think it would work,
did he? Even if I had the aptitude for business, which I
don't. I supposed his family had been giving him hassle
and that's what had brought all this about, but he'd
betrayed himself with the idea of Jay helping with the
accounts. With one breath he was talking of branching out
on his own. With the next, he was still relying on the
family network.

Rather unkindly I retorted, 'Forget it. It's a barmy idea.
It'd drive me round the bend. I certainly couldn't stick
your brother-in-law coming round once a week to audit
the books!'

'You might,' he said touchily, 'think about it.'

'I've got the police on my back right now. How'm I supposed to think about anything else? I can't even think straight about what happened at the house any longer!'

He mumbled a bit and I could see he was annoyed with me. But I couldn't imagine myself, even when the present crisis was over, sitting over the books every evening with or without Jay at my shoulder, trying to make them balance. Worrying about staff and business rates, profit and loss? I think I'd pitch myself out of the window. But it illustrated, if nothing else did, the reason why Ganesh and I couldn't ever progress beyond friendship. When it came down to lifestyles, he was a traditionalist at heart. Me, I was just me, a gypsy if anything, an urban nomad. No fixed abode, no fixed employment, no fixed anything. Another word for that is freedom.

But none of that helped right now. I didn't want to hurt his feelings and tried politely to explain to him how I saw it. He said it didn't matter and took himself off, still looking huffy. Alone, I sat eating the oranges, one after the other. It's called comfort-bingeing.

I did need the extra money so, in the end, I went over to the shop and helped out. I thought the customers would recognise me and ask me questions, but Ganesh had been right. All they were worried about was making sure I didn't sell them any bruised fruit and making me pick all the yellow leaves off the greens.

Going back to the flat in the evenings was something I began to dread.

For the first time in my life I was actually afraid, although I didn't tell Ganesh. I hadn't been frightened in the squat or in any other place I'd lived in and I'd lived in

83

some crummy ones. But that tower block was unbelievable. The winds whistled round it and right through it and when I woke up in the middle of the night I had a dreadful feeling of being lost in some kind of nightmarish desert. I felt that when dawn came I'd find everyone had gone and left me entirely alone in that place. I can't describe it. I wouldn't wish it on my worst enemy.

I took to switching on the light if I awoke and reading till morning. I was getting through Nev's books at the rate of about one a night and getting bags under my eyes as well. I told myself I was at least making up for my missed education. Nev's book choice was on the heavy side.

One afternoon Inspector Janice turned up on my doorstep. With luck I'd at least seen the last of Parry. It was the first time Janice had tackled me in the surroundings of my own home.

I made her coffee and let her have the armchair Euan had got from the Sally Army for me. When she sat in it, the springs collapsed under her. Her knees shot up to chin level and she grabbed the balding plush arms and glared at me.

'I was being polite!' I told her. 'Not playing a practical joke on you. You can sit on this one, if you prefer.' I indicated the tubular aluminium and plastic effort I was sitting on.

She struggled to the edge of the armchair and perched there. Her mug of coffee was on the floor by her feet. 'This is a dreadful place for you to be living in!' she blurted. 'How did you get into all this mess, Fran? You're young, fit and you've got all your marbles!'

For the first time she wasn't wearing her police hat to

ask questions. She really wanted to know, for herself. Perhaps for that reason I didn't resent her words.

'It's a place,' I told her. 'You don't want to know the story of my life. I became homeless. It's easier than you think.'

'Tell me!' she persisted.

'The person I was living with became ill. She had to go into hospital long-term. She was the tenant, not me, and the landlord wanted me out.'

I was telling her the truth but still not telling her how it really was. After Dad died, Grandma Varady and I had stayed on together. But after a while she became confused. I think it was Dad dying. She couldn't really cope with it. She began to talk as if he was still alive and even worse, she began to call me Eva, which was my mother's name. It was as if she couldn't remember that my mother had left.

'Bondi's late this evening, Eva,' she'd say. Bondi was the name she'd had for my father whose name had been Stephen.

She also started getting up in the middle of the night believing it was morning and wandering out of the house and down the street in her nightgown. Her doctor found her a place in a home. I'd always sworn I'd never let Grandma Varady go into such a place but things never turn out the way you expect. I couldn't look after her. She no longer knew who I was. She lived about six months in the home and died there in her sleep. By then I was already living at the first of many 'irregular' addresses.

I said to Janice, 'Look, I've had jobs, dozens of them. But when employers find out you don't have a regular address, they can't get rid of you fast enough. Or else they take advantage of the situation to offer you slave wages. You drop out of the system. You have to fight to get your foot back in the door.'

'So tell me about systems!' she invited. 'All systems exclude you if you don't kick your way in. Try making it as a woman officer in the CID.'

She had a point but I didn't want her to think I was whingeing and I told her so. 'I'll get out of here one day, one way or another, on my own two little flat feet! Getting this murder business behind me would be a start.'

She nodded, picked up her mug and sipped. 'I'm going through divorce,' she said suddenly. 'So I know how you feel, believe me. When I get the divorce behind me, I'll be all right. Right now . . . ' She bent her head over the mug.

I'd never seen any rings on her hand so I hadn't reckoned on her being married. But there was no reason why she shouldn't be.

'Is he another plod, I mean, police officer?'

She gave a rueful grin. 'No, he works for a bank. I'm rather sensitive about living space myself at the moment.' She jerked her head to indicate the room. 'Tom, my soon-to-be-ex, wants to sell up our house and split the proceeds. I'm damned if I'm going to lose my home! I decorated every room in that house! Up a ladder with a tin of emulsion every evening after I got in from work! While he sat in front of the telly or pushed off to play squash with his mates.'

She sounded really fierce. Tom obviously had a fight on his hands. I sympathised with her and made a few encouraging remarks.

We were getting on pretty well together by now. Then

Janice seemed to remember she was there on official business. She put the mug on the floor and sat up as straight as she could in the chair.

'Finding someone who could remember you and Porter in Camden has helped, Fran, but the superintendent still isn't happy. He can't believe that you knew so little about Theresa Monkton. Where she went during the day and other people she met. She lived with you. Even if she wasn't talkative, she must have let the odd comment slip. When you live with people you find out about them by a kind of osmosis. I found out plenty about Tom by living with him. Not because he told me, but because you can't hide from people you're with every day and night. You're either not trying to remember or you're holding out on us. Give yourself a break. Give me a break. Come up with something, can't you?'

I told her I would if I could, but as I'd told her before, even though I'd seen Theresa every day, I just hadn't known her. 'What about her family? They have to have known more about her than I did.'

'She hadn't been in touch with them in months. They had been trying to find her. You can imagine how distressed they are.'

I cast about desperately. 'How about Lucy? She brought Theresa along in the first place. Did you find her?'

'Lucy Ho? Yes. She met Theresa by chance in a pub and felt sorry for her.' Janice looked both irritated and depressed. 'There's a sort of vacuum around that girl and I'm beginning to think it was deliberately created.'

She saw I was about to deny responsibility and added quickly, 'I don't mean it was created by you or the others. I mean, she created it herself.'

Janice hesitated as if unsure whether to confide in me. Then she hunched forward on the chair edge and went on in a rush, 'Fran, think about this. No friends, no visitors, no background details about herself, no attempt to mix with the others and be friendly. To me that's someone trying to hide, terrified of giving clues.'

I did think about it and conceded she might be right.

'She was careful not to leave any trail for someone else to follow,' Janice insisted. I could see it was her pet theory.

I played devil's advocate. '*Someone* followed it. Because *someone* found her.'

I sounded hard-boiled but I wasn't feeling that way. I was feeling guilty. It had never occurred to me that Terry had been scared, living in fear all the time she was with us, and in need of help. None of us had offered it. I reasoned that she hadn't seemed afraid. But then, I hadn't tried looking beneath the surface of the front she'd put up. All right, she couldn't have expected much help from Nev or Squib, and Declan had his own problems and had left. But I could have listened. I could have tried to give her some support.

'I didn't want to know what made her tick,' I said. 'She lived with us, but she was a stranger.'

And that *was* the truth, although I was just beginning to see it myself for the first time.

Janice struggled out of the chair. 'Thanks for the coffee. I'll be in touch.'

I felt even more depressed when she'd left. I realised that I was feeling grief for Terry, something I hadn't felt before. I wasn't proud of myself. I should have felt it before.

Now I knew that I owed her. I hadn't helped her then, but I could still help now if I knew where to start. I gave it a lot of thought without coming up with an answer.

Ganesh came over in the van and took me to our old place, down by the river, where we sat on a chunk of concrete and looked across to the Crystal City and watched gulls picking over debris on the mudflats.

Gan said, 'I wrote a poem, about her, about Terry.'

Gan is a good poet. Generally he only shows his poetry to me, although he has been known to read out some of it to Mad Edna. The last time he did that, she said it was very good and had he thought of taking up the piano?

'I'm not bloody Nöel Coward!' Ganesh had told her.

So he read his poem to me now, the one about Terry. It was strange hearing him read it because he hadn't known her as well as I had, and had no reason to feel guilty as I did. But it was as if he felt what I felt and was able to express it better than I could in words.

When he'd finished, I said, 'Thanks, Gan.'

'Perhaps we aren't meant to know,' he said, tucking the paper away in his leather jacket. 'What happened to her really, I mean.'

'I want to know!' I retorted. 'But short of Edna recovering her sanity and backing up your story, I can't see where to begin!'

That must have been giving Fate a gentle hint. The next day, out of the blue, I had another visitor at the flat.

The doorbell rang as I was trying to block up some of the gaps round the bedroom window with ready-mixed filler.

I'm not much of a handyman but I was making a fair job of it and I was annoyed to be called away.

I peered through the little spyhole and saw a very smart, elderly gent outside. More out of curiosity than anything, I opened the door.

'Miss Varady?' he asked very politely, and raised his hat. 'I'm Alastair Monkton, Theresa's grandfather.' He held out his hand.

I apologised for having Tetrion smeared over me and suggested it would be better if we didn't shake hands.

He followed me into the sitting room, trying not to look too appalled. I invited him to take the notorious armchair, while I washed my hands and brushed my hair.

When I came back I asked him if he'd like a cup of coffee.

He probably didn't fancy coffee made in a place like that. He said, 'I don't want to impose, Miss Varady. You realise I want to talk about my granddaughter. Perhaps you'd allow me to take you to lunch?'

I wanted to talk about his granddaughter, too. He was hoping I could tell him something but I was hoping he'd tell me.

Moreover, any lunch he'd buy me had to be better than anything I had in my kitchen. I said 'yes' straight away.

Chapter Six

Monkton had a taxi waiting downstairs. It must have been building up a terrific fare on the clock but he didn't seem to mind. The taxi-driver certainly didn't, although you could see he didn't much like waiting around in that district.

We went to an Indian restaurant which Alastair Monkton said was very good. It certainly wasn't like the Indian take-aways I knew. It had a carpet on the floor and starched white damask tablecloths and the waiters wore white jackets.

The food on the other tables looked and smelled pretty good too, nearly as good as Ganesh's mother's. The menu was the size of *The Times* and it took nearly as long to read it. I settled for the special fish curry and he chose the lamb curry with ginger.

When we'd had time to settle down and size one another up across the Naan bread, he asked, 'I hope you won't take this amiss, Francesca. But may I ask how old you are?'

I told him, twenty-one. Also that I preferred to be called Fran.

'Twenty-one?' He looked for a moment as if his thoughts had drifted away somewhere. He said, more to himself than to me, 'No age, really. No age at all. Life before you. Everything to do. Everything to live for.'

He must have forgotten the flat we'd just left.

He turned his gaze back to me and rejoined the present. 'Then you're much of an age as Theresa, my grand-daughter. She was just twenty. We had thought, hoped, she would have phoned home on her birthday, but she didn't. We didn't know where she was. We couldn't even send her a card. We couldn't help her at all and she obviously needed help so desperately.'

'We called her Terry. That was her idea.' I hesitated. 'She was doing what she wanted to do. I know that's hard to explain to you. She didn't want help. She wanted to be independent.'

I realised as I spoke how futile that sounded. Independence takes money. Not for nothing is it called 'independent means'. Money with no strings attached. Without it, you can forget independence. I realised I'd been deluding myself with notions of my own independence, when all I was, truly, was at a loose end. Nevertheless it was a freedom of sorts.

Alastair wouldn't have understood. He would have sent Terry money if she'd phoned home on her birthday or any other day. But it would have come with chains, not just strings, attached. For that reason alone, she would never have reached for that phone.

I knew he was going to ask me next if I had any idea how her death could have happened, and I didn't. He was so nice and obviously Terry's death had been such a dreadful blow to him, that I really wished I could help.

'She was very quiet,' I said. 'She didn't talk much about herself. I never saw her with a boyfriend.'

I knew she'd been keen on Declan but that didn't count because it didn't come to anything.

'I've been to Cheshire to talk to young Nevil Porter.'

That surprised me and I must have looked it. He smiled and said, 'I thought he seemed a pleasant young man. Sadly, it was obvious he'd been ill. You too, if I may say so, seem a pleasant, sensible young woman. I'm glad that Theresa wasn't in with a bad crowd, even if you were all living illegally in that condemned house. You and young Porter, you seem to be so, well, normal. A matter of – er – style, aside. Porter's people seemed very decent. I dare say yours, too. I admit I've been forced to reassess my earlier impressions.'

Obviously he hadn't met Squib. I rather hoped he didn't. He seemed to be thinking over something again. He was staring down at his plate and he looked very sad. I felt very sorry for him but a little embarrassed too. I looked away and saw that people at the next table were looking at us and whispering. We must have appeared a strange couple, Alastair and I. The woman at the table looked shocked. She probably thought Alastair had picked me up off the street for lunch followed by a session involving leather and bondage. I treated her to a stony glare and she flushed and looked away.

'Is something wrong?' I hadn't realised Alastair had come out of his reverie.

'No. We were getting funny looks from the next table so I gave them a funny look back.'

'Oh?' He almost smiled. 'I see, quite.'

There was an awkward little pause. The waiter brought

our food. I was feeling very hungry by now so I started on mine.

Alastair pushed a fork into his but didn't eat. 'Theresa first ran away from school when she was sixteen. She came home of her own accord but refused to return to the school. About six months after she came home, she ran away again. We traced her quite quickly and persuaded her to come back.'When she was just eighteen she left again. We had more trouble finding her that time, because she was no longer under age and the authorities were less helpful. They pointed out she had a history of running away. There was no reason to suppose anything had happened to her. We tried every other way we knew to trace her. We even contacted the National Missing Persons Helpline and they managed to get that little magazine to show her photograph, the one the young people sell on the street.'

'You mean, *The Big Issue*?' I couldn't see Alastair poring over the magazine sold by and on behalf of the homeless, and it almost made me smile, the image was so incongruous. Luckily I managed to keep a straight face.

'We'd had no idea,' he was saying, 'until we contacted the helpline, just how many people go missing every year. Where are they all?' He sounded bewildered.

I could have replied that some of them were on the streets and some had turned to crime. A few were probably dead and some others, against all the odds, had made perfectly good lives for themselves elsewhere. But I didn't interrupt. He wanted to tell me about it. He was trying to explain what had happened, not just to me, but to himself.

'As it happened, she came home again by herself, just as she'd done the first time. She had been travelling with a sort of hippy convoy. New-Age travellers, they call themselves.

She was in a pitiful state and had developed a bad bronchial cough. She stayed with us until she was fit again and then, one day – it was so trivial . . . '

He was looking distressed so I finished for him. 'There was a family quarrel of some sort and she left again.'

'Oh, she told you?'

I shook my head and grimaced. It was always the same story.

'The last time I ever saw my granddaughter alive,' he said sadly, 'we exchanged harsh words. I'd give anything in the world to be able to take them back. To have her back. She was wilful and undisciplined. But I just don't understand how anyone could harm her. She was a beautiful girl.'

I mumbled that he wasn't the first person to feel that way after a bereavement. That he oughtn't to feel responsible for anything. Terry had been old enough to make her own decisions.

'I know things weren't easy for her.' He'd listened to me but I don't think anything I'd said had helped. He had to work it out for himself. 'Her parents divorced when she was thirteen. Neither of them was in a position to offer her a home, so naturally she came to live with me. Looking back, I realise she may have felt unwanted, although I assure you she wasn't! I did try, we all tried . . . '

His voice tailed away. I wondered, since Terry's parents had taken off somewhere, who 'we' were. 'We all'. That suggested more than two. I asked, 'What did her parents do? After they broke up, I mean? Since neither of them had room for Terry?'

He gave a little start as if his mind had been drifting off again. Conversation with him was a little difficult in more ways than one. He wasn't one of those elderly people who are confused. His mind was clear enough, but it didn't like focusing on one person, me, for more than five minutes.

'I do apologise!' he said, as if he'd realised what I was thinking. 'I suppose it's one of the drawbacks of age that one wool-gathers! My son, Theresa's father—' Alastair's voice had become stilted and it was obvious relations between father and son were cool. 'He works in America and has remarried there. Theresa's mother took up her former career which involved a great deal of travel. She's in the fashion business.'

I thought of that expensive knitted jacket of Terry's. A conscience-salving present from her mother?

Abruptly Alastair added, 'Marcia – that's my former daughter-in-law, Theresa's mother, has been to see me. She's naturally distressed and some harsh words were spoken. She was offensive. She seems to blame me for the way Theresa kept leaving home. I have taken the charitable view that Marcia's words were spoken in haste and grief. In the circumstances, I shall overlook the unpleasant nature of them!' He gave a snort. 'My belief is that Marcia feels guilty. So she damn well should! I hope she feels as guilty as hell!' He stopped short and muttered, 'Excuse me!'

I thought Marcia was lucky the old chap was so well bred. It now seemed Terry and I had had more in common than I'd thought. At least only my mother had dumped me – and my dad at the same time. Terry'd been effectively dumped by both her parents.

'When Philip and Marcia parted,' Alastair was saying, 'it seemed the only practical solution for Theresa to remain with me. It meant I had the melancholy task of informing both her parents of the dreadful tragedy.'

Unaware of what Janice had told me, he went on to explain, 'We saw it in the newspaper. That is, I didn't see it, but – someone else did. Only a small item, a young woman, police seeking next of kin. We all felt it would be Theresa. We'd been expecting something of the sort. Yet it was still a terrible blow.'

He raised his eyes to peer at me over the table. They were very pale blue, the whites discoloured, the rims watery. He looked frail, for all his neatness and upright bearing.

'She was an innocent. She thought she knew about the world, about life. But of course, she didn't. She didn't see the dangers. I tried to warn her that living as she did, she ran such risks. She wouldn't listen. I was just an old man who knew nothing about modern youth. But some things don't change. Human nature doesn't, more's the pity. Sooner or later she was going to find herself dealing with people who would be stronger, more ruthless, and I have to say, cleverer than she was. One wants to protect . . . one can't. That is the worst of it. I couldn't protect her. Too old. Just too old.'

He rubbed his hands together in a nervous gesture. The skin was thin over the back, paper-like, and the veins stood up corded and thick. I didn't know how old he was and wished I did. But I noticed a slight yellowness to the fingertips. He was a life-long smoker.

I remembered Edna and her golden packet and the matches, too. But this old man couldn't have done violence of the kind I'd seen done to Terry. Nor would he have wished to harm her. He had loved her.

He pulled himself together and began to speak again, more briskly. 'My son is flying over for the funeral. They –

the police – say, we'll be able to bury Theresa quite soon. They'll be finished – all they want to do.' He pushed his plate away and I didn't fancy eating any more, either.

When he spoke again, however, his voice was firmer. I guessed he thought out beforehand what he wanted to say and had it well rehearsed. He didn't look at me as he spoke, but kept his eyes fixed on his hands, clasped on the tablecloth.

'There is a strong possibility that her death came about through murder, not suicide or any other kind of mishap. The police have classed it as suspicious.' It must have cost him, but he went on, 'They believe she was knocked unconscious by someone who stood behind her and a little to one side. Almost certainly someone she knew and had admitted to the house.'

He cast me an apologetic look to show he wasn't accusing me. 'Whoever did it arranged her body afterwards to make it look as if she'd hanged herself. Even if she'd started to come round before he completed his task, it would have been too late to defend herself, to stop him . . . ' His voice faltered but he went on steadily enough, once he'd had a moment to pull himself together. He was a tough old fellow under the outward frailty. 'You saw the body.'

It was a statement, not a question. I nodded confirmation.

'The – ah – fixture in the ceiling from which she – the body – hung wasn't particularly secure. My granddaughter weighed very little. All the same, had she been conscious at any stage and thrashed around, she, the rope, everything, would've come crashing down. It leads the police to conclude that she was unconscious throughout. That, in turn, would seem to rule out suicide.'

It was true that Terry had been an anorexic seven-stoner. Anyone, virtually, could have lifted her. I could have done so in an emergency. To talk of 'he' might be jumping to conclusions. A woman might well have done it. But dead weights are more difficult to handle, or so I'd been led to believe. If Terry was unconscious, would that have made her necessarily easier to lift? I wasn't sure.

He had raised his eyes and was studying my face. I'd been lost in my own thoughts and must have looked startled. He gave a small, dry smile.

'I want to know for sure, Francesca. I want to know what happened. I want to know if it was, after all, suicide. The police have not completely ruled that out. Or if it was murder and if so, who killed her and why. I want your help.' He hesitated. 'This is an unpleasant subject to discuss with you. Perhaps I shouldn't have done so. But I came to you for a particular reason.'

'It's OK,' I told him, trying to disguise my unease.

'I have a proposition to make to you, Francesca.'

The people at the next table clearly thought he had, too. The murmured words, 'at his age...' floated across. I hoped Alastair hadn't heard them.

'The police are working hard on this. I have no criticisms of them. However, they didn't know Theresa and you did. They didn't live in that house with her, and you did. They don't know the world she moved in – and you do. I want to ask you if you would undertake inquiries for me into her death.'

'Me?' I must just have gaped at him. It had been the last thing I'd been expecting. I began to stutter objections, that I didn't know how, hadn't the facilities, that there were private inquiry agencies better placed than I was to do as he wished.

He cut me short. 'Private detective agencies don't handle that kind of investigation. I've been in touch with a couple. They seem to spend their time serving summonses and following errant spouses around town. In any case, I've the same objection to them as to the police. They don't have the first-hand knowledge that you have.'

'The police won't like it,' I said. Janice's reaction didn't bear thinking about.

'They won't have to know.'

That took my breath away. He was a surprise, was old Alastair, in more ways than one. But he was right, the police would have to be unaware of my activities or they'd put a stop to them immediately. With or without a charge of obstruction.

'I'm sure you can be discreet.' He cleared his throat. 'I admit I had some reservations about asking a young woman to do this unpleasant task. But Nevil Porter was clearly in no state, when I saw him, to undertake anything. I understand the third member of your group might be unsuitable. I haven't met him, but from what I've heard, I fancy he would prove unreliable.'

'You think I'm reliable?' I had to ask.

His faded eyes fixed mine with disconcerting sharpness. 'Yes, I do. I thought you would be before we met, and now we have met and talked, I'm sure of it. I will, of course, meet all your expenses and – if you obtain any firm evidence of either suicide or murder – pay you a further sum. Oh, and should you get into trouble with the police over this, I shall naturally come forward and provide any legal representation you might need.'

That was a relief. Of a sort.

He put a hand to his inner breast pocket and took out an envelope which he put on the table, propped against a wine glass. 'Two hundred and fifty pounds on account. There will be a further two hundred and fifty on positive results. Does that seem fair to you?'

It sounded like a fortune to me, but I had to make it clear to him, that he might be throwing money away. 'I may turn up nothing.'

'I realise that. But I sense you are a determined young woman. Perhaps, if you turn up nothing, as you put it – it will be because there is nothing to find? In other words, perhaps my girl took her own life, after all. Will you do it?'

'You're crazy,' said Ganesh with such finality that I didn't feel like arguing with him about it. I'd already worked out for myself that I couldn't be in my right mind.

'It was difficult to refuse him, Gan. Poor old chap. Basically, he just wants to know what she'd been doing in the weeks before she died. He's desperate to fill in the gap between the last time he saw her and – when we found her.'

'It's occurred to you that grief might have unhinged the old fellow?'

'He seemed pretty sane. He gave me his card.' I took it out and put it on the greasy table in the café where we sat discussing Alastair's request. The proprietor was writing up the day's menu on a blackboard. He was having a little trouble.

Sosages and egs
Pissa with toping of choise

There was nothing to suggest that his cooking was an improvement on his spelling. Certainly not the smell of ancient grease coming from the kitchen.

'We're not eating here, are we?'

Gan grunted and shook his head. He was turning the card over and over, although nothing was written on the back. 'Abbotsfield near Basingstoke, Hampshire,' he read aloud. 'And what's this, Astara Stud?'

'Horses, I assume.'

'What sort of horses? Racehorses?'

'I don't know, do I? I've taken his two-fifty on account and I'm going to do my best to earn it, right?'

'Don't look at me,' he said discouragingly. 'I'm not going to help you.'

'Well, thanks. I'll manage on my own.'

We left the café and bought two foil boxes of special fried rice from the Chinese take-away. We sat by the river to eat, looking across at the Crystal City.

'Where are you going to start?' Gan asked.

'I'm going to talk to Edna.'

He tipped out the remains of his rice for the gulls. 'And that's going to be worth two hundred and fifty quid, is it?'

Needless to say, it wasn't. Edna had chosen to obliterate everything from her mind relating to the man she'd seen and the cigarette packet.

'Have you still got it, Edna? Or the packet of matches?'

She pushed her hands into the sleeves of her grubby coat and hunched on a tomb, sulking.

'Come on, Edna, I'll buy you a new packet.'

She wriggled away from me along the tomb. 'Don't want it.'

'Has something upset you, Edna?'

She raised furious eyes. 'They took them all away!'

I didn't understand at first and then I realised that there was a curious absence of cats around the place. My heart sank. 'Who, Edna?'

'Animal charity, called themselves. Came with little cages in a van. I told them, they didn't need any animal charity. They had me! I looked after them! She said—'

'She, Edna?'

'Skinny young woman in charge. Face like a ferret. She said, they'd find new homes for them. Don't believe it. Don't believe anyone. Don't want anyone. Don't want you!'

End of conversation.

I was more than disappointed because I'd already had thoughts I hadn't confided in Gan. The book of matches Edna had shown me had been printed with the name of a wine bar in Winchester. Winchester wasn't so far from Basingstoke, and that, in turn, was near Abbotsfield and the Astara Stud. That book of matches was evidence and it had gone.

It didn't change my mind. The police were looking in London for the answer to the mystery. I had an idea that was the wrong place. Down there in Hampshire was where the story started. And down there in Hampshire was where I might end up having to go.

Having a permanent address of my own now, even if it was only the flat, helped in one way and I was able to find another job. I still had Alastair's money, but it wasn't for day-to-day living. It was for my inquiries, and so far they hadn't cost me anything.

It was a pretty lousy job, waitressing in another café which sold nothing but fry-ups and slabs of bread pudding to truck-drivers and labourers from building sites. My clothes and hair stank of frying oil when I got home but the tips were good if the pay was meagre. I also got free food, which meant eating what was on the menu. I came out in spots but I saved money.

In between I trailed from pub to pub and squat to squat, trying to trace Terry. Sometimes my path crossed one left by the police. Generally they'd been ahead of me every time. I had to give them full marks. Whether they'd found out anything I didn't know, but I doubted it. No one had anything to tell me and they were more likely to talk to me than to the coppers. I even found Lucy again but she had nothing to tell me. She'd met Terry by chance and knew as little about her as I did. Lucy had a job now, child-minding. She seemed happy. I was glad.

this time, I'd heard nothing from Squib which didn't really surprise me. On the other hand I had been to the hostel and in theory, at least, he ought to know that. I wanted to know he was OK; I wanted to know what the police had been saying to him and he to them; and I wanted another talk about Terry. Squib was, after all, one of the few people other than myself who'd known her.

Accordingly, one evening after I'd finished my shift at the café, I went back to the hostel and settled myself on the stone wall outside. After a few minutes a woman came out, smiling, of course. Did they ever stop? She asked if I needed anything. I told her I was waiting for Henry and refused her offer of a nice, hot dinner which, from the smell oozing through the basement grill, was mostly cabbage.

She left me on my wall which was hard. The coldness of it seeped through my jeans. I wondered whether I'd get piles and kicked my dangling legs back and forth to generate a bit of heat. To occupy my mind, I listed my favourite films in order of preference. I'd done that before. It took me quite a long time and *The Good, The Bad and The Ugly* came out on top as it usually did.

As the evening wore on, the residents began to drift past me into the hostel and the boiled greens dinner. There were winos, who left their empty sherry bottles stacked by the door, dropouts and junkies, with the occasional out-and-out psycho, twitching and rolling his eyes, but no Squib. When it was nearly dark and I was about to give up, I saw a small white shape trotting towards me out of the gloom. Squib's dog.

Squib himself emerged from the shadows. I jumped up and nearly hugged him. I can't say he responded with equal enthusiasm.

'Hullo, Fran,' he said, trying to sidle past me.

I told him I'd been before and left a note, had he seen it? He mumbled and tried to get away again but I grabbed his sleeve.

'Listen, you don't want whatever they're dishing up in there. I'll buy you egg and chips. I've got the money.'

'Cafés don't let dogs in,' he muttered.

'Then I'll buy us all a burger from the van along the street there, the dog too.' The van had arrived about ten minutes earlier and was setting up in business, smoke belching from it. 'I've been sitting here waiting for you for ages and my backside's numb,' I added.

He gave in and we went to the van, first customers of the evening and the food hadn't yet got leathery. I bought Squib and myself a burger each with all the trimmings, and one for the dog without onions, mustard or pickle. We sat on a bench under a streetlight to eat them.

'How's it going, Squib?' I asked, licking my fingers.

'I'm going to be clearing out soon,' he said. 'I think I'll go travelling again.'

'They've told you to go?'

'Naw, but they don't like him.' He pointed at the dog which had gobbled up its burger and was eyeing mine. 'And I don't like them.'

'What about the police? They've been in my hair.'

'I gotta report in twice a week and stay at the friggin' hostel. Otherwise, they don't bother.'

I told him there was no justice. They didn't leave me alone. Why didn't they pester him in the same way?

'You're bright, ain'tcha?' said Squib. 'They ask you questions because they think you got answers. Me, I'm thick. They don't bother.'

'I don't know anything, Squib, but I'm trying to find out.'

'Whaffor?' He was getting bored, fidgeting and wanting to get up and walk off.

I wasn't going to tell him about Alastair. I told him, 'For my own sake. I want to know why she had to go and die in our house, like that. I want to know more about her.'

There was a silence. 'There was a bloke asking for her one time.'

It was Squib speaking but the words were so unexpected

I found myself looking round to see if someone else had joined us. 'What do you mean? At the house?'

'No, in the pub, couple of streets down, The Prince of Wales. He had her photo and was showing it around. He showed it me. I don't split on a mate, so I said I didn't know her. He said he was going round all the pubs. I wished him luck. Off he went. Flash feller.'

I suppressed a tingle of excitement. 'When was this, Squib?'

Asking him to be specific was a little like asking Edna. He looked vague. 'Couple of weeks before she topped herself.'

'And you didn't tell any of us?'

In the lamplight his face had an eerie sheen on it and his expression was aggrieved. 'Matter of fact, I did, see? I told her, told Terry. Reckoned she ought to know.'

'What did she say?' Keeping my own tone nonchalant was getting difficult. I had to try not to squeak.

Squib racked what passed for his memory. 'She was scared, I reckon. But I told her it would be all right, because I'd said nothing. She give me a fiver.'

'Five pounds? Terry did?'

'Yeah.' Squib frowned. 'It was more'n I expected. But he'd have given me that, wouldn't he? The bloke in the pub? If I'd told him. So it was fair.'

Both fair and shrewd. Squib hadn't given away information that time, but he might be tempted if the inquirer came back again, brandishing a fat wallet. Terry had been making sure. I was annoyed, though, remembering how she never had any money when it came to household expenses.

'I wish you'd told me,' I said.

He settled his woolly hat over his ears. 'Why should I? Wasn't nobody's business but hers.'

True – at the time. Now it was mine. 'Come on, Squib!' I ordered him firmly, 'what else did she say?'

'Nothing!' he protested. 'I forget.' After a moment, he added sulkily, 'She said her people must be trying to find her. That's where the bloke had come from.'

'Did she name a place?'

'Chuck it, Fran, will you? I forget!'

'Basingstoke?' I tried. 'Winchester? Abbotsfield? Ring any bells?'

'Horses,' mumbled Squib. 'It had something to do with nags.'

'Squib,' I said, 'was it called the Astara Stud?'

He muttered, 'Can't remember!' but he didn't mutter it fast enough. He remembered, all right.

I sat there, both excited and frustrated, because he was still holding out on me.

Suddenly he asked, sounding odd, sort of shy and hopeful mixed, 'Reckon her people got money?'

'Probably,' I said. 'Everyone's got more money than us.'

That seemed to make an impression on him and he sat thinking about it until, without warning, he stood up. The dog, which had been curled up under the bench, jumped up too.

'It's getting late,' he said. 'They close the doors nine o'clock. After that, you're locked out. It stops us staying down the pub late. They don't allow drink, no beer, nothing.'

He was already setting off down the street. I called after him, 'You can still set out your bedroll at my place!'

'Forget it!' he called back. 'I got plans.'

I dismissed that because Squib had never been known to have a plan of any kind, ever.

I should have paid more attention. Especially I should have realised that, being a novice where thinking was concerned, if Squib had finally got a plan, he was bound to screw it up.

Chapter Seven

My life continued on its usual doomed course. After two weeks of dishing out fry-ups by day and sleuthing around the less savoury parts of London by evening, someone left the fryer switched on overnight by mistake and my place of employment burned down. So I was out of work again. I sat in my highly undesirable residence and wondered where else I could go to ask about Terry. I'd reached the end of the road, as far as I could see.

By now I'd read nearly all Nev's books and reached the point where I couldn't stay in that flat another forty-eight hours. The estate's kids had taken to rampaging up and down the staircase. I had to lock and bar the door. The mould on the bathroom wall, despite my washing it down with bleach, was spreading and there were scuttling noises behind the rotten skirting boards which I was sure meant rats. I'd had enough.

Parry hadn't been to see me for a while, nor had Janice been in touch again. I felt a little hurt by that. I wondered if she was still on the case. Maybe she was having problems over the divorce and her mind was on that.

I knew I wasn't forgotten by the police in general. I'd

never be forgotten until they closed the file on Terry. But I didn't see how they ever would. No one knew what happened that Monday afternoon.

I was still thinking about Terry in the way I'd started to think after Janice's last visit. I still felt I owed her and there had to be something I could do. I'd made a start. I had what Ganesh and Edna had told me, added to Squib's story. I wished I also had Edna's packet of matches but, unfortunately, that was lost for ever.

I did go back to the hostel and try to see Squib again. But they told me, still smiling, that he'd cleared out, as he'd told me he meant to do. Everything was pointing me in one direction only.

I took myself to Victoria Coach station and asked about National buses down to Basingstoke. The return fare was cheap enough even for me. I went to see Ganesh and asked if I could borrow a camera. It seemed to me the sort of basic equipment a detective would need, although I wasn't sure what I would snap with it.

'Not an expensive one, just an ordinary one, easy to use. Nothing that it would be disastrous to lose or anything. Though I'll take great care of it.'

'What are you up to now?' he asked suspiciously.

I told him I intended going down to the country, to the Astara Stud, and seeing what I could find out.

He was aghast. 'You can't do that! The old fellow thinks you're investigating up here, scene of the crime. He doesn't expect you down there, stirring up trouble! If you ask me, it's time you called him and told him you're quitting. You have tried and you can't do more than that.'

'I've done nothing, Gan, except trail round in the

footsteps of the police, asking the same questions they asked and getting the same blank looks. I'm nowhere further on and frankly, it's a matter of pride! I *will* get to the bottom of this!'

'You're in enough trouble, already,' he argued. 'You don't know anything about this family except what the old man told you over lunch. Who's to know how accurate that was? You said his thoughts kept wandering off. He probably forgot half a dozen things. That woman inspector would throw a wobbly if she knew you meant to go there. You know sod all about being a detective. What have you found out so far? Nothing! You admit it yourself!'

'All the more reason to try somewhere else,' I growled.

He gave me a superior smile. 'What would you do if you turned up a murderer, down there in the sticks? On top of everything else, you don't know anything about the country.'

'What's to know?' I asked airily. 'It's got fields and cows and people saying *aarrh!'*

'It's different!' Ganesh snapped. 'You won't know your way around there, as you do here. You don't know those kind of people. Here in the city, people are too busy to bother what you do. Down there a stranger will attract attention. You will, that's for sure!'

'Why me?' I was insulted.

'Look at you!' he said unkindly. 'Jeans with holes in the knees and a black leather jacket, Doc Martens boots. They'll barricade the doors when they see you coming.'

I was sorry I'd asked to borrow the camera. But his attitude made me more than ever determined. 'Don't be so negative! Have a little faith in me, can't you? I took his money and I'm trying to earn it.'

'There's more to this than taking the old man's money!' he retorted suspiciously.

'All right! I have a stupid feeling that somehow I let Terry down, when she lived with us. I was mean to her.'

'No, you weren't. She was mean to everyone else. You used to moan about her all the time! And even if you were, there's nothing you can do about it now!'

I lost my temper. 'That's a cop-out of an attitude! I'm not just giving up!'

Ganesh yelled, 'This isn't about her at all, is it? Or old Alastair! This is really all about you and *your* father! You think you let him down. You just want to put this business of Terry right because you wish you could put right the way you think you failed your old man. Do you know what you're in danger of doing? You're in danger of adopting this Alastair Monkton as a substitute father-figure! That's a very dangerous thing to do. It's risky for you and him and it's unfair on him!'

I was in no mood to be psycho-analysed. 'Are you going to lend me a camera or not?'

He went upstairs and came down after some minutes with a really neat little camera in a leather case on a strap. 'Don't lose it! It's fool-proof. A six-year-old could work it. Don't put your finger over the lens.'

As he handed it to me, he muttered, 'I wish I could come with you. But we're busy in the shop and Dad's back is playing him up. He can't lift the crates. But promise me, you'll keep in touch.'

'Promise, Gan.'

Ganesh's remarks about my appearance had hit home. I

had to admit he was right. I'd stick out like a sore thumb around the Astara Stud. I had to look respectable. They were a traditional lot in the country or so I imagined.

I washed my hair and tried to style it. In the squat long hair wasn't practical because we only had hot water if we boiled a kettle. Although I kept it short, it was longer than I had it in my punk days when I wore it cropped down to a quarter-inch stubble and coloured it purple. Now it was back to its normal mid-brown.

At the time I'd been going through my purple phase, I had a gold ring put through the outer edge of my right nostril. I was still at school then. I think that was what finished the headmistress off as far as I was concerned, the day I walked in with my purple hair and nostril-ring. I just wasn't the image she wanted for the school. She told me so. They were trying to turn out ladies, even in these benighted days. She meant, of course, that well-heeled parents, arriving to visit the school with a view to sending their precious daughters there, didn't expect to see a purple-haired, nostril-ringed punk lounging along the corridor. There was a barney. I was told to take out the ring and grow my hair. I refused. About a week later, Dad got The Letter. Goodbye, Francesca. We tried to make you one of us, but you weren't suitable material. No one can make a silk purse out of a sow's ear. It was couched in more official phrases, the letter, but that's what they meant.

A little later, when I was on the drama course which I was also destined never to finish, I swopped the nostril-ring for a nostril-stud, gold with a diamond chip in it which twinkled in the sunlight. I still wear the stud. It fixes in with a fitting like a tiny Allen key. If I leave it out for any length of time, the hole in my right nostril fills up with soap. Sorry, but that's life, full of sordid details.

I sorted through my wardrobe. I'd got my best clean jeans with no holes in them, a clean shirt, a denim waistcoat and my Victorian-style lace-up ankle boots with little heels. All put together it didn't look bad when I studied myself in the bathroom mirror. Although that mirror didn't encourage confidence in your appearance. It had livid patches all over it. If you looked at yourself in the nude in it, the reflection made you look as if you had leprosy.

Apart from the nostril-stud, I'm not one for jewellery. But I have Grandma Varady's gold locket so I put that on. I used to babysit for Lucy while she was out job and flat hunting. When she left the squat, she gave me her good jacket because I'd always admired it. It was blue-grey loose weave with a pretty silver-grey satiny lining. She'd always kept it in a polythene bag away from the children so it was quite smart. It was a bit on the big side for me, so I turned the sleeves up and the satin lining showed on the outside but it looked quite good.

So that was what I would turn up in Abbotsfield wearing. I wasn't sure how long I'd be staying. (Or if I'd be thrown off the place as soon as I got there.) *Hope for the best and plan for the worst*, said William of Orange, or somebody. I got out my green and purple duffel bag and put in a towel with my toothbrush and soap. Then I put in three pairs of clean knickers and a spare pair of opaque black tights and spare shirt. There was still room so I added a sweater in case it turned chilly and finally my one blue cotton button-through skirt, because I wasn't sure quite where I'd end up and it might be somewhere that jeans didn't suit. That skirt was handy because it didn't need ironing, it was meant to look crumpled.

I managed to get it all in and just do up the zip. I've always carried my money in a purse on a cord round my neck under my shirt. The places I'd lived in, you kept your money on you and you didn't let anyone see it.

Amongst Nev's books was one called *Three Plays* by Turgenev. One of the plays was entitled *A Month in the Country*. That seemed an omen so I put the book in my pocket to read on the bus.

I'd got that far when the doorbell rang. It was Ganesh.

'I thought, if you hadn't left yet, I'd come to Victoria and see you off.' He picked up my duffel bag. 'What on earth have you got in here? A crowbar and a hammer?'

'Ha-ha! My overnight essentials. I might stay a few days.'

He was frowning at me, studying the outfit. But he didn't say anything and I asked, nettled, 'Something wrong?'

He shook his head but still didn't say anything.

I couldn't be bothered whether he approved or not and turned away to check I'd not left anything I'd need.

From behind me, Ganesh said very loudly, 'I wish you weren't going down there on your own. You don't know a thing about the place. Or who will be there.'

'It can't be worse than this flat!' I pointed out snappishly.

'Have you got my camera?'

'Here.' I picked it up and slung it across from one shoulder, bandolero fashion.

'Want me to show you again how it works?'

'Thanks, but I remember! I'm not totally simple! And you don't have to come to the coach station!'

'If I have to come looking for you,' he said. 'I want to know which bus you went on, where it was going, and what time it was supposed to get there. It'll give me something to go on when I report you missing to the police and we start tracing your last movements.'

It wasn't exactly an expression of confidence.

At Victoria I got a seat on a bus going to Basingstoke. Ganesh went off somewhere and came back with a plastic carrier containing two packets of crisps, a box of orange drink with a straw and a tuna sandwich in a triangular box.

'In case you don't get a chance to buy lunch.'

I knew Ganesh was the best friend I had, more than that really. But all I said was, 'Thanks!'

When I actually got on the bus, sat in my seat by the window, I found I was really suffering a bad case of butterflies. My stomach was just a quivering jelly mass.

I could see Ganesh standing by the side of the bus with his hands shoved in the pockets of his black leather jacket. His long black hair curled loose round his face. He has nice hair. I can understand why he doesn't want to cut it off, even if his dad does believe it would be the first step on the pathway to success. He looked worried. I smiled brightly and waved to him. He took one hand from his pocket, waved back and gave a thumbs-up sign.

Then we were off. I was on my own, just me and Turgenev.

I wondered if Ganesh was right and I would find a murderer down there in the country. And I wondered what I'd do, if I did.

Chapter Eight

The coach crawled through mid-morning traffic out of London. I'd brought along a little notebook and I thought I better start off straight away being organised, the way a proper detective would be. So I began to write down all I knew about Terry under the heading 'Lines of Inquiry'.

But it was difficult to write clearly as the bus wove in and out of traffic. There wasn't much room and an old woman next to me took out her knitting. She was doing some sort of complicated stitch which meant that every other minute she threw the wool over the needle with a flourish and her elbow stuck into my ribs. When this happened, she said, 'Sorry, dear!' But then she did it again.

I squashed myself up in the corner of my seat, which was by the window, put the notebook away and decided to think it through. But that didn't work, largely because I'd been sleeping so badly the last few nights. My brain was sluggish. It was the warmest day for weeks and it was really hot in the bus with the sun beating in through the window. We were stuck in a traffic jam. I decided perhaps

I'd better leave it for a while, and come back to it when I had my head together.

The jam was building up. The old lady next to me was unscrewing her vacuum flask. She was obviously a seasoned coach traveller and preparing to sit it out. I took Turgenev from my jacket pocket and made a start on *A Month in the Country*.

I wish I could have completed that college drama course. It was just getting interesting when I quit. I remember being told to think myself into a part as I read it. So I cast myself as Natalia and set myself the intellectual exercise trying to be her.

I admit the first thing which struck me was that it must take Russians ages to carry on even a brief conversation, what with calling each other by such complicated names all the time.

Leaving that aside, I found the play was about a group of people shut up in a country house in the wilds of Russia in the 1840s, all bored stiff and trying to get off with one another. Not very successfully, I might add, which considering how long it took one character to ask another character to go for a walk, wasn't surprising.

Was I going to find life like that when I got down to the country? The heat was overpowering. I closed up the book and I fell asleep with my head propped uncomfortably in the angle between the back of the seat and the window.

When I woke up we were belting along the motorway. I drank Ganesh's orange drink and ate a packet of crisps. I still hadn't worked out what I was going to do when I got to Abbotsfield. I hadn't planned this at all well. Just borrowing a camera wasn't enough. And now, before I knew it, we'd reached Basingstoke and I had to get off the coach.

Like most people, I suppose, I'd always vaguely thought that 'going abroad' or to a foreign country meant crossing the borders into another nation's territory. Some foreign countries appear more alien than others, to the mind. I, for example, have never thought of Hungary as a foreign country because Grandma Varady talked of it so much. Yet I've never been there and, were I to go now, it wouldn't be the Hungary Grandma remembered. It would be somewhere else, resembling nothing I'd ever imagined. Perhaps that's the reason I've never made a serious effort to get there. I want to keep my image of it intact.

The truth is subtler. It usually is. None of us has to travel very far to find a different tribal territory, certainly not outside the boundaries of your own country. You need only travel a few miles, or streets. A mere block away and hey presto, you're a foreigner. That's what Ganesh had been trying to tell me and he was right.

I realised that as soon as I set foot to the ground in Basingstoke. I didn't belong here. I didn't know where to begin. I pottered around for a while and bought a paper bag of vinegar-drenched chips and ate them in the street while I wondered whether to go on, or just find a coach back to London. It hardly seemed possible that only this morning I'd been in my familiar surroundings of boarded-up houses and crumbling blocks of flats.

Basingstoke, on the other hand, had an air of depressing respectability, a pleasantly dull sort of little place, busy enough. It must have been just a market town to start with but some years ago, the modern world had hit it and now it even had a couple of shiny office blocks, giving it a foot in both camps. The people scurried about, mostly looking ordinary and harassed. In the crowd was a scattering of women in calf-length skirts teamed with knitwear-over-a-blouse. Some of them wore headscarves, expensive headscarves, which made them look like off-duty Royals. Me, tie a headscarf on me and I look like a babushka.

Time was getting on. I still didn't know what I was going to do when I got to Abbotsfield, or how I was going to get there, or find the Astara Stud, or where I was going to sleep that night or anything.

I thought about telephoning Alastair Monkton and letting him know I was on my way, but I chickened out when I got to the callbox, and anyway, I didn't have the right change. Besides, if I rang, anyone might answer and whoever it was might be far less welcoming than I hoped Alastair would be. If Alastair were there. Suppose he was away? What did I do then?

By now I was muttering like Mad Edna as I talked myself out of going to the stud. But if I turned back now, after coming this far, I'd lose all self-respect. Ganesh would crow over me for weeks.

I got a grip on my nerves and went in search of a local bus to take me to Abbotsfield.

I was lucky to find a bus which went to Abbotsfield at all. It arrived there late afternoon, around five o'clock. A couple of women with shopping bags got off and disappeared quickly. I was left staring round me.

It had been a pleasant drive if you like countryside. It was pretty, I suppose, but it might just as well have been on the moon as far as I was concerned. I'm a townie, through and through, and was realising it with horrible clarity, even more so than in Basingstoke which had at least offered a jumble of streets and shops. I like bricks. You know where you are with bricks. You turn a corner and there are more of them. Turn a corner in the country and you never know what you're going to find. You can hide in a town. You can't hide in the country, or I couldn't. It was all too open. Miles of empty fields. On the other hand, you could bury a body out there and who'd find it?

From that it was only a step to thinking, who'd find *me*?

Abbotsfield was a sprawling place, bigger than I'd imagined. It had a centre of terraced cottages, a church, two pubs, a post office cum general store, a garage and *Lisa Marie, Ladies and Gents Hairdressing*. Beyond this was a sizeable estate of elderly council housing and a primary school. There was a newer estate of brick bungalows on the outskirts of town.

When I'd explored all this I made my way back to the general store which was still open. It looked the kind of place which stayed open as long as anyone was interested in buying anything. Mr Patel operated on the same principle. I went in and bought a carton of milk and asked the woman for directions to the Astara Stud.

She was obviously curious. She must have heard all about Terry's death. But she told me which way to walk, down the hill out of Abbotsfield, following the signpost for Winchester. Then to look for a turning which indicated Lords Farm.

I asked, puzzled, 'Is that the stud?'

She told me no, it was just a farm, but the stud wasn't marked on the main road. They didn't believe in making it easy for visitors down here.

I thanked her and made my way to the church. I couldn't get into the building itself, as it was locked. But the doorway was interesting, a rounded Norman arch carved with strange geometric designs, resting on corbel heads which had blunted with time and weather into faceless things. The tombs in the churchyard were also old, mossy, the lettering mostly obliterated, although in the far corner was a patch with newer headstones. The sun was going down and it was warm and pleasant here. I sat on a tombstone and ate the tuna sandwiches, feeling, and perhaps looking, a little like Edna. The sandwiches were threatening to go off by that time, they'd turned warm and squishy. Perhaps I'd get food poisoning. I drank the milk and decided what to do. In fact, I didn't have a lot of choice. I had to head for Alastair's place and see what turned up. Although I'd be the one turning up. Or, after the sandwiches, throwing up.

There's a general assumption these days that everyone has transport. I didn't, except my feet. By the time I started walking, it was six o'clock. I'd passed a public loo in a carpark on the way out of town and cleaned myself up, but I still felt sticky, dusty and a mess. The boots weren't made for walking, unlike the ones in the song. I was soon starting to hobble a bit.

I felt conspicuous going along the road, not only because of my increasingly dot-and-carry-one gait, but because no one else was walking. It wasn't like a London pavement where you're shoving or being shoved out of the way all the time. There wasn't any pavement, only a narrow beaten track along the verge. There weren't any houses so no obvious reason to be wandering along. You just weren't supposed to be walking here.

Cars passed, one or two slowing as the drivers – men – took a look at me. I realised I looked like a hitch-hiker. I stuck my hands resolutely in my pockets to show I wasn't thumbing. Grandma Varady used to read the *News of the World* and newspapers of that sort. They were great on tales of rape and murder of young girls. She would read the details out with gusto.

'You never do this, darr-link!' She'd peer over her spectacles at me, shaking the paper under my nose, and making hitching motions with her thumb. 'These men are out there – everywhere! Devils! They are lying in wait for young women!'

Despite this I have, on numerous occasions, hitched. I always applied the rule taught me by a chance acquaintance, a girl I met at a Salvation Army coffee stall near King's Cross one cold winter evening. She was working the area professionally. I was just passing through. She was a cheerful sort of girl, friendly once she'd established I really had just stopped for a hot drink and wasn't aiming to work her patch. She wanted to give up the game on account of her varicose veins but her boyfriend wasn't having it and beat her up when she complained.

'Standing about down here in the cold in a mini-skirt with your arse freezing is no joke!' she said. 'And it does in your legs and ankles.'

Her advice was, 'Never get in a car with any man under the age of thirty-five.'

I remembered that as I walked along the verge. I also remembered her other advice which was never wear a skirt so tight you can't run or kick. Also, have steel tips on your high heels so that you could kick out the windscreen if you did get in the wrong car and things got really tough. I never had to take that kind of action though I had a few wrestling matches with sweaty truckers. On the whole they weren't serious. They nearly all had wives and kids and just wanted company in the cab. The worst thing was being bored to death with tales of the kiddies and their photos taken on Spanish beaches.

I was thinking of all these things as I hobbled along that verge looking for the turning to Lords Farm. I was beginning to think I'd missed it and was about to retrace my steps and check, when one of the cars swooping past screeched to a halt. The driver got out and called to me, 'Want a lift?'

It was a big smart car, a Volvo. He was a big, smart bloke. He wore a shirt patterned in small green check and one of those sleeveless jackets with pouch pockets, coloured khaki. He looked self-confident and was clearly trying his luck.

I told him no thanks, I wasn't going far. I really hoped that last bit was true – I couldn't make it much further in these boots.

He smirked. 'Come on, girlie, hop in!'

No one, but no one, calls me 'girlie'.

I said sharply, 'You deaf or something, *laddie*? I said no!'

He pulled a face, still grinning. 'Oh, a feisty lady? Where do you want to go?'

'Shove off!' I said wearily. I couldn't be bothered with him.

'No need to be like that,' he said. 'I'll take you anywhere you want. We can stop off for a drink on the way.'

I couldn't believe it, that anyone could be that dim, to think I'd fall for a line like that.

'You must be off your trolley,' I said. I must have sounded as though I believed it because it annoyed him.

'Look!' he said nastily. 'You're walking here, hoping to be picked up, right?'

'Wrong! I'm going to call on someone.'

He glanced round in an exaggerated way, drawing attention to the dearth of dwellings. 'Where?'

I was wasting time. I started walking again and although my feet really hurt I was determined not to hobble while he was there to see. After all, if Chinese noblewomen could make it on bound feet, I could make it in pixie boots.

He got back in the car and drove alongside me with a practised ease which suggested to me he'd done his share of kerb-crawling. King's Cross is full of cars like his, doing slow motion manoeuvres, until they see a copper and then they speed off like it was Silverstone.

After we'd gone a little way like this he stopped the car again, just ahead of me and got out, confronting me on the verge.

'All right!' he said. 'You've made your point. What's the name of these people you're looking for?'

I suppressed the first retort to come to my lips. It occurred to me he was probably local and if I told him I was looking for the Astara Stud, he'd know where it was. So I told him where I was bound and added Alastair's name for good measure.

The reaction was extraordinary. It wiped the smirk right off his face. 'Then we're headed for the same place. I'm James Monkton.' He scowled and looked nonplussed. He wasn't sure what to do next.

Oh shit, I thought. It would be!

'But I don't know you,' he said doubtfully. His manner suggested that he was used to a better class of acquaintance.

I told him, 'I'm Fran Varady. I knew Terry – Theresa.'

For a moment he was reduced to silence. A couple of cars rocketed past. Then an ugly look crossed his face and he said, 'You're that girl Alastair talked to in London. You lived in that place where Theresa died! What the hell are you doing down here?'

'My business, all right?' The road was empty now and we were alone by the verge. I hoped I didn't look as nervous as I felt.

'And I'm making it mine!' he told me. 'You can just turn around and go right back where you came from!'

'Alastair told me to come and see him. He gave me his card!' I stood my ground and hoped the half-truth would work. James wasn't to know exactly what had passed between Alastair and me.

He thought about it for a moment, then decided to accept what I'd said. 'Then I'll take you to see him. And there'd better be no funny stuff. I'll be watching!' He gestured at the car and added sarcastically, 'Go on, get in. On the level!'

'Thank you!' I told him. I slung my holdall on to the back seat and we set off.

'Alastair didn't say anything about expecting you.' He glanced sideways at me.

I felt rather foolish. 'We hadn't fixed a date. He said to come when I – wanted. It was a spur-of-the-moment thing. I meant to phone from Basingstoke. But I hadn't any tenpence pieces.'

It sounded weak, not to say the height of bad manners.

But James wasn't worried about my lapse of etiquette. He didn't expect any better from me. His mind was running in a different line.

'So, you came down here without even tenpence for a phone call? Really up against it financially, are you?'

It was clear what he was thinking and I felt my face burn. 'I came to talk to Alastair. I told you that.'

'Not to touch him for a hand-out, by any chance?'

I said, very coldly, 'You don't have any right to suggest that. You don't know me. You don't know why I'm here and you don't have any business to know, as far as I can see.'

'Quite a little Daniel, aren't you? Running into a den of lions. Or did you think Alastair lived alone?'

As a matter of fact, I had assumed that. It had been stupid of me. Obviously he didn't. Indirectly he'd mentioned others. But I hadn't thought they all lived under one roof. What I wanted to know now was whether James here beside me was a permanent member of the household or, like me, a transient visitor.

When I didn't reply, he treated me to a smirk of satisfaction. I tried to pretend I hadn't seen it.

We'd reached the turning marked Lords Farm. James spun the wheel and we slewed off left and then right. We were now following a single-track road, very badly surfaced, and slowly climbing through rolling pastureland. Horses grazed peacefully behind the neat fencing. This must be part of the stud.

I sneaked another look at him. I supposed him to be in his late twenties. He was good-looking in a solid, healthy outdoor way. The solidity was muscle, not fat. I was pretty sure he could take care of himself and probably anyone who got in his way.

I could see he was thinking about me, too. I caught him giving me a couple of sidelong glances, just as I was doing to him, and there was a mean set to his mouth. Our glances collided at last and we both looked away. He was wondering what to do about me. For two pins, I think he'd have pushed me out of the car while rounding a corner at speed. But he *was* curious to know what I wanted.

Suddenly a wooden board appeared by the roadside. On it was painted a horse's head and the words ASTARA STUD. There were a couple of fir trees either side of an entrance. James turned into it with another flourish and roared down a long drive, bordered with overgrown purple-blossomed shrubs which I recognised as buddleia. Buddleia grows anywhere at the drop of a seed and has a liking for the sides of railway tracks in and out of London. James drew up in a shower of grit, before the principal block of a cluster of buildings.

'Here we are then!' he said.

I stared through the windscreen. This must be the main house directly before us. It was red-brick, with sash-windows in white-painted frames, and looked Georgian. A newer extension had been built to the left, forming a separate wing. The ground floor of that looked as though it might be kept for offices.

The really intriguing part lay on the other side of the house. What had been a stableyard had been considerably expanded. I could glimpse the stabling, built around a square yard. Between it and the drive a garage block had been added, standing by itself. Behind that I glimpsed a modern bungalow. In addition to the buddleia, rhododendrons had been planted, either to give the bungalow privacy or to shield the main house from the sight of the humbler dwelling.

James was watching me as I studied all this. He still thought I'd come to see if I could shake some money out of Alastair. He was sure he could take care of it, if so. I found myself wondering if they kept any dogs – the sort which could be set on unwelcome visitors.

I just said as sweetly as I could, 'Thanks for the lift! I didn't realise it was so far out of town.'

He just gave a dry little smile and got out of the car. I hopped out too, grabbing my holdall off the back seat. The front door of the house was on the latch which shows you how different it was to London. Leave your door on the latch where I came from and when you got back either all your belongings would have disappeared, or someone you'd never set eyes on before would be sitting in front of your fireplace drinking lager out of a can, all his kit stowed round the room.

James walked in, leaving me to lug the holdall in by myself which wasn't very gentlemanly. But I had the funny feeling James Monkton wasn't entirely the country gent he took so much trouble to appear.

We were in a wide hall with a polished parquet floor and a staircase running up to a landing. James pushed open a door to a room on the right.

'Why don't you go in and make yourself at home? I'll see if Alastair is anywhere about. He might be out back in the garden or over in the yard.'

The room was a sitting room. The evening sun was shining in the bay window and it looked very comfortable and pleasant. The chairs were old and chintzy and soft. There was a big new TV set in one corner and it gave me quite a surprise to see it there. I was beginning to imagine they'd sit round all evening playing the piano or cards or reading to one another out of leather-bound tomes, like all those characters in Turgenev. I sank down on a sofa and took another look around. If this was where Terry had lived, she must have found sharing the squat with us about as big a change as she could have made.

I guessed I had time to look around. James would want to find out from Alastair as much as he could before he let the old chap anywhere near me. He was probably trying to persuade Alastair to let him, James, send me off back to London forthwith.

There was a big marble fireplace and, over it, a shelf crowded with photos and knick-knacks. I got up and went to have a look. I didn't know most of the people in the photos. I recognised one of Alastair in tweeds at some sort of gymkhana or show. He looked as if he were judging. He had a rosette pinned on his jacket. There were a couple of women standing with him. They had weather-beaten faces and were grinning away at the camera with teeth which wouldn't have disgraced a respectable horse.

In one large silver frame was a studio portrait of a remarkably beautiful girl, all done up in a party dress and looking like a million dollars. It was with shock that I suddenly realised I was looking at a picture of Terry. For a moment, I doubted it and thought, perhaps a relative looking a bit like her? I took it off the shelf for a closer look and it was Terry. I was holding it in my hand still staring at it when I heard a footstep behind me. I just had time to put it back before Alastair came into the room. James was just behind him. I knew that he meant to hear for himself what I had to say, how I'd explain my being there.

But old Alastair forestalled us both. He came straight over to me, took my hand and said, 'Francesca! My dear, why didn't you let us know you were coming? I'm really so pleased to see you. What a good thing Jamie passed you on the road. This house isn't the easiest place to find.'

I could see James looking a bit miffed at all this. It made me feel quite cheerful to think his nose had been put out of joint. I apologised to Alastair for turning up unannounced and so late.

He asked where I was staying. That embarrassed me, and I mumbled that I'd have to go back to Basingstoke, unless there was anywhere in Abbotsfield which offered rooms, perhaps one of the pubs?

'Nonsense, you must stay here!' he said at once, ignoring negative signals from James. 'Stay as long as you like, my dear! I'll get Ruby to make up a bed for you. I dare say you could do with a cup of tea. Jamie, why don't you go along to the kitchen and see if you can rustle one up?'

James didn't like being dismissed, certainly not to fetch the tea, but he went. I think the phrase for it would be 'in high dudgeon'. It occurred to me he'd chalk it up against me as a score to settle. That stopped me feeling so chirpy about it. He was the sort who made sure he always got his own back on anyone who crossed him.

When the door had closed, Alastair leaned forward.

'Have you something to report, Francesca?' He looked anxious, but hopeful too.

I explained to him that to be honest, I'd discovered nothing in London and even worse, had found myself following the police around. 'They're doing a good job,' I said. 'If you want your money back, I've brought it, less my bus fare. But I've been thinking – and maybe you won't agree with this . . . ' I waited but he said nothing, forcing me to plunge on. 'I haven't had much luck following her backtrail in London, so perhaps I ought to start here, where she lived before she came to London. Or just seeing where she came from might give me some ideas. You see, I know she shared the house in Jubilee Street with us, but that doesn't mean any of us knew Terry well. To tell you the truth, we found her a bit of a pain and we tended to ignore her. I'm sorry.'

Alastair didn't seem to find that rude. He nodded. 'I quite understand. Frankly, Francesca, if you'd said you and Theresa were bosom pals I'd be sceptical. I know my granddaughter had difficulty in forming relationships. She didn't make friends. Or at least, not what I would have called real friends.'

'But I do want to know what happened,' I insisted. 'I wish I had talked to her more. I wish I'd been a better friend to her, someone she could have confided in. I promise, I mean to do my best by her now and by you. I don't want more money. That's not why I'm here. James thinks that's why I've come, but he's wrong.'

Alastair frowned. 'My dear, Jamie is not the arbiter of who may visit here and who not! Incidentally, although he knows I called on you in London, he doesn't know about our little arrangement and I see no reason to tell him. The money I gave you on account is yours to keep and, as I promised, I'll pay an equal amount upon result.'

'I may not get any results,' I pointed out.

'I feel sure you will!' he retorted optimistically. 'Now you're here, we'll put our heads together, eh? Work it out!'

He sounded quite enthusiastic and I began to feel a lot better. He was such a nice old boy. If there was a fly in the ointment now, it was Jamie Monkton who clearly thought I was up to no good.

Suddenly Alastair said, 'As for getting to know poor Theresa, I wonder if any of us ever did that?'

Before I could answer that one, the door opened and a middle-aged woman came in carrying a tray with teacups.

'There you are, my dear!' she said, putting it down on a little table. 'So you're Theresa's friend! Really nice to have you here. I'll make up her old room for you. I think you'll be comfortable there!'

Alastair said, 'Thank you, Ruby!'

I hadn't really expected to find a family retainer and I certainly hadn't reckoned on being given Terry's room. But if it still had some of her stuff in it, there might be a clue amongst it all.

Jamie had come back and looked more miffed than ever. He said sharply, 'Theresa's room? Isn't that a bit – a bit depressing for Fran?'

'No, it'll be fine, thanks!' I said quickly, which earned me a dirty look.

I decided to take the initiative and asked, 'Are you a cousin?' because that seemed the most likely.

'Sort of!' he said shortly. Or, at least, I think that's what he said.

'Jamie is actually the son of a cousin of mine,' Alastair said. 'Rather a complicated relationship. But cousin's a fair enough description. Theresa always called you a cousin, didn't she?'

Jamie grunted and began to hunt through his pockets. A tingle ran up my spine. He'd produced a familiar-looking gold packet of cigarettes. Relax! I ordered myself. It's a popular brand. It doesn't have to mean anything.

He'd looked up and saw how I stared. 'Do you mind if I smoke?'

'No,' I told him, honestly. I wanted to see if he also used a book of matches. But he didn't. He had a lighter, one of those disposal ones in coloured plastic. I resolved, at the earliest opportunity, to hunt through any waste-paper baskets in the house.

We drank our tea and made small-talk about the countryside and then Ruby appeared to take me up to my room.

As I passed by Jamie's chair he murmured so that only I could hear him, 'Don't make yourself too comfortable!'

Chapter Nine

I tried, as I followed Ruby upstairs, to get some idea of the layout of the house. Living in an old house, the squat, had given me an eye for the architectural features of yesteryear. They liked a lot of plaster moulding then, picture rails, arches, that sort of thing.

Even a quick glance round here told me that serious alteration had been made to this house, probably a century ago. To begin with, no one would be allowed to mess with the interior of a building as old as this one nowadays. Even the alterations had a permanent look. The tell-tale clues were the arches which began and never finished, chopped off by a partition wall. The rectangular uneven tracks across the plastering of walls marked where once doors had been blocked up. Other doors, and windows, were the wrong proportions, added later where they were never meant to be. There were hazardous drops in the level of the corridor, so that one suddenly had to step down a pair of flights, just to continue in the same direction. All this in the main part of the house, not the additional newer wing I'd noticed from outside. I mentioned it to Ruby.

'The house seems very old. Has it been much altered?'

'Not in my time,' she said, without turning her head, her broad rump plodding on ahead of me. 'But I do believe that originally it was two houses, back to back, as you might say. This corridor,' here she paused and pointed vaguely up and down the dusky passageway. 'This was where one house met the other, do you see? These doors were knocked through to make the two into one. Doesn't make it an easy place to clean, I can tell you!'

We'd reached our destination. She pressed down a polished brass doorhandle and light streamed into the corridor. 'Little Theresa's room,' she said. 'Can't seem to believe she'll never use it again. You'll be all right, then, will you, dear? Let me know if there's anything you need. The family usually eats at seven, but I'll hold up everything till seven-thirty to give you a chance to settle yourself. There's plenty of hot water if you want a bath.'

I understood immediately why Ruby couldn't believe that Terry wasn't ever coming back. The fact was, she had never left. I knew, as soon as I walked into the room, that Terry was there with me. I even glanced at the white-painted Lloyd Loom chair as though I would see her sitting there, in her grubby knitted jacket, peering at me through spaniel's ears of tangled blonde hair.

But there was one difference. Before, in life, she'd always appeared to resent me. But this had changed. This time, she didn't mind my being there. I had the even stranger feeling that she was pleased, that she knew why I'd come and approved. She expected me to do something. I hoped I didn't let her down again.

Alastair and Terry both pinning their hopes on me.

Ganesh was right. I'd bitten off more than I could chew.

The room itself was pretty, an adored little girl's room. A collection of stuffed toys, all rather worn and damaged, huddled together on the top of a white-painted chest of drawers. All the paintwork was white. There was a floral-patterned duvet and a kidney-shaped dressing table with a matching flounce round it. The curtains matched, too. Someone had taken a lot of trouble with this room. It was very feminine, just a bit twee, and definitely not my sort of scene. In fact it made me feel a tad uneasy. There was an obstinate clinging to childhood innocence in it. Terry, whatever else she'd been, couldn't have been described as innocent.

But that was my view of her. Alastair, in our talk over the Indian meal, had clearly clung to the view that his granddaughter had no idea of the wicked ways of this world. She'd been his little girl, she'd always be that. Death had done him a favour, did he but know it. It had preserved his image of her, always young, always beautiful. Not a human being with failings and the right to make her mistakes, but a doll, preserved in Cellophane so that her clothes would never get dirty and her hair never mussed. My unease increased.

I went to the window. I was at the back of the house here, which meant that, at some point, Ruby and I had stepped through what had once been the dividing wall between two dwellings, and I'd passed from the front one to the back one. It would be quieter here, away from the stableyard which would be a noisy, busy place from early in the day till last thing at night. The view from here was down the garden behind the house, a tangled, unkempt affair of grassy paths, overgrown shrubs, unpruned trees and uncut lawns. Attractive, though. A place to wander in. Kids would like that garden. A great place for hide-and-seek, cops and robbers, all the rest of it. Cops and murderers, even.

Someone could stand out there and watch the house from the shrubbery and no one here be any the wiser. He could stand only some fifteen or twenty feet away, invisible. He might be there now, looking up at this window, watching me.

I moved away. I did feel like a bath and, looking at my watch, I saw that it was already ten to seven. The bathroom had been pointed out to me, just along the corridor. I didn't have much time. A faded quilted dressing gown hung behind the door. I took it down.

There was a Cash's woven nametape sewn in the neckband. *T E Monkton*. It took me back to when I was eleven years old and just starting at the private school my father hoped would educate me into a success. Grandma Varady had sat sewing nametapes just like that into all my new school uniform, even on my socks. They were sticklers at that school for that sort of thing. I wondered who had sewn in Terry's nametapes. From what Alastair had told me of her mother, she hadn't sounded the type to do that, even if she was in the fashion business and ought to be able to manage a few stitches. This old dressing gown reminded me Terry had been at boarding school. Mine had been a day school. I was glad I hadn't been sent away to school. I'd hated the school I was at, but at least I got to come home at the end of each day.

I pulled the robe on and hurried along to the bathroom. I nearly fell headlong when I opened the door, because the bathroom marked one of those unexpected drops in level. I stepped in and plummeted down two steps, saving myself only by grabbing the door jamb and swinging on it, like a chimp. Ruby might have warned me.

The bathroom was the size of a bedroom and probably had once been one. Modern plumbing had come by degrees into this house. I ran three inches of water in a massive old-fashioned cast-iron tub standing on lion's paws. I hadn't time to run more. I'd taken my skirt with me and I hung it up so that the steam would help the creases fall out. Then I clambered up the side of the tub and down inside it into the water. I felt lost in depths of it, and began to wonder just how many people it was designed to accommodate at one go. I hadn't imagined the Victorians going in for merry jinks altogether in one bath. I wished I'd run more water. When I lay back, bits of me stuck up above the tide-line, knees pointed up like twin atolls, my stomach a low flat island which would be submerged at high tide and nipples lurking like coral reefs. I was splashing water over these dry-land bits of me, when I heard a curious noise outside the bathroom door.

It was a low whine accompanied by a faint rumbling. It sounded as though a very small milkfloat was going past. That was unlikely, but that's how it sounded. Then I heard a clang like a metal gate and – and there was no doubt about this – the noise of a lift.

A lift? In a private house? It looked as if the evening was going to be full of surprises.

I felt better as I climbed out of the tub, freshened up. I'd been afraid I'd discover my toes rubbed raw from the hike in the pixie boots but they were all right which was a relief. I couldn't afford to be laid up lame now. I let myself out of the bathroom, wrapped in the dressing gown, and turned to shut the door.

The corridor was dark here. As I fumbled with the handle I heard a step behind me and a hiss of indrawn breath. A man's voice whispered, 'Theresa?'

I turned. It was Jamie, white as a sheet as even I could see in the gloom.

When he saw who it was, colour flooded back into his face. He snapped, 'What the hell do you think you're doing wearing my cousin's clothes?'

'The robe?' I twitched at the dressing gown. 'I didn't bring one with me. It was hanging in the room. I didn't think anyone would mind.'

'Well, I mind!' He sounded really shaken.

I felt I ought to apologise. It must have given him a bit of a shock. I said I was sorry. 'I didn't think anyone would see me. I've only come along the corridor in it.'

'Don't let anyone else see you! The old people – Alastair. The old boy would have a heart attack! Even if he didn't, it would be distressing . . .'

He turned and strode off, still visibly shaken, and leaving me by the bathroom door. Something he'd said had lodged in my brain. Old people? Who else, then, other than Alastair?

Back in my – in Terry's – room, I opened the drawer in the kidney-shaped dressing table and found a jumble of odds and ends of makeup. There was a pink lipstick which wasn't too lurid. I smeared some on and rubbed the pad from a box of pancake powder over my nose, put on the skirt and my tights, polished up my dusty boots with a tissue from a box on the dressing table, and set off downstairs.

But first I went exploring up to the end of the corridor. Sure enough, just round a corner in a little nook, there was a lift. A lift in a private house? An old house, which didn't even have modern bathroom fittings? I thought about getting in and pressing the button but decided that might be thought presumptuous. I went back to the staircase.

As I walked down I could hear voices coming from the sitting room. Jamie was making a speech in a hectoring tone. I could hear Alastair murmuring some kind of protest. Then Jamie said quite clearly,

'But you don't know a thing about this girl! She says she knew Theresa. But we all know what kind of company Theresa kept! This girl is probably some heroin-shooting drop-out from God knows where! We'll be finding needles in the flowerbeds and we'll have to keep everything locked away!'

I thought it was time I made my entrance. I threw open the door and marched in. I was going to make a little speech about how I didn't do drugs and never had, nor was I a thief, so they needn't worry. I wasn't going to make off with the family silver. But before I could speak, a deep but female voice boomed out,

'So you are the young lady my brother met in London?'

I hadn't seen her when I first went in and so when she spoke it gave me quite a start. I fairly leapt round.

I saw a very stately old lady in a ruffled blouse and long skirt which covered her legs. Her hair was white, blue rinsed, and very neatly waved. Her eyes were deepset, but very large, dark and clear with a look which seemed to see right through me. She was in a wheelchair which explained the lift and the noise I'd heard outside the

145

bathroom door. She was also so obviously Alastair's sister that even if she hadn't said 'brother' I'd have guessed it. She had the same large strong features but looked a year or two older than he was.

Alastair had risen to his feet as I came in but Jamie stayed seated, glowering at me. He knew I'd overheard what he'd said about me. He was glad. It saved him having to say it all to my face.

Alastair said courteously, 'Yes, this is Francesca, Ariadne. Fran, dear, this is my sister, Mrs Cameron.' Then, really throwing me, he added, 'This is her house.'

I'm not the sort of person who's easily embarrassed. But I felt really embarrassed then, because if this was her house, I ought to have been invited to stay by her and not by Alastair. I hadn't even known about her and here I was, a real gate-crasher, someone who had just marched in and wangled an invitation. I couldn't meet Jamie's eye. I must appear to be confirming every doubt he had about me.

However, Ariadne said, 'It's very nice to meet you, Francesca. I hope you'll be comfortable in that room. It was Theresa's, as I expect they told you.'

I mumbled 'Yes', adding, 'Please call me Fran. Only the teachers at school ever called me Francesca, so when I hear it, I always feel I'm in trouble.'

'Hear it often?' Jamie asked silkily.

Mrs Cameron gave him a look which would have stopped anyone in their tracks. But she spoke quite mildly. 'Now, Jamie, behave. Fran's made a long journey to come down here and visit us!'

She made it sound as though they'd really invited me and I was doing them some sort of favour so I was truly grateful to her. She must have noticed how red my face had turned. She and Alastair both seemed so nice, it hardly seemed possible that they and Jamie could be genetically connected.

Ruby came in and told us all to, 'Hurry up and get to the table, it's all going cold!'

The meal was traditional, grilled lamb chops with tomatoes, mushrooms and the best mashed potatoes I'd ever eaten, followed by treacle tart and custard. Mrs Cameron didn't have the pudding, only a small piece of cheese. The rest of us fell on the food and ate it all up. I hadn't realised I was so hungry.

We all went back to the sitting room afterwards and the coffee was there on a tray, ready for us. It was getting late so I asked, 'Would it be OK if I rang someone in London and let them know I've arrived? I'll pay for the call.'

'Of course you must ring and let your friends know you're safe!' Alastair said. 'The phone's in the hall.'

I went out into the empty hall. From somewhere in the distance I could hear crockery rattling. Ruby in the kitchen. There was a grandfather clock by the phone, ticking softly. But there wasn't anyone to overhear.

I rang the Patels. Ganesh answered. He said, 'Thank God, I've been worried sick! Where are you?'

I explained I was staying at the Monktons and he needn't worry.

'I'll be the judge of that!' he said grimly. 'Look, don't hang around down there. You don't know those people!'

'They're dead respectable, Gan! Don't make a fuss. Look, I can't hang on the phone and run up a bill. I just wanted you to know I'm all right.'

'Fine, but if anything odd happens, anything, right? Get on the phone and I'll bring the van down and pick you up! Otherwise you might wind up very dead and not very respectable.'

'I promise. Cheers, Gan.'

I put the phone down and turned round. I was wrong about not being overheard. Jamie was lounging by the closed sitting-room door with his arms folded. He must have made an excuse to go out, just so he could eavesdrop on my conversation. I was furious.

'Heard enough?' I snarled.

'Who is Gan?' he countered.

'What's it to you? A friend.'

'Male or female?'

'Male. You don't mind asking questions, do you?' I stormed at him. 'How dare you snoop on me?'

'Not snooping, sweetie. Came out for a smoke. Ariadne doesn't like it. Makes her cough.' He produced his Benson and Hedges packet and held it out to me.

'I don't!' I said coldly.

'Got at least one virtue, have you? Lost the rest?' He lit up and grinned at me. 'As for snooping, I bet you're no shy violet when it comes to asking around, Fran! Isn't that what you came down here to do? Or one of the things you came here to do, anyway.'

He'd scored a point over me. I snapped, 'So what?'

'So mind your own business!' he snapped back. 'This Gan, is he a boyfriend?'

'Let's both mind our own business, shall we?'

I'd had enough of him. Besides my relationship with Ganesh was no concern of his.

Jamie and I locked stares but he backed down first. He opened the sitting-room door for me with mock politeness and I stalked past him to join the others.

Mrs Cameron didn't have coffee. There was a glass of water on the tray. Her brother handed her that and she took a couple of tablets with it. I wondered if they were painkillers. Her face had that drawn look which people have when the pain never quite goes away.

Directly after she'd taken the tablets she said she would 'go up now' and bid us all good night. That left me and the two men. Alastair opened a drinks cabinet, but I didn't want anything else. I was fit to drop with tiredness. I said goodnight too.

I was sure that, once I'd left, Jamie would start trying to persuade Alastair to get rid of me. They were going to have a whisky apiece and were clearly settling down for a talk. Alastair had produced a pipe and tobacco pouch and was fumbling with it. I waited hopefully to see if a book of matches would appear, but he got up, took a paper spill from a jar on the mantelshelf and lit it from the hearth. Jamie had produced his Benson and Hedges again together with his plastic disposable lighter. I was beginning to think the match booklet was going to prove a non-starter as a clue.

I wasn't worried about what Jamie would say in my absence. I was sure either of the old people could handle him. I did wonder, if he was such a distant relative, just what he was doing there.

But I was glad they were settled for a while. I knew that if I meant to do my detecting properly, I must lose no time making a search of Terry's room. I was well aware that if there was anything to be found there, which anyone in the house thought I oughtn't to see, tonight might be my only chance of finding it before it was removed.

But I just felt so sleepy. I knew I'd make a rotten job of

looking and probably would miss anything significant. I decided to get up early and search the room before breakfast. I pulled back the curtains so that the early morning sun would wake me.

It was pitch dark outside. Not the sort of darkness I was used to in the city where there's always a glow above the rooftops from the street lights in the main roads. This was just a solid wall of black night. If there was a moon up there, it was behind cloud.

It was so quiet. In the city there is always the faint background hum of traffic or trains. People stay up later and go out at night to have fun. Here it was only nine-forty-five, but Ariadne was already in bed. I was about to go to bed and, judging from the lack of any sign of life out there, everyone else round here, with the exception of the two men chatting over whisky downstairs, had also turned in early.

As a child, Grandma Varady had lived in a village out on the *puszta*, the great Hungarian plain. She'd described nights there as being like black velvet, dotted with the dancing orange fires of the herdsmen who tended the horses and cattle. Perhaps I will go to Hungary one day, if I ever have the money. There are lots of things I'd like to do if I ever have the money. I could seek out my roots. Not that I feel I have roots there. All my roots are in London. I don't even speak Hungarian. I've often wished I had learned when I was a child from Grandma Varady and Dad. Learning languages is a doddle to kids. But I hadn't. Another opportunity missed. The story of my life.

Nothing broke this darkness. We were an oasis in the middle of a sea of nothingness. I wished I could see the stableyard because that must have security lighting. But from here, nothing. I pulled myself together and told myself it was the lack of 'purple' in my eyes. Someone told me once that city-dwellers lack 'purple', whatever that is, and that's why they can't see so well in the dark. Country-dwellers are used to darker nights and manage better. I didn't know if that was true. And I didn't know whether someone who didn't mind the dark, as I did, was out there. The watcher, still watching. I had begun to believe in him by now, try as I might to convince myself he was only the figment of my imagination.

As if I didn't have enough worries about possible events inside the house. I turned the big old key in the door, locking myself in.

I fell asleep as soon as my head hit the pillow. I woke up just as suddenly. I'd no idea what time it was and, for a moment, didn't even know where I was. The moon had appeared to shine through the undraped window and the room was bathed in clear white light. I could see every-thing now, all the furniture, my clothes lying over a chair where I had thrown them, too tired to hang anything in the wardrobe, the battered collection of stuffed toys sit-ting on top of a chest of drawers, the pattern on the wallpaper.

And the door handle. I'd sat up and that made me stare directly at the door, and the handle which was twisting downwards ever so slowly as someone on the other side pressed it down. I watched it fascinated. I ought to have been scared but, in a way, I'd been expecting something like this, and in my own mind I was prepared for it. I wasn't altogether prepared for anyone actually getting into the room, but what I'd do then would depend on a lot of things.

Besides, I reasoned, the door was locked.

The handle went up again. The person outside was having a rethink. He – I was pretty sure it must be Jamie – realised I'd turned the key. The floor boards creaked. I thought he'd given up and relaxed.

I was wrong. After a moment or two, he was back. He had only gone to collect a sheet of cardboard. He slid this under the door where there was a sizeable gap. I guessed what was coming next but I watched, just to see if he could do it. The key rattled in the lock. He was pushing it through from the other side. It fell out and landed with a click on his cardboard. He began to inch it back, under the door.

The thing to do was leap out of bed, grab the key before it disappeared from sight and foil him. But I'd left it too late. It slithered under. The lock scraped. The doorhandle turned.

I was naked and didn't fancy offering Jamie Monkton a free show. I jumped out of bed and ran to snatch up the robe, pulling it on, as the door opened.

'Come in, why don't you?' I invited.

He walked in with as much composure as he could muster in the circumstances. He wore tennis shoes, jeans and a sweater. Burglar's kit and keeping burglar's hours.

I wasn't worried how to handle him because I was sure he wouldn't want to start a shouting match which would bring Alastair to investigate. But I did want to know what he was after. It wasn't my body, I was almost sure of that. I must have made it clear how I felt about him. But you never knew with men. They're loath to take no for an answer and big handsome Jack-the-lads like Jamie here can never get it into their thick heads that any girl doesn't fancy them, no matter what she says.

'If you're going to tell me I'm the sexiest thing you ever saw,' I told him sarcastically. 'Skip it.'

'You've got to be joking,' was his reply, expressed with considerable feeling. So much feeling that it really wasn't flattering and although I'd asked for that, I felt quite offended. He went on, 'I wouldn't touch you with a barge-pole with a rubber glove on it, as the saying goes.'

'Kinky!' I said.

He just gave me a disgusted look. 'As far as I'm concerned, you're just a piece of garbage which blew in here off the city streets. God knows what I'd catch. You might even be HIV positive, for all I know.'

'Thanks.' If nothing else, I really knew for sure now he hadn't come here looking for nookie. 'So what do you want?' I asked.

'You've got a confounded nerve!' His tone was almost one of wonder, as if he really couldn't understand it. 'You come here, get yourself invited to stay, run rings round the old people, even old Ruby, help yourself to my cousin's bathrobe, her room . . . anything else of hers you can find, I guess.'

Remembering the lipstick, I felt my cheeks burn and was glad of the moonlit room which meant, I hoped, he couldn't see it.

'I don't creep around at night trying to get into other people's rooms while they're asleep!' I snapped.

He just grinned, holding up the key and waving it slowly back and forth like a metronome beating time. 'Expecting me?'

He still laboured under the misapprehension that I must find him attractive and had been lying here hoping he'd appear. I suppressed the impulse to deny it, because he wouldn't have believed me, and would have taken my protest as proof.

'What do you want?' I asked as coldly as I could.

'A little talk, nice and private. And keep your voice down! I've taken care not to make a noise and disturb the household. You'll oblige by doing the same and not shouting your head off, as if you were still on your street corner!'

'Drop dead!' I invited him. 'You're out of your tiny mind if you think we've got anything to discuss. Right?'

Even in the pale light, I saw him glower. 'Wrong! We're going to straighten out this situation here and now, before you see Alastair at breakfast and get another chance to play little girl lost.'

That made me wild. But I realised that if I reacted to the jibe, I'd be playing this his way. It was time to set a condition of my own.

'You can do all the talking you want,' I told him. 'I'm not saying a word unless you give me that key.'

I saw him debate that with himself. It was no use his being my gaoler if I just heard him out in silence. No situation was ever 'straightened out' that way.

He didn't want it to look as though I'd won a point, however, so he decided to be amused by my request. 'Here!' He chucked the key at me. I just managed to catch it and, I have to admit, to have the small piece of metal pressing into my palm was comforting.

Preliminary negotiations settled, we moved to the next stage. Jamie swivelled the dressing-table chair and seated himself.

I took the Lloyd Loom chair, wrapping the bathrobe round me as much as I could. It was on the skimpy side, being tailored to fit, at a guess, a fourteen-year-old. I held it together over my thighs, but my boobs threatened to pop out the top which didn't quite wrap over enough.

He watched me wriggling uncomfortably and offered, 'If you want to put some clothes on, I'll turn my back. Although I'm surprised you're so shy.'

'Just a moment!' I snarled. I got up, sidled my way over to the bed, grabbed the duvet, wrapped that round me and returned to my chair, swathed like a chief attending a pow-wow.

When I was settled, he cut through any more ceremonial with, 'How much?'

'How much what?'

'How much do you want to go back to London, first thing in the morning? I'll pay a reasonable amount.'

'Why are you so keen for me to go?' I countered.

'Fifty quid? Eighty? That's my final offer.'

The man was determined to insult me. Not just by offering the money, but so little! I wasn't even worth a decent amount! But offering at all? He was worried.

'My, you're really keen for me to go! I'm just a bit of garbage, right? Why should you bother about me? Or have I got you rattled, Jamie?'

He couldn't take mockery.

He leaned forward, his face twisted in anger. 'Listen, you little bitch! Alastair doted on Theresa. Losing her was, for him, like losing an arm or a leg. He's been eaten up with guilt, too, poor old devil, because he believes he could have saved her, as he puts it. No one needs to be a shrink to work out what's going on now. You walked in

155

and, as you no doubt hoped he would, he's seized the chance to work off some of his guilt and loss. But you're not going to play that little game. I won't let you. Think yourself lucky I'm offering to pay you off! I could just as easily take you out of the house and beat you to a pulp.'

I fought the instinct to flinch before the venom in his voice and managed to sit steady and meet his eye. 'You'd have a job explaining that to the old people, as you call them! And you'd have a job explaining to Alastair what you were doing in here if I screamed.'

'You? Scream? When did you last scream to defend your honour?' He gave a hoot of laughter. 'Go ahead. I'll tell Alastair it was all your idea. You invited me here, then tried to get money out of me for sex. He doesn't know you well, but he knows your background. He might just believe it.'

'He still wouldn't consider it gave you the right to be preparing to fornicate under his, or Ariadne's, roof. Alastair's old fashioned. He probably imagines you're a gentleman, Jamie, and somehow I don't think you want to disillusion him. As for money, forget it. I came all the way here after giving it a good deal of thought. I'll leave when I'm ready or Alastair tells me to go – whichever happens first. Either way, you don't come into it.'

He got up, towering over me. 'You're going to be sorry you turned down my offer,' he said. 'I won't make it again. You're a fool, Fran.'

He walked out. The door swung closed behind him, leaving me wondering if he wasn't right.

I didn't think he'd be back. I returned the duvet to the bed and clambered back under it. Thumping the pillow, I tried to settle down, but it was hopeless.

Detectives oughtn't to leap to conclusions. Just because I didn't like Jamie, didn't mean he was a complete villain. Perhaps he was just worried about the old people and wanted to protect them from me. Perhaps he had just come here tonight to offer me money to leave – or try and frighten me into leaving. But the more I thought about it, the more dissatisfied I became.

Was it my being in the house he didn't like? Or my being in this room in particular? If so, was it just sentiment? Or perhaps he feared there was something in here amongst all Terry's stuff, which might give me a clue. If so, a clue to what?

My earlier intention had been to search the room before anyone could tamper with the contents. Perhaps I oughtn't to put that off any longer.

Wide-awake now, I got out of bed and switched on a lamp. I didn't want to make a noise and waken the whole house so crept about barefoot, as sneakily as Jamie had done earlier.

First I went to close the curtains in case anyone *was* outside in the darkness. I could see a black frieze of tree-shapes moving in the night breeze against an indigo sky. The moon slid out for a moment and bathed the garden in a light which bleached out all the colours. My eyes, too, were becoming accustomed to the dark. Now I could see the outline of shrubs and paths. As I watched, the bushes moved, leaves shivering. The wind, I told myself. But I couldn't be sure. Was that a shadow down there, darker than the surrounding ones? Was it long and thin, not round and stubby like the shrubs? Did it stoop and shrink into the box hedges? Was it only shreds of cloud floating by the moon's face? Was I hallucinating? One thing was

157

certain, I was clearly silhouetted against the lamplight.

I dragged the curtains to. This was a time to keep my imagination firmly under control. Detectives had to be businesslike. I began to work over the room systematically, slow and steady.

I tried the drawers of the dressing table. They contained the items I'd already seen there. Make-up, crumpled tissues, a manicure set. A couple of old bus tickets. They were similar to the one I'd bought to come from Basingstoke to Abbotsfield. So Terry had taken the bus into town a couple of times. I had to find something more significant than that. I abandoned the dressing table and turned my attention to the chest of drawers in the corner.

I took all the stuffed animals off the top and pulled it away from the wall. Nothing behind it. Nothing of interest in the top drawer, just a couple of sweaters. Second drawer empty. Third drawer filled with old schoolbooks and paperbacks. I took them all right out, each and every drawer, because there are good old reliable tricks like taping things to the reverse of the frame.

Declan told me that once, when a landlady threw him out of a furnished room he'd rented in Bayswater, he'd tacked a kipper to the reverse of a drawer frame before he left. He'd reckoned it would have stunk the place out before they found it.

But there was nothing behind any of these. I sorted through the books but I didn't see what relevance a bunch of old Agatha Christie's or *An Introduction to the Poets of the First World War* could have to any of this. One of the Agatha's had a picture of Hercule Poirot on the jacket. I fancied he was looking at me in a smug way, clearly thinking my 'little grey cells' were vastly inferior to his. No doubt he would have worked all this out in five minutes, assembled everyone downstairs and pointed at whom? It would be nice to think he'd point at Jamie.

I checked through all the other books to see if anything had been slipped inside, but there was nothing. I put them all away and turned my attention to the wardrobe. No luck. I looked under the bed, under the mattress, under the carpet. I remembered reading a book where the heroine had sewn love-letters into the lining of the curtains so that her wicked uncle couldn't find them. But these curtains didn't have any lining and who did that sort of thing these days, anyhow?

I sat down on the bed, discouraged. It was nearly five. It was light outside now and the birds were singing. Several times I heard a horse whinny. They were already at work over in the stableyard.

I'd forgotten to put back the stuffed toys which all sat on the carpet in a row gazing at me with their glass eyes. I felt that Terry's ghost was sitting with them, fixing me with the same reproachful look. I was supposed to have found it and I hadn't. I still didn't even know what it was!

'It's no use looking at me like that, you lot!' I told the toys. I got up and picked them up in one armful to replace them on the top of the chest of drawers. As I did, one of them crackled.

I thought: if I had to hide something small, I could do worse than hide it in one of these toys. If I couldn't sew it into the curtains like the heroine in that book, I could sew it in one of these animals.

I examined them all one by one. I ran a thumb along all the seams, tugged at their limbs and heads, prodded them all over.

Bingo! It was a blue and white rabbit and when I pushed its tummy it crackled again. Someone had definitely resewn the seam up his back, and not very well. The stitches were big and lumpy. I got a pair of nail scissors from the make-up drawer and snipped away at a few of them. It pulled apart easily and I pushed my fingers inside. They encountered a piece of paper, folded into a tiny wedge.

I eased it out, my palms sweating with excitement. It was two pieces of paper, not one. Two sheets of letter paper folded up together. After all, was this going to turn out to be an outpouring of purple passion? If so, I'd no right to read it.

I flattened it out and took a look at the signature.

It had been written by Ariadne Cameron.

Chapter Ten

I sat on the edge of the bed and placed the two rectangles of
thick cream writing paper side by side beneath the bedside
lamp. Each sheet was written on one side only and the
letter was headed with the Astara Stud's address and dated
three years previously. It began, *Dear Philip* . . .

The only Philip I'd heard mentioned so far was Terry's
father, Philip Monkton. All I knew about him was that he
was absent, unpopular and parted from Terry's mother.
Why this letter to him from his Aunt Ariadne should be in
Terry's possession and why she thought it necessary to
hide it away, I'd only find out by reading it. I quashed any
twinge of conscience at reading someone else's private
correspondence and scanned it with indecent curiosity.
The writing was cramped but clear, an educated hand but
an elderly person's. Frankly, few younger people
nowadays could write that beautiful even copper-plate.
My handwriting looks like the tracks of a drunken spider.

The letter began with a general query after Philip's
well-being and some remarks about Ariadne's own
none-too-good state of health. Then came the nitty-gritty
of the affair.

I am writing, Philip, to tell you that I've now settled details of my new will and Watkins, the solicitor, is drawing it up. I shall be signing it on Monday. The future of the Astara Stud is, naturally, my first consideration.

Until recently, my entire estate was bequeathed to my brother. But the passing of time and the corressponding change in circumstances has necessitated some different arrangement. Alastair is getting on in years, as I am, and would not wish the responsibility. Besides which, the Grim Reaper is as likely to call on him as on me! You have never shown any interest in the stud and you are, in any case, busy with your own very successful career. Neither you, nor Alastair, is in need of money. With the exception of a few personal bequests, therefore, I've left everything to Theresa. By everything, I encompass the stud, all property including this house, and the residue of my estate after the individual bequests and other outgoings have been settled. I've discussed it with Alastair, who thinks it the best decision. I hope you will also be happy with the arrangement. It will leave Theresa a wealthy young woman. That in turn will relieve you of any future financial burden in her regard. In view of your remarriage (which may in time produce a new young family for you), it will be, I'm sure, a great relief.

Theresa has been a little wild of late and caused us some anxiety. But it's to be expected of youth. God willing, I shall hang on for a few more years yet, so that by the time she inherits, she will be older and wiser, ready to settle down. She has a good head on her shoulders and I don't doubt she will cope.

I have told Jamie. He is perhaps disappointed, having worked so hard. But he is not so close a relative and, besides, he is one of those, I feel, who needs direction. Left entirely to his own devices and completely in charge, the temptation to realise a large sum of money could prove too much to resist. He might simply sell up. I don't believe Theresa would do that. She knows how much the Astara Stud has meant to me. It's a pity we are such a small family.

The letter concluded with a few more general phrases.

I sat back and thought hard. There was a waspish touch to the letter which rather appealed to me. Clearly Ariadne disapproved of Philip's remarriage and hadn't the slightest intention that a penny of hers should ever fall into the hands of the new wife and any children she might bring Philip. Poor old Phil had been cut off with the proverbial shilling. It was put more politely than that, but that's what had happened and he'd know it.

The letter was dynamite. It was reasonable to suppose Ariadne had no idea it had come into Terry's possession and that was why Terry had taken such trouble to hide it. How had she come by it? Had Philip shown it or sent it to her? Had she come across it by chance amongst her father's papers and simply taken it? Had Ariadne – or anyone else – ever told Terry openly that she would be heiress to Ariadne's entire fortune? And fortune it certainly must be. Or had Ariadne and Alastair deemed it unwise to tell such a young girl she was going to be very, very rich one day?

I pulled myself together. Speculation was dangerous. Nevertheless I was sure I had a valuable piece of information in my grasp. It opened a whole new aspect on the affair. Janice would certainly like to know about this letter.

I had to keep it safe. Above all, I had to keep it out of Jamie's hands.

Ah, Jamie! I thought. He, too, had been cut out of the will. Too unreliable, Ariadne thought him, though he'd 'worked hard'. Worked here, presumably, at the Astara. Someone must run the place. Neither Alastair nor Ariadne looked up to it. Nevertheless, she believed that given a chance, Jamie would sell up and blow the lot on a couple of years' fast living. She knew him better than I did, and nothing I'd seen of him so far, made me doubt her judgement.

I tried to make the rabbit look as if no one had touched him. I couldn't sew up the slit in his back but I pulled the cloth together and he looked intact. I folded the letter up as it had been in a tiny wad and put it in my purse. Then I thought, that was stupid, because if I had to open my purse in front of anyone, they'd see it. So I took it out again and smoothed both sheets out flat. The book of Turgenev plays was on the bedside table. I eased off the wrapper, smoothed the two sheets round the boards, and put the original wrapper back over it. It wasn't perfect, but it would have to do until I could think of something better.

I went back to bed quite satisfied and fell fast asleep.

When I went down to breakfast at eight-thirty in a clean shirt and jeans, only Alastair was there.

'Good morning, Fran! Sleep well? My sister breakfasts in her room. Jamie might join us later. He's been out since six in the yard.'

I sat down and Ruby bustled in and put bacon and eggs

in front of me. I hadn't had bacon and eggs for breakfast for so long, I'd forgotten what it was like.

'Glad to see you've got a decent appetite!' Alastair said, meaning it kindly. 'It's going to be a nice day. I'll take you out in the yard when you've finished and show you around. Do you ride?'

I confessed I only rode a bike.

'Well, we might be able to find a nice quiet animal to put you up on. I'll ask Kelly.'

I wasn't very keen but thanked him, adding, 'I thought I might try and get to Winchester and have a look round there, if that's all right with you. If I go back to Basingstoke, I'll be able to get a bus from there to Winchester, won't I?'

I'd two reasons for trying to reach Winchester. One was to try and track down the wine bar which had been the origin of the book of matches Edna showed me. The letter was important and suggested a motive for someone. But the match book was my only lead. My other reason was to phone Gan and get his opinion on my discovery. I'd already found I risked being overheard if I tried to phone from inside the house.

'Look at the shops, eh?' said Alastair cheerily. 'Or King Arthur's Round Table? They've got that in Winchester. Fake, of course.' He chuckled. 'They painted up an old table to please Henry the Eighth! I think Jamie is going in later this morning. He can give you a lift.'

My heart sank. I mumbled that I didn't want to bother him.

Alastair said heartily, 'Oh, it won't be any trouble for him!'

I'd have liked to hear what Jamie had to say about it. Later on, I probably would.

* * *

Alastair led me out to the stableyard after breakfast. Jamie hadn't appeared by the time we finished and although I looked for him in the yard, I didn't see him. With luck, he'd already left for Winchester. Perhaps I'd been wrong in assuming he ran the place for Ariadne. Perhaps Kelly, whoever Kelly was, ran it.

It was now about half past nine and clearly, most of the morning chores had already been completed. Lie-abeds like me wouldn't be much use around here where everyone was up with the lark, shovelling muck.

The yard was clean and tidy except for a stack of haybales in one corner. A girl was grooming a chestnut horse, working like a Trojan over it.

'Ah,' said Alastair, 'come and meet Kelly.'

I had been supposing Kelly to be a wizened Irish groom in a check cap. But Kelly was also a first name, a girl's name. I'd overlooked that.

She straightened up as we approached and came round the horse, holding a couple of brushes, one in either hand.

'Morning, Mr Alastair!' she said cheerfully, and gave me a curious look.

She was hefty in build, thighs like hams in tight jodhpurs and a bust like a ship's figurehead bouncing around beneath a knitted pullover. Her sleeves were pushed up over her thick forearms and wrists. She had bright ginger hair, plaited into a single long braid and, as often goes with such hair colour, a pale skin which had freckled alarmingly in the sun. Alastair performed introductions while she rubbed the two curry brushes one against the other to clean out the hairs. She wasn't hostile, but she didn't know what to make of me. She smiled a little uncertainly and when Alastair mentioned finding a quiet animal for me to ride, said, 'I'll see what we can do.'

At that moment a man I hadn't seen before came out of a loose-box and looked across at us. He was middle-aged, stocky and tweed-capped.

Alastair murmured, 'Lundy, I wanted a word with him. Excuse me, won't you?'

He set off towards the other man and left me with Kelly.

I took the opportunity to explain I wasn't all that keen on being turned adrift on horseback.

'If you've never ridden before,' she said, 'we might have a problem finding something suitable for you. There's old Dolly, she might do. She can be a bit moody, though, and on her off days she goes on strike. She'd realise you were a novice straight away and play up. We aren't a riding stables, you see. This is a breeding stud.'

'What are they, racehorses?' The question was probably foolish but not knowing one end of a horse from another, I could be allowed it.

Kelly shook her head. 'No, future competition animals. Show-jumpers, dressage, eventers . . . We've a good reputation. The top riders come here to look over our stock.'

'Who runs the stud?' I asked. 'I assume Alastair doesn't.'

'Oh no, Mr Jamie does. Has done for about six or seven years. Joey Lundy is head stud groom and I'm dogsbody. But Mr Jamie makes all the business decisions and does all the paperwork. Deals with buyers, that sort of thing. He's fantastic – and the only one who can use the computer. The place was starting to go downhill before he came but business has picked up terrifically.'

I thought about this. 'It's been here some time, then, the stud?'

The horse stamped a hoof and looked round inquiringly. Kelly patted its rump. 'The stud's been here thirty years.'

That surprised me and I must have shown it.

'Mr and Mrs Cameron founded it,' she explained. 'Then Mr Cameron died and Mrs Cameron carried on until her accident.'

It was beginning to fall into place. I asked, as tactfully as I could, whether the accident had put Ariadne in the wheelchair.

It had, said Kelly. But Mrs Cameron had continued to run the stud until just a few years ago. Then Mr Alastair, as she called him, had taken over for a few years. Then, as it got too much for him, Jamie Monkton had come along.

All this was fascinating but Kelly, as well as the horse, was getting restless. She wanted to get on with her work. I thanked her, apologised for taking up her time and for not being able to stay and lend a hand, and walked over to where Alastair talked with Lundy.

Lundy shook hands with me. He had a vice-like grip which mangled my fingers and he didn't smile. He looked an ugly sort of customer closer to, his eyes small with yellowed whites, as hard as pebbles. I decided I didn't want to tangle with him. He smelled strongly of horses and, I suspected, whisky, certainly not of cologne ... but he looked just the sort of person to hang a body up as easily as a butcher does a side of beef. I wondered whether he smoked and resolved to look around the yard for the odd crushed packet or dog-end. But no doubt smoking was forbidden here for fire hazard reasons. All that hay and straw.

I told Alastair I was going back to the house. On the way I saw Kelly had finished grooming the chestnut and was walking towards a loose-box. She glanced across and waved. I returned the salute. She continued on her way, pausing only to stoop and heft a bale of hay which she carried before her into the box. I couldn't have lifted it, at least not without ricking my back. She was the first person I'd met who heartily approved of Jamie. And that might be significant.

I thought that if I was quick about it, seeing that Jamie hadn't yet shown his face, I might get out and catch the bus before he set out by car. But as I walked into my room, I knew Jamie was quicker off the mark than I'd been.

The reason he hadn't been anywhere I'd been that morning was because he'd been in here, going through the room. Don't ask me how I knew it had been Jamie, I just did. Well, it wasn't likely to have been anyone else.

I was mad with myself, aside from being mad with him, because I should have expected this.

My holdall had been turned inside out. I'd left Gan's camera in it and he'd found that and taken out the film. The celluloid reel sprawled in a tangle across the carpet. The film hadn't been used, but he wasn't taking any chances. I wondered what he'd been afraid I might have photo-ed. Himself, perhaps. It was a thought – another one which hadn't occurred to me before. I was a really lousy detective, that was for sure.

The wardrobe door, which I'd closed, swung open. My skirt had fallen off the hanger on to the floor. I picked it up, muttering what I'd like to do to the culprit. He'd even gone through the pockets of the jacket, leaving them pulled out.

He'd also searched around in the dressing table and the chest of drawers. But he hadn't touched the stuffed animals and – when I checked – I found he hadn't touched the Turgenev. The letter was as I'd left it, wrapped round the boards.

He was determined, was our Jamie, but skimped detail. He didn't know how much I knew and he wasn't sure exactly why I'd come down here. He wanted to get rid of me, but not before he found out. He wanted to know exactly what I planned to do. But there'd been nothing he could find to tell him except—

I gave a screech. My notebook! Yes, he found it. He'd sat on the bed and read it, I could see the dent in the duvet. Then he'd thrown it down. I picked it up and looked through it. I hadn't written much. Just a few key words with question marks. 'T's parents?' 'The last quarrel at home?' 'The man Gan saw?' That sort of thing.

It told him enough. It told him I was playing detective and 'playing' was the right word for it. Had I been half way competent I'd have made sure the notebook was where no one could lay his hands on it or at least invented some kind of code instead of writing it out so plainly.

I tidied up, muttering to myself, put on my jacket and went downstairs.

Jamie was in the hall, standing before a mirror and adjusting his cap to a rakish angle. He thought himself quite something, that was clear. He'd also splashed around aftershave, one with cologne scent. It was trapped in the hall, the same cologne scent I'd noticed when Nev and I had come back from Camden, and which had told me we'd had a visitor in the squat.

Reflected in the mirror, he could see me and see the furious glare I was giving him.

'Something wrong, Fran? Sleep badly?' He grinned and turned to face me. 'Bad conscience, perhaps.'

'Tell me about it,' I growled at him.

'My conscience is clear, sweetheart. Alastair told Ruby to tell me you want a lift into Winchester.'

'I don't. I'll go to Basingstoke and find another bus. Alastair had the idea I could go with you, but the bus seems much more attractive.'

'Bad-tempered little tyke, aren't you?' He shrugged. 'It'll take you all day to do it by bus both ways. Anyway, Alastair wants me to give you a lift. We need to keep him happy, don't we?' He gave that nasty grin again. 'Both of us.'

Alastair was walking back from the yard as we left. He waved at the car as it passed him. I waved back, trying to smile brightly.

'That's the ticket!' Jamie said.

He succeeded, as he probably intended, in irritating me. 'You think you've got all the answers, don't you?'

'Not all, Fran,' he retorted. 'Not as far as you're concerned, but I reckon I can make an informed guess.'

'Guess away, it won't do you any good. You wouldn't last five minutes where I come from, let me tell you that!'

'Spare me the tales of your seedy lifestyle, Fran. If you don't like it here, go on back to the smoke. Keep out of our way.'

'You mean, keep out of your way. Why did you search my room during breakfast?

He glanced at me, eyebrows raised. 'Did I?'

'You know you did!' I snarled. 'Don't play stupid games! Ruby wouldn't need to sneak in. She could go in there openly to vacuum out or something, if she wanted an excuse. It wasn't likely to be Ariadne and Alastair was with me!'

'My, what a clever little sleuth! And that's what all this is about, isn't it? You fancy yourself as the great detective! Notebooks, camera, all the trimmings.'

He was laughing openly. Anything I said would only encourage his mirth so I seethed in silence.

I had another reason to keep quiet. I had remembered how Alastair had insisted on taking me to the yard after breakfast and talking to Kelly about finding me a horse to ride, even though I'd made it clear I wasn't keen on that idea. Was he giving Jamie time to go through my gear? I hoped not. But it was Alastair who'd suggested Jamie take me to Winchester. Was that so Jamie could keep an eye on me?

I was feeling miserable by now. I had trusted Alastair. But that was no attitude for a detective to have. From now on, I trusted nobody.

Jamie planned a cross-country route. We took the lane which had been sign-posted 'Lords Farm' and bumped along over its potholes. There were high banks to either side and no passing place that I could see. Jamie drove at a fair pace and I hoped we met nothing coming the other way, say a tractor.

Even as I worried about this, we rounded a corner and Jamie slammed on the brakes, cursing. I shot forward, was jerked back by my seat-belt, and grabbed the dashboard. The road ahead was filled with cows. They'd just come out of an open gate from a field on the right and were plodding down the narrow track ahead of us.

We inched forward but it was no good in this narrow defile. They'd more or less come to a stop and we had to stop, too. There were hairy bodies and big soulful eyes all around us. They peered in the windows and swung their mud-caked tails against the car's sides which obviously drove Jamie wild.

'Blasted animals! I only had the car cleaned two days ago! Who's in charge of them?'

'No one,' I said, slumping down in my seat. A huge bovine was investigating the door on my side. The creature's breath was misting up the outside of the window as it snuffled around trying, for all I knew, to get it open, and its gungy muzzle left yucky smears on the glass. You could understand Jamie being so mad.

'This is ridiculous!' He was building up a nice head of steam. 'Fran, get out and clear a way through the brutes!'

'What? You're out of your tiny mind!'

He glowered. 'Go on, you wanted to visit the country. All you have to do is chivvy them a bit. They'll move for you.'

'Forget it!'

'They're making a helluva mess of my car! What's the matter, afraid of them? I thought you were the tough sort. All that streetwise guff. I wouldn't last five minutes where you come from, eh? Well, you don't seem to be making out very well here!'

I know I should have ignored it. I shouldn't have risen to it. He was needling me into doing something I shouldn't. I knew all this but I still took the bait. 'All right!' I slipped off my jacket, I couldn't afford to get that messed up, and got out of the car.

I had a job even to get the door open because the cow which was so interested in it wouldn't move. I kept pushing the car against it, even though Jamie got very hot under the collar about making the mess on the outside worse, and at last the beast backed off.

Once I was out, I was marooned. The cows were all around me. There was one thing even I knew cows did a lot of, and it made me very careful where I put my feet. Have you any idea how large a cow is? It's enormous. Like a tank. You do not argue with a cow. It does what it wants and goes where it likes. Not only did they show no sign of moving out of my way, but they seemed to find me some sort of interesting novelty and they all wanted a closer look at me. I was pinned against the car by steaming, smelly, dribbling monsters.

It was a matter of honour, although it felt more like a matter of life and death. I couldn't get back in the car. Jamie'd never let me forget it. So I edged my way round to the front and clapped my hands.

Zilch. The cows ignored it but the flies which had been buzzing around the cows, now began to investigate me. I flailed my hands around my head to drive them away. When I looked behind me, Jamie was watching through the windscreen, laughing himself sick.

That made me mad. I slapped the nearest cow on the back. 'Come on, Bluebell, you've got to help me! It's you and me against him!'

It turned its head and gazed at me. There was a black and white one coming up on my left with a moody look in its eye. I had to act as though I was in charge and hope the bluff worked.

I gave a piercing whistle and yelled, 'Move it!' Cowboy stuff.

Funnily enough, they did try to move. They shuffled a bit sideways, bumped into one another and started lowing noisily. It was pretty clear to me by now, because I stopped panicking, that something up ahead was preventing them from going on. I shoved my way between them, and sure enough, just around the next bend was the farmyard and the gate was closed. They were all waiting for someone to open it.

I unhitched it and dragged it open. The cows began to plod through at quite a brisk pace and mill about in the yard.

Then a dog ran out and started barking at me. I was trapped between gate and cows so there was nothing I could do but get behind the gate as the dog ran up and began growling at me. The cows didn't like it much, either, and one of them put down its head and made a little rush at the dog. The dog backed off very sensibly and joined me behind the gate.

We were both rescued by a man in a pullover and gumboots who came out of a barn and shouted, 'What's the matter?'

'The gate was closed, they couldn't get in!' I yelled back.

'Oh, right!' He began to push the cows around and they ambled off towards the barn and disappeared inside. The cowman or farmer or whatever he was came towards me. He was a big fellow, built like a brick barn. He rested broad, calloused worker's hands on the top rung of the gate.

'Who're you, then?' he asked.

His voice was educated and he didn't ask it impolitely, just curious. The dog wasn't bothered about me now it saw the man didn't object to me. It sat down waiting, with its tongue lolling out.

I explained about being stuck in the car behind the herd. I'd just finished when there was a beep of a horn and we both looked round to see that Jamie had driven up as far as the gate and was gesticulating to me to get back in the car.

The farmer's friendly manner cooled distinctly. 'With him, are you?' The tone of his voice told that he'd met Jamie before and had much the same opinion of him I had.

'I'm not with him!' I denied. 'I mean, yes, he's giving me a lift. But that's as far as it goes. I'm staying at the Monktons as Alastair Monkton's guest.'

'Oh, yes?' He looked at me thoughtfully. His face was sunburned and he had rather nice blue eyes with little crow's-feet lines at the corner which crinkled up as he squinted into the light, studying me. He was wearing one of those tweed caps they all liked so much, but from beneath it escaped a mop of untidy light brown hair. There was something about him I liked. He was looking at me as though he rather liked the look of me, too.

'My name's Fran Varady,' I decided to establish the acquaintance on a formal basis. 'Is this Lords Farm? I saw the signpost further back.'

'Nice to meet you, Fran. Yes, this is Lords Farm. Welcome to it, if you take my meaning!'

He grinned and wiped one of his shovel-hands on the front of his sweater before offering it. 'I'm Nick Bryant.' It was pretty obvious he was deliberately ignoring Jamie who was grimacing at me and signalling I should rejoin him.

I tried turning my back on him. Jamie opened the car door and leaned out, yelling, 'Fran! Are you getting back in this car or are you going to stand there all day gossiping?'

At that point Jamie saw my companion and said loudly and sourly, 'Oh, it's you, Bryant? Your wretched beasts have made a mess of my car!'

'My, my,' said Nick amiably. 'So they have. You'll have to get the brush and bucket out, Jim!'

'Don't call me Jim!' yelled Jamie. He made an obvious effort to regain control. He looked at me and then back at Nick. 'And how is Mrs Bryant?'

Jamie's gaze slid maliciously towards me again as he asked. Damn, I thought. The nice ones are always married.

'She's fine. Old Mr Monkton and Mrs Cameron, they all right?'

Jamie told him ungraciously that they were, and as there appeared to be no more family members left between us to inquire after, conversation came to a natural end for the time being.

'I'd better go,' I said apologetically to Nick. I wanted to talk to him more than ever, now that it was clear he knew Jamie and the Monktons. 'Look,' I said quickly in a low voice. 'This may sound odd, but I need to come back and talk to you some time.'

Jamie squawked, 'If you don't get back in this car straight away, I'm going to drive on without you!'

'I've got to go!' I urged.

Nick glanced at Jamie in no very kindly way. 'Watch yourself!' he muttered. 'And come back any time you like.'

I got back into the car. Jamie was scowling and now he sniffed the air and said, 'You stink of cows! Open the window!'

'So, whose fault is that?'

He drove off with a squeal of tyres. I waved farewell to Nick who raised a hand in salute and set off towards the barn and his charges.

'Shouldn't have thought Farmer Giles there was your type!' said Jamie sarcastically.

'At least he was polite!'

Jamie muttered. After a little while he spoke again, quite calmly, sounding almost polite himself.

'Look, Fran. We can go on like this, sniping and snarling at each other or we can put our cards on the table, come clean. Last night was a mistake, I admit it. But we really do need to talk.'

He must have thought me simple. It was obvious that he'd realised that I'd made a possible ally in Nick Bryant and he was reformulating his own tactics accordingly. After trying to bully and frighten me, he was trying being nice to me.

'I don't have anything I want to talk to you about,' I told him. 'And there's no reason I should. Alastair came to see me in London. He sought me out. I returned the compliment. It's between him and me.'

Jamie gave a hiss and we swept round a corner. 'It concerns me too. I *am* family. In fact, I'm the only family they've got left apart from Alastair's son, Phil. I feel responsible for the old people. I am responsible for them. I carry the responsibility for everything round here and I take it seriously!'

I didn't want to give away anything I'd learned from the

letter. I asked casually, 'Why doesn't Phil run the stud?'

Jamie hooted. 'Phil? Hates horses, for a start! Anyway, he doesn't get on with Alastair. Alastair is a loyal old bird. He tries hard to welcome Phil whenever he shows up. But it's not easy. If you'd been here when they both – I mean Phil and Marcie, Theresa's mother – turned up for the funeral, you'd have understood. Talk about undercurrents. Of course, they divorced some time back and Phil's remarried. He didn't bring his second wife. I wondered whether he would. But even Phil didn't have that much nerve.'

That had given me a jolt because I hadn't realised that Terry had been buried in the time between Alastair coming to the flat and my coming down here. I said so and asked, rather miserably, whether she was buried in the churchyard at Abbotsfield. I'd sat there to eat my tuna sandwich and perhaps she'd been only a few feet away beneath the turf. I didn't tell Jamie that last bit.

He said she was buried there which made me feel pretty grim. The police had given permission, he said, especially as it was an interment and not a cremation. He didn't explain that but I guessed the reason. They could always dig her up again if they wanted to.

'What's Terry's mother like? Marcia, you said she's called?'

He nodded. 'She's a gold-plated bitch but I like Marcie. To be fair, she was genuinely cut up at the funeral, so was Phil. I don't want to give you the wrong impression about that. But neither of them could wait to get away afterwards. Phil back to the States and Marcia back to the new man in her life.' Jamie gave a short laugh. 'She probably doesn't trust him enough to leave him for too long.'

I gave it a minute or two, then asked, 'And that's the whole family, there's really no one else?'

'Not a soul.' We had reached a junction with a more important, busy road. Jamie drew up, waiting for a break in traffic.

'I don't want you down here asking questions. Ariadne's sick and Alastair is far more frail than he looks. Theresa's death knocked the stuffing out of both of them. Don't go making things worse.'

'I'm not thick!' I told him crossly. 'I'd be tactful.'

'I won't! If I find you've been talking to either of them about it, I'll break your grubby little neck!'

We didn't talk again until we reached Winchester. He parked in a public carpark near the town centre.

'If you want a lift back with me, be here at four. If you're not here, I'll assume you've caught, or mean to catch, the bus.'

'I'll take the bus!' I told him.

I hadn't put my jacket back on again when I'd got back in the car after talking to Nick. Now I picked it up. Loose change I'd kept in my pocket for phone calls spilled out and rolled over the well of the front passenger seat, most of it disappearing under the seat itself.

I cursed and scrabbled for it, watched impatiently by Jamie. I pushed my hand under the seat feeling for the coins and my fingertips touched something else, small, pyramid shaped and with a familiar, but momentarily unidentifiable, dusty feel to it. Instinctively, I scooped it up with the coins and withdrew my clasped fist and shoved the whole lot into my pocket.

Jamie slammed his door and locked up. We parted at the top of the road and I was able to look at my hand, the one I'd reached under the seat. The fingertips were smudged with blue colour. I reached in the pocket and took out the small, pyramid-shaped object.

It was an end of blue chalk. One of Squib's chalks, I was almost sure. And it tied Jamie into the squat along with the cologne smell and the fact that his general description was a match to that of the man seen by Ganesh. The chalk scrap must have been trapped in his shoe or maybe he'd worn trousers with turn-ups that day. Three things were too much for coincidence.

So it *was* you, Jamie! I thought and it was followed by a even more alarming thought. The note I'd stupidly made about 'the man Gan saw'. If I was right and Jamie was the man, that put Gan in real danger. It was quite possible Jamie was a killer, and I had kindly suggested his next victim. Supposing the next not to be myself.

Chapter Eleven

Winchester came as a surprise to me. I hadn't expected it to be so busy but it was obviously on the tourist trail. The pavements were crowded, the streets blocked with traffic. There were a number of expensive boutiques and any number of places to eat or drink. Seeking out one wine bar wasn't going to be so easy as I'd imagined.

Now that I had even less reason to trust Jamie, I had to make doubly sure he wasn't following me. In these crowds it wouldn't be difficult to do it unobserved. I dodged in and out of pedestrians, nipped across the road between cars risking my neck and getting a fair amount of abuse, and eventually decided that I must have given him the slip, if he had tried to trail me. If he saw me now, it would be just bad luck.

I couldn't remember the exact name of the wine bar on the match packet, but it had been something to do with ecclesiastical architecture, Crypt or Vault or Cloister, something of that sort. There had been a thumbnail sketch of a gothic arch on the packet. I decided it would be located centrally, where most tourist trade was. But it took me a while, trudging round (it goes without saying, that everyone I asked turned out to be a visitor). Eventually I stumbled across it in a narrow side alley. It had to be the one, not only because I was exhausted and there had to be a limit to the number of watering-holes in this place, but it was the only one so far with a name remotely in the category I sought. *Beneath the Arches*, it was called. I'd been near enough.

I went in. It looked old, and certainly had arches. It was nearing lunchtime and already pretty well packed out. I squeezed into a corner and ordered a glass of red wine and a cheese sandwich, that being the cheapest thing on the menu. There was an ashtray on the table and, propped in it, an identical packet of matches to the one Edna had so proudly displayed. I pocketed it. I was in the right place.

I wasn't quite sure how much further on that would take my investigations. The sandwich and wine arrived. As I ate, I reviewed what I'd learned so far and came up with several theories, each of which I discarded two minutes after deciding that it must be the right one.

I paid my bill and went along to the Ladies Room. I discovered, as I'd hoped, that just outside the toilets was a public pay-phone and, thank goodness, one which took coins, not cards. I rang the Patels.

As bad luck would have it Mr Patel answered and, although I asked him to fetch Ganesh, he started talking to me himself. I didn't want to upset him, but I did try and get across to him that public phones eat money and I didn't have that much loose change.

Eventually he fetched Ganesh when I was nearly out of coins.

'Listen!' I ordered Ganesh before he could start. 'I'm nearly out of money so can't waste time. I'm in Winchester in the wine bar which advertised with that book of matches Edna had.'

'What's this about a book of matches?' Ganesh asked. 'You told me it was a cigarette packet.'

Down the line came a tremendous crash of falling crates and voices upraised in dispute, somewhere behind Ganesh. I hoped he could hear me.

'There was a match book, too! Don't interrupt, Gan, please! I told you, I'll run out of money. I believe the man you saw in the street is down here and his name is Jamie Monkton. He's also the one who dropped the cigarette packet. I feel sure of it. And Gan – Jamie knows you saw him, so take care! He's a nasty bit of work. I've also found something else, a letter. I think all of this has to do with a will.'

Someone at Ganesh's end of things had now begun bashing some metal object with a hammer. 'Will who?' he shouted.

'A will!' I yelled. 'Testament! Saying who gets your goods and chattels!'

'Now you've found all this out, come back!' He didn't sound particularly impressed.

'Can't. Met someone today who might be able to tell me more. A farmer.'

'A what?'

'A farmer—' Peep-peep-peep. 'I've got no more money.'

'Fran—!'

The phone went dead.

I had a cup of coffee in order to collect more coins in change. This time I rang through to the police station and asked for Janice. They tried to stall me and find out what I wanted first, but I wasn't having that. I told them, either I'd talk to Janice or no one. If she wasn't there, I'd call back when she was.

Eventually they put me through to Janice.

'Fran!' Janice's voice, howling down the line, nearly dented my ear-drum. 'What on earth do you think you're playing at? You had no business to leave town without telling me of your intention and giving me your new address! Where are you?'

I'd learned something from my call to Ganesh. I told her I only had a few coins, so would she ring me back? I gave her the number of the pay-phone and hung up.

The phone buzzed almost at once. I picked it up. 'Janice, listen. Don't yell. You can yell at me when I get back to town.'

I told her what I'd told Gan and explained why I was in the wine bar, that Edna had shown me the match book, and had probably seen the same man as Ganesh had spotted. 'I smelled cologne in the squat when I got back that evening. Didn't I tell you that? Jamie Monkton uses a very similar cologne.'

She stopped shouting and became quiet and business-like. 'Fran, you could cause us all a tremendous amount of trouble. You're intelligent enough to know you shouldn't be blundering around in police investigations. As for the letter, you're not authorised to remove anything from that house and, if you do, it's theft.'

'I've got this gut feeling it's the key to the whole thing!' I was beginning to get exasperated. She really didn't have to be so dense. Was someone else listening in at the cop-shop? Yes, I thought, someone probably was.

'We need more than your gut feelings, Francesca. I've already got more than enough cause to charge you with obstructing the police. As for Jamie Monkton, I can't proceed on your flimsy evidence. The baglady's testimony is useless. She's certainly not mentally competent. As regards the so-called identification of an after-shave scent, all those male toiletries smell more or less the same. Tom uses them. They all stink.'

'Not like this one! How is dear old Tom, anyway?' I asked because she was being awkward and I wanted to needle her.

'Still being a shit. He wants to move back in.'

'You're going to let him?'

'He wants to rebuild our marriage. He's made an appointment for us to see a Relate counsellor.' She changed her tone. 'However, this is nothing to do with the matter in hand! I can't go by a smell you think you can identify. This isn't some party-game. As for a vague description made to you by your chum, Ganesh Patel! *You* didn't see this mystery man in the street! You don't know it was Jamie Monkton. You're *guessing*, Fran. That's all.'

She was beginning to give me doubts. I could be wrong.

'The chalk . . . ' I said desperately.

'Fell out of your jacket pocket with the coins.'

'It didn't! There was no chalk in the pockets, I know that!'

'Prove it. You can't. Look, I'm engaged on police work here, not kid's games. If you want to play detective, go and buy yourself a box of Cluedo.'

'But I may have put Ganesh in danger!' I bellowed into the receiver. Two women passing by on their way to the loo gave me alarmed glances.

'*You're* in danger,' Janice said silkily. 'You're in danger from *me*! Get yourself back here to London *pronto*? Understand? And no nonsense. If you try any more playing at detectives, I'll see you really are charged with obstructing police inquiries!'

'Stuff your police inquiries!' I said. Her ingratitude had really got to me. I hung up the receiver before she could reply.

I stomped back into the wine bar in a rage and it was nearly my undoing.

Jamie was there, sitting at a table, making a start on what looked like steak and kidney pie and talking to a pallid man in a business suit. The pallid man was sipping soup and looked as if he was making it his meal. A bottle of mineral water stood by his glass. Perhaps he had an ulcer. He looked depressed enough. Although having to sit in a cramped room full of tourists, watching Jamie munch through pie and chips and knock back half a bottle of plonk by himself would depress anyone. They must have come in just as I left to find the phone. It was a bit of luck because if I'd been at a table, they'd almost certainly have seen me. Equally, if I hadn't gone to find the phone, or if Mr Patel hadn't kept me talking, I might have left and missed them. But there he was, Jamie, large as life. This must be one of his favourite eating spots.

I wished I had the nerve to go back and call Janice again. Because here was another coincidence, and even she would have to admit it was one too many. If Jamie hadn't dropped that match book, someone else had, who'd been in this Winchester wine bar. The likelihood of that was nil.

I hadn't asked Jamie his reason for coming to Winchester

today, in any case it was unlikely he'd have told me. Clearly it was a business lunch of some kind. I wished dearly I knew what they were discussing. Jamie was doing most of the talking, the pallid man pushing the spoon around his bowl and crumbling a bread roll in gloomy silence as he listened. I hoped that Jamie was so intent on getting the point across that he'd be oblivious to all else around him. I had to walk past their table to get out into the street.

I edged past, trying not to look at them. If someone is looking at you, you sense it. I got to the door without anyone calling after me and glancing back, saw that Jamie was still talking away, and refilling his own glass at the same time. Even from the back, the man in the business suit looked depressed.

I reached the street. Safe. I set off. I had some shopping to do.

I went to the nearest chemist and bought a new film for the camera. I wanted to get back to Astara Stud quickly and the bus services would be too slow. Nothing for it but to hitch.

I was in luck. A middle-aged woman stopped for me, concern on her face as she peered at me through the window.

'My dear? You really shouldn't be doing this. It's very dangerous. Anyone could offer you a lift, just anyone!'

'I wouldn't go with just anyone, honestly,' I told her. 'And I wouldn't be doing this if I wasn't desperate. My boyfriend dumped me here. We had a quarrel. He'd pushed me out of his car on this road and just drove away and left me. I don't even know where I am. I need to get to a place just outside Basingstoke, Abbotsfield.'

She was shocked. 'How callous! What an irresponsible young man! Really, there can be no excuse for that sort of behaviour!' Indecision showed on her face. 'I don't normally give lifts to hitch-hikers. One never knows . . . '

She peered at me again and I tried to look innocent, harmless and hard done by.

'I suppose it's all right,' she said. 'I'm going near Basingstoke. I can drop you on the main road in.'

I hopped in the car before she had time to change her mind, thanking her profusely.

'What did you quarrel with your young man about?' she asked as we drove off.

This was a tricky one. But I noticed a mascot swinging from the key-ring holding the ignition key, a little plastic dachshund.

'He made me get rid of my dog,' I said. 'He wouldn't let me keep her.'

'What!' The car swerved. Perhaps I shouldn't have picked on something she felt so strongly about. 'What did you – he – do with your dog?' she demanded sharply.

I had to get this right. 'A friend took her. A good home, I know that. In the country and everything. It's not that any harm's come to my dog. It's just, I had to give her away. I was very fond of her. She used to sleep on my bed. That's what he didn't like. He said he was allergic to her. I don't think he was. He just wanted rid of her, you know.'

She sniffed. 'Couldn't you have compromised? Bought a dog basket?'

'He wouldn't,' I said firmly. 'He said she had to go.'

'What sort of dog is she?'

One can over-egg the pudding. I turned my eyes from

the dachshund mascot, bobbing on the key. 'Part retriever, part German shepherd.'

'Goodness, wasn't she rather large to sleep on your bed? I must admit, dear, I can see why your young man might object.'

'But she'd slept on my bed since she was a puppy,' I said pathetically. By now I'd begun to believe all this myself. I felt quite aggrieved.

She sighed. 'I know how it is with animals. It's so easy to spoil a puppy. Such adorable little creatures. Bad habits set in. And if it grows into a really big dog ... You were rather unwise, dear.'

'Yes, I know that now,' I said meekly. 'I won't make the same mistake again.'

'You're going to get another dog?'

'Yes. And another boyfriend.'

'Perhaps you should get a smaller one,' she said thoughtfully.

'Yes, this one was a body-builder and it was hopeless arguing with him.'

'No, dear, I meant a smaller dog!' She frowned. 'A body-builder? Sharing a bed with a German shepherd-retriever cross and – er – and you? It really couldn't have been very comfortable.'

She had been intending to stop just outside of Basingstoke, but in view of my predicament, as she termed it, and the distress I was obviously feeling over parting with my dog, she insisted on taking me right into town and putting me down at the bus station.

'You are sure you've got money for the bus fare, dear?'

I promised her I had. I was feeling as guilty as sin by now, but the deception was in a good cause. Plus she drove off with the glow that comes from having done a good deed.

I jumped on the Abbotsfield bus, reckoning that I'd be home before Jamie. I knew he planned on leaving Winchester at four that afternoon and I knew how long it had taken us to drive there. Arithmetic told me what time to expect him home. And sure enough, there was no sign of his car at the Astara Stud. I looked in the garage. Empty. I'd cut it fine, but I'd done it.

I wanted to know who else was out and about in the vicinity because I didn't want to be observed when Jamie got back. I walked over to the stableyard. It had a sleepy late afternoon look about it. I wondered where Kelly was. As I stood at the entrance, looking around, a horse whinnied inside a loose-box near at hand, a male voice cursed it, and a moment later, Lundy came out.

He saw me and stopped. 'Can I help you?' The words contrasted markedly with the way they were expressed. The only help he wanted to give me was help on my way out, probably with his boot.

I told him, I was looking for Kelly. I didn't particularly want to find her and get into conversation, because I hadn't to miss Jamie's return, but I had to give Lundy a reason for hanging about there.

'She's not here.' He came closer and instinctively I took a step back. That was a bad tactical move because it encouraged him to think he'd got me at a disadvantage.

'I want a word with you,' he said ominously.

'What about?' I stood my ground although my instinct was to run. He couldn't harm me, I told myself. I was Alastair's guest.

'What are you doing here?'

'Looking for Kelly,' I repeated nonchalantly.

'Don't mess me about!' He pushed his ugly mug at me. 'I don't mean in the bloody yard. I mean here – at the Astara. What's your game, eh?'

'I'm a visitor!' I said grandly.

He spat to one side, expressing his opinion of that.

'Ask Mr Alastair if you've got doubts', I added.

His pebbly little eyes bored into me. 'Clever, think yourself, I dare say. Well, you be careful. I got my eye on you!' I was aware of it, both of them.

I chose to say nothing, largely because I couldn't think of anything. He seemed satisfied he'd delivered his warning and turned away, going back into the loose-box and cussing the unfortunate horse in it again.

I scurried away and hid in the tangle of buddleia bushes by the garage. The sweet smell was overpowering and reminded me of honey. There were any number of butterflies fluttering about the mauve blossoms and perched on them. A small bird of a kind I didn't recognise (I can only recognise sparrows) was darting about catching the butterflies and gobbling them up. I felt sorry for the butterflies but admired the agility of the bird.

He hunted. I waited, camera ready. I was a hunter, too.

Jamie didn't stand me up. He turned up about ten minutes later than I'd estimated. Perhaps he'd waited a few minutes in Winchester, at the carpark, to see if I was coming home with him. The car swept up to the garage and he got out. I took a snap of him closing the car door. Then he walked round the car to inspect the muddy marks left by our encounter with the cattle. That gave me a chance for another couple of shots. Then he looked back down the drive which gave me a beautiful profile.

I was getting careless by then and must have moved because the buddleia rustled and Jamie's head snapped round. I held my breath. But my little friend, the hunting bird, chose that moment to fly out. Jamie relaxed and set off towards the house, whistling.

I waited a few minutes and then followed, entering the house through the kitchen. Ruby was there, mixing batter. A woman I'd never seen before was tackling a pile of ironing in the corner.

'Hullo, my dear,' Ruby said. 'You came back with Mr Jamie, then?'

'No, I came earlier. I was finished in town.' I glanced curiously at the other woman, who hadn't looked up from her work or shown any sign she was aware I'd come in.

She was a shapeless sort of person, looking rather as if she were made of dough. Her straight grey hair was parted centrally and pinned back with a couple of kirby grips and she wore the sort of wrap-over apron I hadn't seen in years.

'Mrs Lundy,' said Ruby, nodding towards the woman. 'She comes over a couple of times a week to give me a hand.'

Assuming Mrs Lundy would acknowledge the introduction, I said hullo. But she carried on ironing without any reaction at all, although Ruby had spoken in a normal voice.

'Is she, I mean, is it—'

'Joey Lundy's wife,' Ruby anticipated me. 'They live in the bungalow, behind the yard.'

She still spoke quite normally, clearly audible to the

ironer, and still Mrs Lundy took not the slightest notice. She paused long enough to sprinkle water from a small basin on to her ironing, then carried on. It occurred to me she might be deaf.

As tactfully as I could, I lifted a hand, tapped my ear and raised my eyebrows.

'Oh, no,' said Ruby cheerfully. 'There's nothing wrong with her hearing. She's not one for chat. A bit slow on the uptake, but a good worker. Makes ironing a real art.'

An awful thought struck me. 'Kelly, the stablegirl, she's not their daughter, is she?'

'Oh goodness, no!' Ruby chuckled. 'She just lodges with them.'

Lodging with the Lundys must be about as comfortable as a Tudor traitor would have found himself in the Tower.

Ruby tapped her spoon on the edge of the mixing bowl. 'There, that's done!' She began to spoon the contents over a Pyrex dish part-filled with stewed fruit. Then she handed me the wooden spoon with batter smeared on it. 'Do you want to lick it clean, or are you too grown-up for that? Theresa, when she was little, she always did hang round to scrape out the bowl. And when she grew older, too!'

'I'm not too grown-up!' I took the spoon. 'I used to do this when my grandma made cakes. She used to make a wonderful chocolate cake.'

Ruby put the dish in the oven and began to clean the worktop. Mrs Lundy folded a pillowcase, put it on a pile of finished ironing and took another from a daunting pile of dampwash. Ironing might be an art with her but it appeared to have turned her into a zombie, or living with Lundy had. But she wasn't deaf and, despite what Ruby had said, she might understand more than expected,

enough to repeat anything I said to her husband. On the
other hand, it was a good opportunity to talk to Ruby. I
just had to gamble.

'Ruby,' I said carefully, 'you know I shared a – a house
with Terry, Theresa, don't you?'

'So they told me.' Ruby straightened up, expelling
breath with an 'ouf!'. Her face was kind but her eyes
were sharp. 'Was she in some kind of trouble, poor lass?
Because seems to me, she must have been.'

'I don't know, Ruby. If she was, she didn't talk about
it. Honestly, I'd tell Alastair if I knew.'

'She was headstrong,' Ruby shook her head. 'Mr
Alastair and Mrs Cameron, they both doted on her. But
she made life very difficult for them. They're getting on
in years, you see. They couldn't cope with the sort of
problems young people have. Not today's youngsters,
anyway. It was beyond them. They wanted to help, but
they didn't know how, most likely.'

'What sort of problems?' I asked guilelessly. Mrs
Lundy splashed water and ironed on accompanied by a
faint hiss of steam. It was a pity she was there, but it
couldn't be helped.

Either Ruby had remembered Mrs Lundy or she
wasn't going to gossip with a stranger, and that's what I
was. 'Bless you, don't ask me!' was all she said.

She wasn't going to say any more. I thanked her for
letting me finish the batter and walked past Mrs Lundy
out of the kitchen. As I passed by her, she looked up. I
had a fleeting impression of a flat, vacant face, heavily
coated with face powder. But no lipstick or any other
effort to make herself presentable. It seemed odd. I
smiled at her and she looked down again at once, but not

before I'd seen a momentary reaction in her eyes. Not any return of greeting. But fear.

I had plenty to think about as I went upstairs to my room. Once there, I set about adding to my photographic record. I snapped a view of the room, showing the toys on top of the chest of drawers. Then I snapped the rabbit, showing his back pulled open the way I'd done it to find the letter inside. Then I snapped both pages of the letter, although probably the writing wouldn't come out well enough to be legible, and returned it to its hiding place inside the book wrapper.

When I'd done all that, even though the film was far from finished, I ran it on to the end, took it out and rolled it up in some cottonwool from the make-up drawer. I wrote a note to Ganesh, telling him to get it developed by the one-hour service locally and take it straight away to Inspector Janice, because it would back up what I'd told them both on the phone. I especially wanted him to study the photos of Jamie to see if he could identify him as the man he saw hanging around the house the day Terry died.

When I'd done all that, I stepped out into the passage.

There was a gasp. Mrs Lundy was outside the room, standing by my door. I'd opened it suddenly and she stepped back, looking so confused and frightened that I automatically assured her, 'It's all right!'

She shuffled her feet. 'I been to the linen cupboard,' she said.

'Lots of ironing.' There wasn't much I could say to this poor creature.

She still seemed to think I was going to scold her for being in the wrong part of the house. 'I come upstairs to take it all to the linen cupboard,' she repeated. The flat face looked into mine, then she turned and hurried away.

But not before I'd had time to realise the reason for the layer of face powder. Beneath it, her doughy features were puffed and bruised. Joey Lundy was a wife-beater.

I walked slowly down to the kitchen. I knew I was very angry but I felt quite calm. Ruby was at the table, enjoying a quiet cup of tea and looking at cookery pages in a woman's magazine, waiting for her own fruit sponge pudding to be ready to come out of the oven.

'Joey knocks his wife around,' I said. 'Why doesn't anyone here do anything about it?'

She looked up from the brightly coloured pictures of perfect cakes and complicated desserts. 'One can't come between husband and wife,' she said reproachfully.

'Rot.'

She flushed. 'Mr Alastair has spoken to Lundy about it. Lundy's a good worker.' She leaned forward. 'Would you want Mr Alastair to sack Lundy?'

'I'd throw him off the premises!' I told her.

'Yes, you would. And then what? He'd blame that poor creature, take it out on her. She wouldn't leave him. Wherever he went, he'd drag her along with him. Away from here, it'd be worse. Mr Alastair, he keeps an eye on things. There's a limit. Lundy knows it. Leave it to Mr Alastair, dear.'

She was right, of course. Lucy had been bright, articulate, young, and she'd found it hard to break away from a violent husband. Mrs Lundy was never going to be able to make the break. Here the situation was controlled. It was the best to be hoped for. I hated to admit it but there didn't appear to be any way out of it.

I asked Ruby if she had any stamps and an envelope, preferably a strong manila one. It didn't have to be new. I could strike out the old address.

She did better. She found a little padded Jiffy bag. I bought two first-class stamps off her. Out of her sight, I put my letter to Ganesh and the roll of film in the bag and stuck it all down with Sellotape. Then I slipped out of the house and grounds and walked down the road to where I'd noticed a brick postbox by the roadside.

I posted the package with relief. Once it had left my fingers and fallen down inside the postbox, there was no way Jamie could get it back, even if he found out about it. It was on its way to Ganesh and, all going according to plan, from Ganesh to Inspector Janice.

As a detective, I was improving. I was at least getting a bit more organised.

Tomorrow, I'd tackle the farm. I knew now what time the cows pitched up for milking and I'd avoid that. I hoped Nick Bryant would be there at other times. I had an idea I could talk to Nick . . . and to his wife as well, of course.

There was an hour to go before dinner. I didn't want to go back into the house just yet and, anyway, there was something else I had to do.

I didn't really want to do it, but it had to be done. I walked on down the lane, turned into the main road and set off back to Abbotsfield. Now that I knew the way, it didn't seem so far. It took me a quarter of an hour. I went straight to the churchyard and sought out the corner where recent tombstones indicated the modern burials were taking place.

Theresa's was very recent and they hadn't got a stone fixed up yet. Instead there was a white-painted wooden cross with just her name and the date of her death. There were flowers on the grave, fresh ones.

It was getting late and the churchyard deserted and very quiet. Occasionally a car went past up on the road but it made little impression here. It was timeless. The white cross had slipped slightly to an angle. The soil was settling. That was partly why there was no stone yet. It seemed to be suggesting a time limit to me, as if I had to get this all worked out before the soil was finally packed down enough for the permanence of a marble slab. Right now the grave was neither one thing nor another, neither new nor established but half way in between. Unfinished business, I thought.

A curious feeling ran over me, as if I weren't alone. It felt as though someone stood behind me, had perhaps been behind me for some time, watching. I whirled round. But there was no one.

'Imagination again, Fran!' I said aloud. I glanced at my wristwatch. Time to go back.

'Don't worry about it, Terry,' I said to the white cross. 'I'll find out who it was and I'll see he gets what's due him!'

I hoped I could keep the promise. Even more now, because I couldn't do anything about Lundy's treatment of his wife. So many things were wrong and I had to be able to put at least one of them right.

Moreover, I was remembering the bruises on Terry's

body to which Janice had drawn my attention. Until this moment, I'd been concentrating on Jamie Monkton. But Joey Lundy liked beating up women.

Chapter Twelve

The best-laid plans of mice and men are apt to gang awry. My plan didn't go wrong but it did get unexpectedly delayed.

I was down promptly for breakfast the next morning, meaning to make an early visit to the farm. Alastair was already there, reading his newspaper, and after a few minutes Jamie walked in. This meant that at least he wasn't searching the room again and messing up my few possessions. We said 'good morning' to one another and exchanged frosty looks, just so that each of us knew nothing had changed.

'What are you planning today, Francesca?' Alastair asked, emerging from behind his newspaper. Jamie looked up from his chipolata sausages, mushrooms and tomato.

'I'll walk into the village,' I said casually. 'Just to take a look around.' I saw no reason to tell them I'd visited Terry's grave the previous evening.

'You'll need some different footwear,' Jamie said with a grin. He was remembering how I'd hobbled along the verge at our first meeting.

'Pair of wellies around somewhere, I dare say,' Alastair said. 'All kinds of odd pairs in the back porch. One of them should fit you.'

It was a good idea. I said I'd take it up. Jamie was still watching and listening and I wasn't sure whether he'd guessed I meant to go to the farm. He couldn't stop me, even if he did, but I didn't want him to know my plans, even so.

I went down to the kitchen after breakfast and dried up the breakfast dishes for Ruby before asking her about the boots.

'That shouldn't be a problem,' she said. 'Now, let's see—'

A bell above the door jangled. She glanced up. 'That'll be Mr Watkins, come to see Mrs Cameron. He said he'd be early but it's a little bit too early, I fancy. She mightn't be ready yet. Just wait a moment, will you, dear?'

She bustled out into the hall, heading for the front door.

Watkins was the name of the solicitor mentioned in the letter. It might be a coincidence, but I fancied not. I sneaked out after Ruby and lurked in a dark corner of the hall, behind a hat stand.

'Perhaps you'd just like to wait a moment, sir,' Ruby was saying. 'I'll run up and see if she's ready. Or Mr Alastair is about somewhere.'

'That's quite all right,' said a dry, gloomy voice. 'I'll just wait in the sitting room here, and if Mrs Cameron isn't ready to see me yet, I'll go and take a look round the stableyard.'

Ruby's feet pounded up the stairs. Faint shuffling and breathing told me Watkins was moving towards the room into which Jamie had shown me when I'd first arrived.

I peered out. The hall was empty, but the door to the sitting room was open. I crept out cautiously and peeked round it.

He was standing by the fireplace, his back to me, rearranging the photographs in the mantelshelf in a pernickety and, I thought, interfering way. Even from that angle he was clearly recognisable as the pallid man who'd been lunching with Jamie.

As bad luck would have it, he glanced up, having got everything neatly set out, and looked in the mirror above the mantelshelf. I jumped back behind the door jamb, but too late. His pale features froze and he turned.

'Who is that? Come!'

I trotted into the room as nonchalantly as I could. 'Sorry, I didn't mean to disturb you. I was coming in here to read the paper.'

He glanced round, sparse eyebrows lifted. 'I don't see any newspaper.'

'Alastair must still have it. He had it at breakfast.'

Watkins was still eyeing me with deep disapproval. Perhaps it was his normal expression. 'Are you the young woman who has come down from London?'

Jamie must have told him about me. I confirmed it.

He said, 'I see!' but looked puzzled. 'Have we by any chance met before?'

I told him I didn't think so, but I was cursing. Jamie may have been too intent on his lunch and his argument yesterday to notice me, creeping out of the wine bar. But Watkins was the sort of person who missed very little and no doubt owned a mental filing system. Lodged somewhere in his subconscious was a little card with my face on it and sooner or later, he'd connect it with a location.

'You seem, forgive me, familiar.'

'A lot of people look like me,' I said feebly.

'Indeed?' He had doubts about that. He took a watch from his waistcoat pocket and consulted it. His time was money.

'I am rather glad to have the opportunity of a word with you.' He tucked the watch away. 'You're not in a hurry?'

I began to explain that I was, actually, just on my way out. But there was something about his dry pale face and professional manner which overruled objections. I told him I had a few minutes to spare.

'Good, perhaps you'd be so good as to close the door.'

I closed it and perched on the edge of a chair. He had the kind of presence which made it impossible to sit back and relax.

He took his own seat in a cautious way, as if not sure the chair mightn't buckle beneath him, and hitching up the knees of his shiny trousers to reveal wash-shrunk wool socks and an expanse of dead white shin. He placed the tips of his bony fingers together. 'I understand that you were one of the young people who shared a house in London with Miss Monkton?'

'With Terry, yes, I did.'

'The police have spoken to you, of course.' His manner suggested I'd be the first one they'd haul in for questioning.

'Several times,' I assured him.

His features twitched. 'The police are aware that you are here?'

Thanks to my phone call to Janice, I was able to assure him heartily that Inspector Morgan was fully aware of my movements.

He tapped the tips of his fingers together and looked at me without speaking for so long that I began fidgeting.

'Were you a very close friend of Miss Monkton's?'

'I was one of the people closest to her in London,' I told him and had a fair idea it was true.

He didn't like that answer. The tapping hands were stilled. He pressed his thin lips and pinched his nostrils. 'Did she talk to you about her home? Her family?'

Fully aware he couldn't check on anything I told him, I said, 'Quite often.'

I wondered whether he played chess. He was watching me as if contemplating his next move and assessing my likely counter-move. I got the impression he'd be a good chess-player. He said delicately, 'However, I gather you told the police that you knew very little about Theresa.'

Yes, he'd be a good player, good at finding the opponent's weakness, while giving nothing away himself.

'Nothing relevant to her death, no. We thought she was out of the house, when in fact she—' I gestured at the ceiling. 'To think that we sat there while she – she was hanging there. To find her like that.'

'Yes, yes!' he said curtly. 'Quite. The whole affair is most distressing. She didn't, at any time, speak of the future? She didn't, for example, speak of the Astara Stud itself?'

'In the vaguest terms,' I said.

He wasn't sure what to make of that and sat staring at me with his gimlet eyes sunken in bags of unhealthy white skin like badly cooked poached eggs. 'And your own personal interest in this matter?'

I was spared having to find an answer which would satisfy this modern Torquemada by a welcome tap at the door, followed immediately by the appearance of Ruby.

'Mrs Cameron's ready to see you now, Mr Watkins. Would you like to go up?'

Watkins rose to his feet – I swear his knees creaked – and gathered up an ancient scuffed leather briefcase which he must have bought when he first joined the firm as junior clerk. He gave the barest nod and walked out.

'Right,' said Ruby, expressing no surprise at having found me there, tête-à-tête with the solicitor, when she'd left me in the kitchen. 'Let's see about those boots, shall we?'

Since she hadn't asked any explanation, I didn't offer one. I followed her back to the kitchen, feeling that I hadn't handled the interview very well. Watkins was suspicious of me. When he succeeded in placing me, as he surely would, he'd tell Jamie immediately.

Jamie would be furious to think I'd been spying on him. But he might not, I thought, be in a position to do much about it. It all depended on what he'd been discussing with Watkins. Watkins, too, might have something on his conscience. He wouldn't be the first solicitor to bend the rules and I had a funny feeling that's what had been happening in that wine bar yesterday.

I inspected the collection of ageing gumboots in the back porch to which Ruby directed me and found a smallish pair which I suspected had belonged to Terry. Ruby joined me as I was putting my foot alongside one of them, to check the size. I didn't put my foot inside it because of the cobwebs festooning it. If there's one thing I cannot stand, it's putting my foot into a shoe of any sort and encountering some kind of beastie. In the squat it happened fairly frequently. Woodlice mostly, and spiders with the occasional silverfish, my particular phobia because they slithered around so quickly. I'd got into the habit of tapping my shoes to see what fell out before I put them on.

Ruby was bearing a dreadful-looking waxed jacket 'in case it rained'. I accepted it gratefully, hoping that between the elderly Barbour and the wellies, I'd at least look more the part than I had yesterday.

I took the boots outside and bashed them against the wall to dislodge the creepie-crawlies. As I suspected, they were full of dust and dead spiders. When I was sure they were uninhabited, I tugged them on. They were on the tight side, I discovered, as I clumped round the front of the house. A blue Mercedes was parked there. Watkins's clients must pay well. Then, as I paused to admire it, another car drew into the drive and pulled up by me. The door opened and a blonde got out.

She was in her forties and wore an outfit even more out of place than mine had been when I'd first arrived here. It consisted of a short black skirt and sheer black tights, both a mistake because although the pins were shapely, the knees were on the knobbly side. Her fitted jacket was tangerine in colour with large ornate gold buttons and looked expensive. On her feet she had slip-on flatties, presumably for driving. The rest of the outfit called for stiletto heels. Her thick shoulder-length hair had faded slightly but she wore it brushed back and secured with an alice band. I guessed she dieted as a way of life. Her face was good-looking, but had that pared-down look. Her expression was sharp. In every way she so resembled Terry that I knew this must be Marcia Monkton.

She was giving me equally close scrutiny. 'Who are you?' she asked without preamble.

Since it was the second time I'd faced interrogation by a stranger that morning, I was quicker with my reply.

'Fran Varady,' I told her, adding, 'You're Terry's mother.'

She blinked. 'Theresa's mother!' she corrected icily.

'Sorry. We called her Terry because we never knew her as anything else.'

'Who are *we*?' Without pausing for breath she answered her own question. 'You're one of those awful drop-outs from that ghastly house!'

Even making allowances for her distress, I felt that was gratuitously rude. I tried to explain I, at least, had always struggled to hold on to some kind of a job, and the house had been our home and we'd liked it.

She shrugged. 'Perhaps it suited you and your friends. From what the police told us, it wasn't the sort of place I like to think my daughter lived in.'

I thought it was time to express some form of condolence. But it didn't go down well.

'Sorry? So you bloody well should be, all of you! God knows what went on there—'

There was a crunch on the gravel behind us and I turned. Jamie had appeared. 'Marcie?' He started forward. 'We didn't expect you!'

'Hullo, Jamie.' She walked past me and they exchanged a chaste kiss. 'I'm on my way down to the coast to catch the ferry. I thought I'd better call in on my way. Make my peace with the old chap. We had a bit of a barney when I was here for – for the funeral.'

'He understood, Marcie. Don't worry about it. He knows you were upset.'

Jamie looked from the Mercedes to Marcia and back

again. Her arrival had complicated things. He was no longer worried about me. Marcia was a bigger threat to upsetting whatever little applecart he and Watkins had been stacking in the wine bar. But he was putting a good face on it.

'You're staying for lunch, Marcie?'

The tangerine shoulders twitched. 'Can't, I'm afraid. I'm already pushed for time. All the same, I thought I ought to see him.' She glanced at me. 'What's she doing here?'

'Wouldn't we all like to know that,' Jamie sneered.

Suspicion, probably her natural expression, increased on her narrow features. 'Isn't that Sammy Watkins's Merc?'

'He's come to see Aunt Ariadne.' Jamie was looking uncomfortable.

'Are you pulling one of your stunts, Jamie?' She wasn't one to mess around. She was asking the question I'd have liked to put.

Jamie wasn't going to answer it in front of me. 'Family business, Marcie!' He jerked his head angrily in my direction.

'You carry on without me,' I said. 'I'm just going for a walk.'

It was working out rather well. If Jamie was busy with Marcia, he wouldn't have time to follow me. But Marcia had her own ideas.

'You're not going anywhere,' she said unpleasantly, 'until I've had a word with you!'

I was about to decline this pleasure when I recollected that a detective wouldn't pass up an opportunity to talk to her. I wouldn't get another. Jamie mumbled that he'd go and tell Alastair of Marcia's arrival. He set off indoors with such alacrity that I wondered whether he also meant to try and get the message to Watkins. It left Marcia and me facing each other like a couple of wary cats about to squabble over ownership of a stretch of pavement.

'What happened?' she demanded.

'I don't know.'

'Don't give me that crap!' she retorted. 'You must know. You were there!'

'Not when—' I broke off just in time. This was, after all, a woman whose daughter had been murdered. 'Not when it happened,' I finished.

Her features had become even more pinched with anger and the resemblance to Terry had increased. It gave me a strange feeling. It was like seeing Terry there, before me.

'How did she ever get to be there, with you?'

'She needed a place to live,' I pointed out.

Her voice rose to a wail, part rage and part, I realised, despair. 'She had a place to live!' She flung out a well-manicured hand to point at the house behind us. 'She lived here!'

'She didn't want to live here.'

'Why not?' she shouted furiously.

'Why ask me? Why didn't you ask her when you had the chance? Did you ever ask her if she wanted to be dumped here?'

'She wasn't dumped!' she practically spat.

'Wasn't she?' I ought to respect her grief, but she was a street-fighter, underneath that designer chic, and I recognised the type. She'd give no quarter and any attempt at niceness on my part, would be seized on as a weakness.

'You know nothing about it!' She'd moved slightly

towards me and looked as if she'd attack at any moment. Those manicured nails were long and pointed.

I got ready to get out of the way. 'Perhaps I know something about being dumped. My mother walked out on me. I know how it feels.'

She paused, looking me over, and thinking it out. When she spoke next it was more calmly but the voice was still steel-hard.

'I don't owe you any explanation. My marriage broke up. I needed to earn a living. I was offered an opportunity to get back into the only job I know. I couldn't turn it down. Theresa was well looked after. Her father paid the fees to send her to a good school. When she left school, I tried to get her to take up a place at art college. She turned it down and ran off somewhere. We were worried sick, and after a lot of trouble, found her and brought her home here. She did it again. More than once. On one occasion, she went traipsing across country with a band of hippies. I tried talking to her but I couldn't get through. She just seemed hell-bent on—' Her voice wavered. 'She seemed hell-bent on her own destruction. We should have seen it coming, what happened.'

I realised that what she was telling me was true, but only partly so. There was a lot more she wasn't telling possibly because she considered it none of my business. She was right: it wasn't. But perhaps she was leaving out anything which didn't fit with the picture she was anxious to paint of a caring parent, who'd done her best, everything she possibly could in difficult circumstances. She wasn't painting that picture for my benefit, but for her own. She needed to believe it. How could I blame her for that? What would I have done in her place?

I still didn't like her but I'd begun to feel some sympathy for her and it hampered my side of the conversation. I mumbled something to the effect that not every runaway finished in such tragic circumstances.

She picked up the words as though they represented a foreign phrase she hadn't heard before, rolling them experimentally round her mouth.

'Tragic circumstances. Which, of all the utterly wretched circumstances, would you dignify as *tragic*? Her death? The waste of her talents? The miserable life she was leading in London? The sordid acquaintances who dragged her down with them – eventually to her death?'

She waited, as if I'd give some precise answer to this unanswerable list of woes.

I would've objected vigorously to the last, but I was beginning to understand Janice's dread of speaking 'to the family' in cases like this.

I floundered with, 'She didn't see her lifestyle the way you see it. The house in Jubilee Street was home to us and we were comfortable enough there. Terry was really very capable and knew what she was doing.'

She cut me short with a look which was pure vitriol. She didn't want to hear any of this.

I'd been a fool to try. Her grief had put her beyond reason. I compounded my errors by repeating my regrets. Since I didn't now know what to call it, I ended lamely with a reference to 'the accident'.

'Accident? You call it an accident?'

She was back on the offensive. 'My daughter was *murdered* and I'm by no means convinced that you and the others in that squat weren't involved! More to the point, right now, what are you doing here?'

'Alastair—' I began weakly.

'Don't bother!' She moved in close. 'Just pack your bags and get out! You're trouble. You were part of Theresa's problems and you've brought yourself and your street manners with you down here. Alastair and Ariadne don't need that. My hope is that, one day, someone will catch up with you. If not the police, then someone else, the sort of person who caught up with my daughter. My daughter's life was wasted. She could have done so much. No one would miss you. You're nothing.' Her voice rose again, wavering, 'Why couldn't it have been you? Who would have missed you? Why had it to be my lovely daughter? It's so unfair!'

She turned on her heel and almost staggered. I stepped forward to grab her elbow and steady her but she gave me a fierce look and made her own way indoors, head high.

Jamie had reappeared at some point during our talk. I hadn't noticed exactly when. He must have overheard a good part of it. He met my gaze now and chuckled.

'You think you're so tough, don't you, Fran? But you can't begin to match Marcie.'

'Get lost!' I told him. I tramped off towards the gate in my borrowed wellies, hearing him laugh behind me.

I knew he was wrong. Marcia was finding out she wasn't as tough as she'd thought she was. None of us is.

Chapter Thirteen

I had to admit that the conversation with Marcia had shaken me. Not just by her grief or her expressed wish I'd been the one found hanging from the light fitting. It had disturbed the way I'd felt until then about my own mother's desertion. Perhaps I'd also judged her too quickly. When she went, she must have had good reason. Much as I'd loved my father, obviously my mother and he had troubles which couldn't be resolved. If she hadn't taken me with her, possibly it was because she, like Marcia, had needed to begin her life over again from scratch, without the encumbrance of a young child, or had had nowhere to go remotely suitable for a kid.

Then I thought about Lucy and her children. Even reduced to living in the squat, Lucy had never once envisaged parting from the children. No matter how bad things got, she'd told me once, the three of them stayed together. No way would she ever let the kids be taken into care, and, as for the father having them, 'I'd kill him first!' she'd said. I think she meant it.

It was complicated and, to be fair, not having faced a similar situation myself, I was in no position to judge. But

I liked to think that, like Lucy, I'd have hung on to my children. Or at least tried.

The dog saw me coming as I walked into the farmyard and ran towards me. It barked once, then sniffed at my feet and wagged its tail. It was nice to be recognised. I hoped Nick remembered me and that he'd asked me to call.

He came out of a barn at that moment, dressed in grubby dungarees and wiping his hands on an oily rag. He looked more like a mechanic than a farmer.

'Old truck's just about given up the ghost,' he said. 'Have to be replaced. I just about manage to keep it ticking over from day to day. Nice to see you again. Have a good trip into town?'

'Fine, thanks. Nice place. I'm a true townie, as you can probably see.' I waved a hand around. 'Never been on a farm before in my life.'

'No? Really?' That seemed to puzzle him. He glanced at the buildings around. 'Not much to see. This is a working farm, not someone's tax dodge. Come inside and we'll have a cup of coffee or something. I could do with a drink.'

I hesitated. 'I don't want to trouble your wife.'

'Wife?' He looked surprised.

'Jamie asked after Mrs Bryant . . . '

'Oh, my mother!' he grinned. 'Not married. Haven't yet found a woman willing to take on the farm! It's a tough life.'

I hadn't counted on his mother and felt apprehensive. Respectable old mothers and I seldom saw eye to eye. I was glad I wore the boots and Barbour. At least I wouldn't be teetering along in my pixie boots.

As I followed Nick to the house, I tried to prepare myself. I imagined 'mother' as rosy-cheeked, in an apron, baking scones after a hard morning feeding chickens.

Nick took off his boots at the back door, using an ancient wooden device which I guessed was a 'boot-jack'. I followed suit and the pair of us padded indoors in our socks. The floor was stone-flagged and uneven, and the kitchen had an untidy, cluttered and comfortable look. Nick led me into an equally untidy sitting room where a woman sat at the desk, muttering to herself as she stabbed at the keyboard of a home computer. She swivelled round as we entered.

Nick's mother was surprisingly young. She had long hair, wore jeans and an old sweatshirt and I liked the look of her on sight.

'Hullo,' she said. She didn't seem surprised to see me. 'Do you know how these things work?'

'Sorry, no.' After all, I'd been living in a house which didn't even have electricity. When would I get to learn about computers?

'Never mind.' She sighed.

'This is Fran,' Nick told her. 'She's come to have a cup of coffee. She's staying with Mrs Cameron.'

'Penny,' she said.

I wondered if that was what she meant to charge me for the coffee, but even in the country things couldn't be that cheap.

'My name is Penny,' she explained. 'Let's go into the kitchen and I'll put the kettle on. I'm fed up with this machine. I want to get out of sight of it for a bit.'

Nick made an excuse and went off to clean up. In the kitchen, Penny rattled about in a cupboard and apologised for not having any proper coffee. 'Only this stuff in a jar. I've got to go shopping this week. I never seem to get any time. That machine in there—' She jabbed a finger viciously towards the distant computer. 'Is supposed to save me time. It takes me four times as long to do anything! Nick says I'll get the hang of it. Wish I felt sure.'

It seemed she didn't bake scones, either. She produced a tin, looked inside it, grimaced and said, 'And I haven't got any biscuits, either. You must think I'm a lousy hostess.'

I assured her I didn't need biscuits. I really appreciated being offered coffee. 'It's not just a social call. I'm – I'm on a sort of fishing trip, for information.'

I had decided that with Penny it would be best to be quite straightforward.

She clanged the empty biscuit tin back on the shelf. 'What about? Not computers, I hope? Farming? Ask Nick.'

'Do you and Nick farm here alone?' I asked, curious. I'd always thought farms abounded with dairymaids and shepherds and so on. I said as much and she burst out laughing.

'Not these days! Everyone has to be a Jack of all Trades! There's only Nick and myself and Jeff Biles who comes when an extra pair of hands is needed. He knows more about farming than either of us. My husband bought this place and had ideas.' She hesitated just fractionally. 'He didn't live to carry them out.'

'I'm sorry,' I said awkwardly.

'Yes, it was a pity. I wish I were more use. I can run the book-keeping side of it. Farming is a business, after all.

I'm used to that, dealing with the financial side of things. I've got a little antiques shop in Winchester. The trouble is that I have to spend a lot of time there and can't always be here.'

'Antiques?' I asked. That sounded interesting.

Very quickly she said, 'It isn't grand. It's more what once upon a time would have been called a junk shop. But I try to keep it looking decent and it doesn't do so badly, especially in the summer. The tourists, you know. A lot of people want a souvenir which isn't modern tat. They're happy to buy what, frankly, is often Edwardian tat. However, the deal leaves everyone happy.'

I remarked that it must be difficult, keeping the place stocked. She said she went to house sales, of which there was usually one somewhere in the area most weeks.

'Remember,' she said, 'I'm not after valuable stuff. Just old photo frames, odds and ends of china and ornaments, scrapbooks, period clothes which are still in good condition. Best of all, if I can get them, are toys. But old toys of all kinds are highly collectable and the dealers usually get there before me. There's a strict cash limit on how much I can pay for my stock because I have to price competitively when I sell on.'

'Who runs the shop when you're not there?'

'A friend. She's actually a partner who put up some of the original money. But she doesn't do any of the business side of it. She says she's got no head for it. She likes being in the shop, meeting people and selling things. Only she's been in poor health recently so I've had to spend a lot of time in town. I've hardly been out here at the farm at all the last few weeks.'

Penny looked glum. I realised she did have a lot of

worries and I felt badly about coming here and with the intention of pestering them about Terry.

But Nick's mother obviously wasn't one of those to brood on things. She dismissed her personal problems with a brisk shrug. 'I can offer you some tips on how to run a business on a shoestring!' She grinned at me.

Nick came back just then looking much more presentable, in fact, really rather handsome, in a clean sweater and jeans. We all sat round the table, very cosy. I didn't know why he had so much trouble finding a girl interested in the farm and in him. I was beginning to get quite interested myself.

'Everything all right at Mrs Cameron's?' Nick asked.

'That's it,' I said. 'I don't know.' They were watching me. Obviously they were both pretty bright and I felt I might as well tell them everything. One thing I'd already realised was that Nick didn't approve of Jamie Monkton. So I wasn't taking too much of a risk confiding in them. The fact was, I was too much on my own out here. I needed allies of some sort. The Bryants looked as if they were the sort of people to have on my side.

'You know the circumstances of Theresa Monkton's death?' I began and they nodded, both silent, both watching me and waiting.

'I knew her in London,' I said. 'We all shared a squat. We called her Terry, not Theresa. She preferred it.'

Penny stirred and sighed. 'Poor girl,' she said. 'She really had rotten luck. I used to urge her to call by here sometimes, when she was at home, just to have a chat and – I don't know – get away from the house. But she was a funny girl. She never came here. I don't know whether she was shy or it was just that she didn't want to talk. She was very – closed up. It was as if she was frightened to talk about herself.'

Nick asked, watching me, 'Did she talk much to you, Fran?'

I shook my head. 'No, it was just the way your mother described it. She didn't talk to anyone.'

I plunged in and told them all about the squat, the discovery of her body, Alastair's visit to my flat. I didn't tell them that just possibly Ganesh had seen Jamie hanging about outside the house before Terry died, or about the cologne smell or the scrap of chalk in the car. Nor did I tell them about Jamie's searching my things or my turning over the room and finding the will.

They were both of them clearly upset when I described finding the body. Penny looked quite pale and Nick got up to make some more coffee. He probably noticed that his mother was taking it badly and I hoped he wasn't annoyed with me for upsetting her. I apologised because I hadn't come to ruin anyone's day, just to find out if they could help.

Penny leaned across the table and patted my hand. 'Don't worry about it, Fran. Obviously it's not pleasant to hear about it. But it must have been even more unpleasant to be the person who found – who found her.'

Nick clashed the coffee mugs together and refilled them from the kettle.

'Don't take this wrongly,' he said, over his shoulder. 'But before we met you – well, we had a different idea about the people Theresa knew in London. We'd gathered she was living in a way Alastair and Ariadne Cameron wouldn't approve of. We imagined you all as down-and-outs. Obviously, you're not, weren't. Highly normal, I'd say.' He gave me a wry smile which quite made my heart hop.

'I can imagine what you've heard,' I told him. 'Believe me, she was safe enough with us! *We* didn't kill her!'

This time they both apologised, speaking at the same time. That made me feel I'd been rude so I apologised again and we all apologised together until it became funny and we all started to laugh.

When we stopped giggling, Penny said in a contrite voice, 'It's not something to be light-hearted about in any way, that's the worst of it. It's wicked and terrifying and – and it makes me so angry. What on earth happened to her? It must have been just—' She gave a gesture of despair. 'We can't imagine how awful it must have been during the last moments of her life.'

Nick grunted and buried his face in his coffee mug. I guessed he was upset too, but he had a different way of showing it. Strong, male, keeping it to yourself stuff.

They probably didn't know the details, how poor Terry had been knocked half unconscious and strung up, perhaps aware of what was happening, perhaps not. It was better they didn't know.

I just nodded. 'I want to know what happened to her. Alastair was nice to me and said to get in touch, so I did and here I am. I didn't know about Ariadne until I get here. I didn't know it was her house. It was embarrassing, I can tell you. I really wouldn't have barged in the way I did if I'd known about her.'

'Ariadne's fine!' Penny assured me. 'Just a bit formal in her ways. She's in a lot of pain most of the time. She hurt her spine some years ago in a riding accident. She was a very active woman before that. Being stuck in that chair must be unbearable for her.'

'Someone mentioned it to me. I understand her husband had died before that, so it must have been a terrible blow to find herself disabled as well.'

'It was more than that,' Nick said unexpectedly. 'She took the fall from his horse, Cameron's. The horse's name was Astara and they called the stud after him. Cameron had bought the horse with the intention of breeding good competition horses out of his bloodline. The horse was worth a packet to them. After Cameron died, Ariadne used to ride Astara around the place. Then she had the bad fall. You can understand it if she's a bit tetchy sometimes.'

'Basically she's a very kind-hearted woman!' Penny insisted. 'She gave a home to Theresa when her parents split. And to Alastair, come to that. He had nowhere to go so she took him in. He ran the place for a while for her, but he wasn't the ideal person. She could've taken on someone more efficient. Then there's Jamie. He was at a loose end until he came to the Astara Stud. Admittedly, he's turned things around there and made a go of it.'

'She took me in, too, in a manner of speaking.' I was thinking about it. Some people took in stray animals but Ariadne Cameron seemed to collect stray human beings.

At the mention of Jamie, however, a distinct *frisson* had been felt in the atmosphere.

I trailed a lure. 'I have to admit I don't like Jamie much.'

'Jamie Monkton cares about no one but himself!' Penny said crisply. 'I've known him since he was a boy. He was a little stinker as a kid and he's not improved.'

Nick was watching me carefully. 'Fran? Do you think Jamie had anything to do with Theresa's death?'

'Nick!' his mother exclaimed, shocked.

'Oh, come on, Ma! Fran's investigating. She told us so. And she's come all the way down here so she doesn't think the killer is in London, does she?'

He was right. I didn't. But this wasn't the moment to start making accusations I couldn't back.

Penny was going to argue about it. 'They were cousins, Theresa and Jamie. Near enough cousins, anyway. I know he's pretty well capable of most things but he wouldn't – not *family*, surely?'

It hadn't struck me that Jamie would let a relationship put him off his stride. But it would be undiplomatic to take sides in an argument between Penny and Nick. I stuck to my part of the conversation.

'I feel the more I know about Terry, the nearer I can get to *her*, then the nearer I get to the answer to all this. That's why I'm here. Alastair told me she'd run away several times before – before the time she came to London and ended up living with us. On one occasion she went off with some New-Age travellers. I know that's true because she did mention it once.'

The Bryants looked at one another uneasily.

'It didn't last long,' Penny said. 'A few months. Just during the summer. When the weather turned chilly and wet she came back. Her health had quite broken down, I think she was quite ill. I used to see her sometimes, wandering up and down the lane. She was as white as a sheet and I was worried she'd pass out somewhere and fall into a ditch, lie there for ages with no one any the wiser. Both Nick and I took her home a couple of times in the old pick-up after we'd found her wandering about. Her manner was always very odd, most unfriendly and withdrawn. I don't think either Ariadne or Alastair could cope with it. Poor child, she needed help, but there was none to be had at the Astara.'

I sipped at my coffee. 'She had parents. They could have been asked in to help. I met Marcia just this morning.'

'She's at the Astara? Theresa's mother?' Penny and Nick spoke together. Nick whistled.

'She doesn't lack nerve! There was a hell of a bust-up with Alastair at the funeral.'

'I think she's come to make up.' In fact, interesting though it had been to meet Marcia, I'd dismissed her from my investigations. Since her divorce and Terry's death, Marcia had no interest in what happened to the Astara Stud. But someone else did. I asked, 'What about Philip Monkton, Terry's father? If Terry was ill, shouldn't he have been told?'

Penny considered the question. 'He's a successful man in his own line of business, and I think there's some ill feeling between him and his relatives. He didn't come often to see his daughter. I fancy that if there'd been a problem, Phil wouldn't have wanted to know about it. He has remarried, too, and that always makes a difference. I understand his new wife is quite young – nearer his daughter's age, if you see what I mean, than his. It's not something he'd want to be reminded of.'

There was a silence. Into it came a clip-clop of horse's hoofs outside and a bark from the dog. A girl's voice called out.

'That sounds like Kelly,' Nick said. He raised his voice. 'In the kitchen, Kell!'

She came in a few moments later, her face flushed either from the exercise of having ridden over here, or from anticipation.

'Good morning!' she said happily. 'I thought I'd—'

At this point she saw me and broke off, an almost comical consternation on her freckled face.

'Another visitor!' said Penny hospitably. 'Join us, Kelly. I'll make another lot of coffee!'

Kelly came awkwardly into the room, her former exuberance evaporated. She sat down, her eyes still fixed on me. 'Hullo,' she said dully.

'Fran's seeing life on the farm at first hand,' Nick grinned. 'She's never been on a farm before, can you imagine it?'

'You've always lived in a town, I suppose,' Kelly sounded more resentful than curious.

She was casting covert looks at Nick and the situation was clear enough for me to read. She was sweet on him and in a big way. The thing was, did he even notice? She wasn't unattractive, in a healthy, outdoor way. In fact, I'd have thought she'd have been ideal if he really was looking for a wife on the farm here. But what people need, and what they want, are not always the same.

'I reckon', said Nick cheerfully, 'that she'd settle into a farming way of life in no time at all! You want to give it a try, Fran.'

Kelly was clearly startled and gave me a very unfriendly look. From now on, she'd see me as a rival. It was a pity, because I'd been getting along well with her and she might have been a valuable ally.

Rather too obviously, she turned her back to me. 'I

called by, Nick, because I missed you at the yard the other day. Lundy told me you'd been.'

'Only being neighbourly,' Nick looked momentarily embarrassed. 'I thought Alastair might be in the yard and I'd have a word to let him know Ma and I are thinking about them. But he wasn't there and I didn't want to call at the house in case I ran into Jamie. His car was parked by the garage so I knew he was there and didn't fancy chatting to him. Lundy was as tight as a tick, by the way. How does he get away with it?'

Kelly's features had become steadily more disconsolate as he spoke. She'd hoped he called by the yard to see her. 'I know Joey drinks, but it doesn't interfere with his work.'

'You oughtn't to be lodging with them,' said Penny severely. 'The man's not to be trusted.'

Kelly brightened, hoping, I was sure, for an invitation to lodge at the farm.

I decided the moment had come to make a tactful retreat.

I thanked Penny for the coffee and said I really must start back.

'Come again!' Penny urged.

'Show you around the place properly next time,' Nick chimed in.

Kelly's misery returned. Her day was ruined and I was the cause.

However, as I walked back, I had plenty to think about besides Kelly's troubled love-life.

Ariadne was a wealthy woman. Everyone depended on her. She was old and in poor health. She had no children and her brother, to whom she was close, was elderly. Her nephew Philip she disapproved of heartily and, in theory anyway, he was a successful man who didn't need to inherit wealth. Jamie had worked hard in the business, but she had doubts about him. Theresa, on the other hand, she had 'doted on' in Penny's words. Terry had been her heiress and Terry herself was dead. With no obvious alternative to Terry, Ariadne must have faced a dilemma over the future of the stud. Her choice had been restricted to plumping for one of several candidates, all of whom had less than her wholehearted support. But time wasn't on her side. She'd had to make a choice and make it quickly.

This morning, Watkins the solicitor had called on Ariadne with a briefcase containing, I'd bet my boots on it, a new will. And very likely, this morning, Ariadne had signed it.

But in whose favour? And would it mean that Ariadne herself was now in danger?

Chapter Fourteen

I needed to speak to Ariadne but realised it wouldn't be easy to get an answer to the question which mattered most. There was no way I could casually ask her about the provisions of her will. But I was convinced that the answer to that would provide the answer to everything else.

I set off back to the Astara Stud, turning over the problem all ways in my head as I tried to decide how to tackle it. I hadn't realised detectives had to be so versatile. A course in practical psychiatry might have helped but I didn't have it. All I knew was I had to deal with an iron-willed old lady of the old school, who was ill and on medication. No wonder I was so apprehensive at the thought. I juggled all kinds of approaches in my head, but none of them seemed realistic.

So buried in my thoughts had I been that I hadn't been aware of anything else. Belatedly I realised that a vehicle was following me along the narrow, single-track road. I'd been walking in the middle – there were no pavements and the verges to either side were treacherous obstacle courses of grass-concealed holes and drainage ditches. I assumed the vehicle behind me couldn't get past. Obligingly I moved over to the far side.

He didn't overtake. He seemed happy to crawl along at the same pace, just a few yards behind me. I glanced over my shoulder. It was an old van. The driver seemed to be peering through the windscreen at me. But the screen was yellowed with age and chipped where a flying stone had hit it. I couldn't make out the face behind the wheel. He was dawdling along, almost at a standstill. With a sick feeling in my stomach, I realised he hadn't been held up by me. He was following me!

I began to walk faster. What with all the ideas of family secrets and murderous plots running round my head, I succeeded in frightening myself considerably. Not only Ariadne was in danger. I was. Me. Fran Varady, the great detective. Imagining I was one of the Famous Five and putting my nose into Jamie Monkton's business.

I broke into a lumbering run, hampered by the gumboots which weren't designed for sprinting. Even the pixie boots would have been better. They, at least, belonged to me and were the right size.

The van increased its speed. I couldn't outrun a motor vehicle, even such an old one. Sweat poured off me. My feet were redhot and useless, my calf muscles ached. It was like running in thick mud, a nightmare of pursuit, as to lift one foot and put it in front of the other became increasingly impossible.

My heart was beating like a drum and I felt my isolation in this wilderness more than ever before. Why hadn't I stayed in London? In London I could have ducked down a side street, gone into a shop, jumped on a bus, anything. Out here I was marooned amongst empty fields. I'd have to scramble over a hedge or fencing before I could get into one of those and the driver would be out of his van and have grabbed me before I'd got ten yards.

The one hope was to reach the turning up to the stud. He wouldn't follow me on to the property, surely? Someone might see him from the house. I could see the turn ahead with the wooden sign, promising sanctuary. I made for it like a medieval fugitive, heading for the church door with the mob on his heels. But it was all uphill, very steep. An agonising stitch shot through my side. I doubled over. I couldn't make it. I had to halt.

The van had reached me and stopped. A door slammed. Footsteps grated on the road surface, approaching.

'This is it, Francesca!' I told myself between spasms of agony.

I tried to stand upright, groaning with the pain of the stitch. A hand gripped my shoulder. I wasn't going to give in without a fight, even in my state. If Terry had put up a fight, she mightn't have finished dangling from a light fitting. I struck back with my elbow and there was a yell of pain. Good! I thought. I'd got him where it hurt. I tried another jab and there was another howl.

'Fran! Stop it, will you? What are you trying to do?'

I could hear my name and the protesting voice was familiar. I twisted in his grip, peering up in my doubled-over state, hand clasped to my ribs, panting, sweating – a real sight.

'Have you gone completely crazy?' Ganesh panted. 'I tried to attract your attention and you took off like a rocket! What's is the big idea? Training for the Olympics? Then you tried to use me as a punch-bag. Country living has scrambled your brain – or what brain you've got left!'

* * *

'I thought you were a hit man,' I said.

We'd limped together to the van and driven past the house and down the hill on the other side until we reached a wooded dell. There we sat until the stitch in my side had gone and the pair of us had got our breath back.

Ganesh lounged sideways on the driver's seat, his back against the door, one arm propped on the seat and one on the wheel. His long black hair hung over his face and he was scowling ferociously at me through the tangles. He was probably still suffering from the two punches I'd aimed at him and what I had to say didn't make him any happier. In reality, I was delighted to see him, but at the moment could do no more than gawp at him.

Then he said in the tone which he reserves for pouring cold water on my ideas, 'Hit man?'

'Well—' I tried to sound as if it wasn't a daft idea. 'You might have been!'

'A hit man, in a van like this? Not built for getaways, is it? It only just got here from London! Why didn't you recognise the van, anyway? It's the one belonging to the shop. You've seen it enough times.'

This drew my attention to the fact that the inside of the van smelled of cabbages, potato earth and over-ripe bananas. There was a torn plastic net at my feet with a label reading 'Florida Pink Grapefruit'.

'I know I have!' I snapped, getting flustered. 'But in London, not here! You didn't say you were coming down here! What are you doing here, anyway?'

'Rescuing you,' he said. 'I've come to drive you back to town.'

'Not now! Not now I'm getting somewhere!'

I burst into a recap of my theories. 'Terry was going to inherit the lot. That would have left several people out in the cold. There's Philip, her father. Everyone says he was never interested in the stud and anyway, he's got his own successful business. And I don't really think he'd kill his own daughter. But what about Jamie? He was in London that day, I'm sure of it. You saw him and so did Edna. I found a piece of Squib's chalk in his car and he uses that cologne. He frequents that wine bar. He smokes Benson and Hedges. He's worked hard to rescue the stud from the slide in business while Alastair was in charge. He probably feels that if Ariadne left it to anyone, she should have left it to him. He is a family member, after all. He's probably resented bitterly her decision to leave it to Terry.'

'If he knew about it,' Ganesh pointed out. 'And even if he did, why didn't he just marry Terry?'

'That's the Indian way,' I said. 'Keep everything in the family. That hasn't been done in this country for a hundred years. What's more, I can't see Terry falling for Jamie.'

Ganesh didn't look convinced but I ploughed on. 'There's a very unpleasant groom, or stable manager, called Joey Lundy. He knocks his simple-minded wife around. Alastair and Jamie seem content to let him stay in his job and just drop a word from time to time when poor Mrs Lundy's bruises get too obvious. But Terry might have thought differently. She might have ordered Lundy off the place, once she owned it. So he would have a motive to kill Terry and he's the sort who'd do it.'

'Is there any evidence this Lundy fellow was ever in London in his entire life?' Ganesh punctured another theory.

'Evidence', I told him, 'is what I'm here to find. Maybe he and Jamie were working together. They both had an interest in removing poor Terry from the scene.'

'Only according to you and your theories.' Ganesh could, on occasion such as now, sound irritatingly smug.

'All right, there's something else,' I told him. 'I saw Jamie talking to the solicitor, Watkins, in that wine bar. I'm sure Jamie was trying to find out about Ariadne's new will. He might even have tried persuading Watkins to put pressure on her to make it out in Jamie's favour. Jamie had no business to be with Watkins there.'

Ganesh struck his hand against the steering wheel and swore vigorously, something he rarely, if ever, did. 'I've sometimes thought you were crazy, Fran, but I've never thought you were stupid. I'm beginning to change my mind! This is family business. Monkton family business. The last thing they want or need is a complete stranger like you prying into it! Besides which, you're putting up a load of theories without any proof! Why shouldn't Jamie Monkton meet Watkins? Watkins probably handles all the legal business to do with the stud. They needn't have been discussing the will at all!'

'Watkins came to the stud this morning. If Jamie wanted to talk business with him, he could have done it today, without traipsing into Winchester. He wanted to meet Watkins in Winchester, Gan, because he didn't want anyone at the stud knowing about it! Ariadne should be warned! Look, suppose—'

'You can't go about making accusations like this!' Ganesh broke in hoarsely. 'If you're wrong, you're going to be in a hell of a tight corner! And if you're right – it's not Ariadne you should be worrying about, it's you!' He leaned forward pugnaciously. 'You shouldn't stay here another minute. You've found out all you can. We'll drive back to London right now. We'll go to Morgan and tell her. She can sort it out, right? It's her job. Leave your stuff here. You can phone Monkton and ask him to send it on.'

'No way!' I told him indigantly. 'I've got your camera, amongst other things! Hey! Did you get that film developed?'

'What film?'

Dismay swept over me. 'You didn't get it?' Then I remembered. I'd only posted it the previous day and if he'd left London early this morning – 'It will be at your place now, unopened! Gan—' I grabbed his jacket. 'You've got to drive back, now, pick up that film and take it to the chemist's near your shop. He does one-hour processing!'

'If I drive back, does that mean you're coming with me?'

'No.' He was looking so furious I found myself almost pleading, 'I must stay just one more day. I've *got* to talk to Ariadne.'

'She'll tell you to mind your own business and I for one won't blame her!'

'I've still got to try! Right?'

He glared at me. 'Wrong! This isn't a game, Fran!'

'I know that! Look, I don't know why you have to come. I can look after myself!' I yelled.

It was getting pretty noisy inside the van. My ears were ringing. It was time to quieten down.

We both sat in silence for a few minutes until Ganesh began to speak again, using a reasonable tone which always infuriates me.

'You can't look after yourself, Fran, not this time. I know you can in normal circumstances, but there's nothing normal about this. You're in a strange part of the world, living among people you know very little about. These aren't your sort. They're rich. They've got big houses, land, horses and so on. They may quarrel among themselves but they'll close ranks against outsiders. You're the one who will be sacrificed. You do see that, don't you?'

He waited and when I didn't answer, went on more angrily, 'All right, look at it this way. Just now you thought you were being attacked. Suppose you'd been right? How tall are you? What do you weigh? I've seen twelve-year-old kids as big as you. You haven't got the strength, Fran, to save yourself in a struggle.'

'I know all this,' I told him. 'Because contrary to what you seem to think, I'm not stupid and not unaware of the risk. But I can't give up now, not just at this point. Not after I've come all the way down here and managed to find out so much.'

He sighed. 'How much longer do you think you'll need to stay on?'

'Twenty-four hours tops, I swear. Tonight and perhaps part of tomorrow. Then I'll go back to London. I realise I'm a fish out of water down here. But I don't like leaving something half-finished.'

He scratched his head and scowled. 'All right. One more night. I came prepared to doss down in the van in case I couldn't contact you at once. I've got a sleeping bag and some food. Tomorrow, right after breakfast, I'll come and collect you. If anything goes wrong before that, get out of the house, leg it down here and you'll find me.'

I felt a twinge of guilt at having yelled at him and I told him I really did appreciate his coming to help, and being worried, and all the rest of it.

'Yeah, yeah ... ' he said impatiently. 'Just remember, watch out! If anything – anything at all goes wrong – just start running as fast as you were running away from me just now!'

At the house, both Marcia's car and Watkins's Mercedes had gone. I limped round to the back porch to take off the wellies. They were jammed on my swollen feet by now and I could have done with a boot-jack, like the one they had at the farm. I managed to get them off and thankfully divested myself of the Barbour, inside which I was steaming like a steak and kidney pudding.

I staggered in my socks into the kitchen, carrying my pixie boots in my hand. I couldn't get them on.

Ruby was there mixing up batter again. She was an obsessive cook.

'Hullo,' she said without stopping the beating action. 'You look as if you've been running.'

'Brisk walk!' I told her. I drew a glass of water from the tap and drank it down in one long swig. She gave me a curious sideways glance. My purple face indicated more than a healthy stroll, but she didn't say anything else.

She poured batter into the cake tin and put the whole thing in the oven. This time she just handed me the bowl to scrape without asking.

The batter was sweet and sticky and made me feel about six years old.

'Ruby? Does Mrs Cameron come downstairs during the

day? She doesn't stay up there all day, does she?' I pointed my spoon at the ceiling.

Ariadne obviously had a private sitting room upstairs, but I hardly felt I'd be welcome if I just went up there uninvited and knocked on her door.

'Not generally,' Ruby said. 'You finished with that bowl? Not unless she's having a bad day. A nice day like today, she likes to go out in the garden. She's quite a fine artist. She's out there now with her drawing papers and pens. She's a very talented lady.'

I took off the socks and walked out barefoot into the garden. The grass was blessedly cool under my toes. Ariadne was at the far end in her chair under some appletrees which had seen better days. She had a board propped up on her lap and she was sketching. It must have been a little chilly there despite the sun, but she didn't seem to mind. She had a blanket over her legs and a gauzy scarf wrapped lightly round her throat, the ends trailing down her back *à la* Isadora Duncan. The breeze caught the ends of the scarf from time to time and lifted them gently, only to fall back again, pale turquoise tips trailing across the long grass.

It occurred to me that if anyone meant her any harm, she was about as vulnerable as she could be, sitting out here in her invalid chair, all alone and too far away from the house to shout for help.

'I wish I could draw or something,' I said, sitting on the grass by her.

'Have you ever tried?' She smiled down at me.

I had to confess I hadn't. She pointed to a satchel by her chair.

'Take a sheet of cartridge paper out of that and see what you can do. Try charcoal.'

I got myself a sheet of paper and a piece of charcoal and used the cardboard satchel to lean on. I could just see a corner of the house through the shrubs and old fruit trees so I had a go at drawing that but it looked lopsided when I'd finished, with all the windows too large.

Ariadne inspected it when I finally decided I couldn't manage any more.

'You're too worried about detail,' she said. 'You need to get down just a general impression first. Details can come later.'

That tied in rather neatly with what I was doing here. I wondered how I could get round to Watkins's visit that morning.

While I was thinking it out, she showed me what she'd done. It looked highly professional to me. I told her about Squib and his pavement reproductions. She seemed genuinely interested.

'If he's had no formal training, he must have an exceptionally keen eye,' she said.

I asked her if she'd had lessons and she said she'd had a few. She'd been at art college when she'd been young.

'Did Terry draw?' I asked. 'I never saw her do anything like that.'

'Theresa had no patience.' She began to put her work away. There was something final about the way she spoke. She didn't want to talk about Terry. I persevered, all the same.

'She never talked about her home, this house,' I told her. 'Or the stud. I was really surprised when I found out what was here.'

'Did she talk about anything else?' Ariadne's sharp eyes rested on my face.

I felt myself blush. 'No. She grumbled a lot. I don't think she was very happy with us. I'm not surprised, not if she was used to living here.'

'Obviously,' Ariadne said, 'she wasn't happy here, either, or she'd have stayed with us.' There was bitterness behind the words although her voice sounded calm enough.

I told her I was sure that Terry had simply been going through a phase. That she'd have come back eventually. It was such a beautiful place and there was so much here. The fact that she'd been so miserable in London showed how much she must have missed them all at the Astara.

She made no reply. It was as if I hadn't spoken. I felt horribly embarrassed.

We sat for a while. Ariadne just looked ahead of her at the view of the house. Though she was old her profile showed what a beauty she must once have been. Her skin was still fine, though wrinkled, and her nose, the line of her forehead and her deepset eyes were classical in form. Her hands, folded now in her lap, had long thin fingers and her rings were loose. But the hands were sinewy and I remembered that she'd been a horsewoman before her accident. I knew I was frightened of Ariadne. Not in the way I had been frightened when pursued, as I thought, in the lane. But frightened in a way more difficult to explain. There was no way I could talk to her without seeming crass, and in the presence of this poised former beauty, that appeared almost like a sin.

Nevertheless, I tried again. 'Look, I'm sorry, I know it sounds as though I'm interfering and making this worse for you all. But I shared a house with her. I want to know what happened to her. After all, we – I – found her!' I finished by blurting out.

I was beginning to feel a little aggrieved. After all, the police had grilled me and Nev and Squib and made us feel like assassins. They were still not satisfied now. When I got back to London, Janice would be round to my gungy flat the minute she heard I was there. Perhaps Ariadne didn't feel like talking about it to me. But she had no right to cut me out of the whole affair as if I were not already a part-player in it.

She seemed to be thinking it over. Eventually she said, 'Yes, you did, I was forgetting. How very difficult for you and your friends. I dare say the police were unpleasant.'

'Yes, they were.' Parry, at least. In case she was wondering, I added, 'She was *not* killed by anyone living in the house. I know I didn't do it and I know the others didn't. You must believe me, it's the truth.'

'I believe you, Francesca. I think I am a fair judge of character.'

There was no way I was going to finesse my way into saying what I wanted to say. I blundered in. 'Mrs Cameron, you know, you might be in danger? Whoever killed Terry, he – or she – it might be something to do with this house or the stud.'

She was watching me work up another sweat, this time of embarrassment. 'My dear,' she said, 'you really ought not to worry about me. I am quite capable of taking care of myself, you know.' She sounded faintly amused.

That's what I'd said to Ganesh, about myself. He hadn't believed me and I didn't believe Ariadne. But there was nothing I could do about it. I began to appreciate how frustrated Ganesh must feel about my obstinacy, and how

243

useless. Ariadne didn't want to believe anyone could walk out here to this lonely corner of the garden and, quite unseen by anyone at the house, just reach out and tighten the gauzy scarf which encircled her neck.

As if she could read my mind, she said, 'It is my home, Francesca. I hope I'm safe in my own home!'

I hoped she was, too.

'Lunchtime, I fancy,' she went on. She reached down and released a catch on the side of the chair. She turned it manually with a push of her deceptively thin hands, preparing to return to the house. Only when it was in position, did she press the electric button and start up, whirring quietly as it juddered along the bumpy path. I walked a little behind her as there wasn't room alongside.

'I wish', Ariadne said conversationally, as if I were quite the ordinary sort of visitor to whom she was showing off the garden, 'that you could have seen the house when my husband was alive. The gardens were so much better kept then.' She raised her voice slightly so that I could hear, behind her.

I confessed I'd been told about the origins of the Astara Stud and how it had come by its name. I had no idea how long horses lived but it seemed unlikely she still had the original animal, Astara. I asked, instead, how many foals he'd sired and whether any of them had inherited his name. Were the horses here named like racehorses, which, as I understood it, got names based on their sire or dam's name?

'There has only been one Astara,' she said. 'And after the accident, he was shot.'

I was so startled, I stopped and let out a squawk of dismay.

She braked the chair and looked back at me, eyebrows raised quizzically.

'He was injured, too, unfortunately.'

'I see,' I said and asked whether he'd broken a leg. I had an idea that once horses broke legs, they were put down.

'No, but he was left permanently scarred and temperamentally uncertain. Why are you so shocked? Death isn't the worst thing.' She tapped the arms of her chair. 'There is worse. When one sees an animal which has been so beautiful and which one has cared for so long, reduced to a twitching wreck, would it be better to prolong its miserable life? No. Sometimes, a bullet is kinder. I've never feared death myself. I feel sometimes I've lived too long. The Greeks used to say that those whom the gods loved, died young. Death preserves beauty, strength, grace and innocence. Life has a way of destroying them. A beautiful thing, once damaged beyond recall, is better destroyed.'

The chair whirred into life and trundled on towards the house. I followed silently behind her. I wanted to cry out that she was wrong. That she misunderstood what life was about. That it wasn't a world just for the young and beautiful and rich. It was a world with a place in it for me, Squib and Mad Edna, too. That the faceless planners who had decided to demolish our squat had reasoned as she was reasoning. That it couldn't be saved, wasn't worth saving, was too far gone. But we'd loved that house with all its peeling plaster and leaking rooftiles, and given a chance, we'd have saved it.

But I knew, if I tried to tell her this, she wouldn't listen. I realised now why she scared me so. And was this why Terry had been afraid? Terry, the beautiful doll of a grandchild and great-niece, who had been destined to receive everything which Ariadne and Alastair had to give. But the doll had tumbled from her pedestal and broken, become a sharp-faced, shop-soiled, streetwise brat, 'temperamentally uncertain', unable to be restored.

'A beautiful thing, once damaged beyond recall, is better destroyed.' How terrible those words were. My head was filling with thoughts which froze me with such horror, that I thrust them away from me in revulsion.

Chapter Fifteen

Ariadne didn't lunch with the rest of us. I gathered she lunched in her room and rested until the evening.

Alastair and Jamie were whispering conspiratorially as I entered the dining room and greeted my appearance with an ill-subdued glee. There was absolutely no mention at all of Marcia's visit – and none of Watkins. Perhaps part of Alastair's good humour was due to Marcia having managed to smooth things over. I knew he'd been angry with her before. She must have said all the right things this time.

'Got a little surprise for you!' he chuckled.

I didn't like the sound of that. I looked inquiringly at Jamie. His bland expression made me feel worse. Their manner suggested they'd planned a jolly jape of the sort which generally leaves a third party humiliated and helpless. I couldn't quell the uneasy feeling I was to be the victim.

'After lunch,' crowed Alastair. 'Eat up.' The condemned man being presented with his last meal probably got that sort of grim encouragement.

They ate well at the Astara, three cooked meals a day,

including breakfast, and I was hungry. Lunch was Toad in the Hole, the sausages peeking coyly through the curled brown batter. It was followed by cheese and biscuits. Simple but substantial fare and, after it, I rather felt like going and taking a siesta myself. It wasn't to be.

Ruby appeared, obviously part of the plot, carrying a pair of riding breeches, a hard hat and soft-topped boots.

'They belonged to young Theresa,' she said. 'Seeing as you got her gumboots on this morning, you'll be able to get your feet in these and the jodhpurs will fit.'

My heart sank. It was clear where this was leading.

'Can't let you leave without getting you up on a horse,' said Alastair merrily. 'Kelly will saddle up old Dolly for you. Quiet as a lamb. Jamie is going to show you a bit of our countryside. The way to see it is from horseback.'

I didn't want to be shown the countryside by Jamie and I certainly didn't want to do my sightseeing from the back of a horse, but argument was clearly useless.

Togged up in my equestrian finery (the boots pinched and the jodhpurs fitted like second skin), I tottered out to the stableyard accompanied by my two supporters. Jamie looked the goods in his riding gear, very dashing. Grandma Varady and all those Hungarian hussar ancestors would've approved. I didn't know where Ganesh was. I hoped he wasn't wandering around the place, partly because he might be seen – and partly because he might see me in this ridiculous get-up.

Kelly was waiting in the yard, holding the bridle of a grey mare. She didn't smile. I was still the rival and it was possible she was about to be revenged.

I was slightly encouraged by the fact that Dolly herself appeared to be half-asleep, eyes closed and one hind hoof hitched up in rest position. But my relief, if any, was cancelled by the sight of Joey Lundy, lurking in the background with a smirk on his unlovely countenance.

'Here we are, my dear!' cried Alastair, slapping the nag on her neck. 'Give the lady a leg up, Lundy!' Dolly opened her eyes and twitched her ears. If ever a horse could be said to sneer, she did.

Lundy sidled over and stooped, cupping his hands. They all stood round me, blocking any escape. I had no choice but allow myself to be catapulted into the saddle.

The one and only time I'd ever sat on anything with four legs was when I was very small and was put on a donkey on the beach one summer. I must have been about four years old at the time and I yelled blue murder to be lifted down again. I felt the same way about it now. It seemed an inordinately long way up. Dolly's neck was very narrow and insubstantial, viewed from above, and it and the animal's head appeared way below me. I felt I was sitting up there in the saddle with nothing at all to prevent me pitching forward.

Kelly was fussing around me, giving instructions, showing the correct way to hold the reins and position my feet in the stirrups. Jamie, meantime, had swung into the saddle with the greatest of ease and looked as if he was about to lead the charge of the Light Brigade.

'We'll avoid roads,' he said kindly. 'So you won't have to worry about traffic. We'll cut over the fields.'

This reduced the likelihood that Ganesh would see us, which was a relief.

'You'll thoroughly enjoy yourself!' cried Alastair, waving us away. Kelly raised a hand in silent salute like a gladiator in the arena.

Lundy, I noticed from the corner of my eye, slipped away as we walked sedately out of the yard. His whole manner suggested someone up to no good.

For a while it went rather better than I'd expected. We crossed several fields of pasture, one of them with mares and foals in it. The youngsters were attractive with their spindly legs. I wasn't thoroughly enjoying it, but I was *almost* enjoying it.

Dolly behaved herself impeccably, despite having a novice aboard. She plodded along in her half-asleep way. Jamie, efficiently opening and closing gates as required, continued to play the gallant escort, pointing out local landmarks. I still wasn't quite sure what the purpose of this whole outing was and eventually I asked him, point blank.

'Alastair's idea,' he said briefly.

'I didn't expect you'd volunteered to give me the guided tour, Jamie. But I can't imagine why Alastair thought I'd be keen. He knows I'm no country girl.'

Jamie's horse snorted and tossed its head as emotion communicated itself from rider to mount. 'I hope to God he isn't trying to turn you into one!' Jamie growled. 'The idea's grotesque.'

He turned a direct stare on me. 'And just remember! You may be literally in Theresa's boots right now, but it's as near as you're going to get to taking her place. I've already warned you. No way will I allow you to insinuate yourself into the old people's favour.'

I was furious and told him what I felt about that suggestion. My anger bounced off him. I followed behind him as we progressed Indian file across a field towards distant trees. It occurred to me when I'd simmered down a little, that Jamie himself felt insecure in the old people's affections, or he wouldn't be worried about me. Perhaps, for all his assiduous attention to Watkins, the solicitor had refused to tell him the contents of Ariadne's new will. Until Jamie knew his name was on that document, he couldn't relax.

Sometimes the direct approach pays off.

'Jamie!' I called out. 'What will happen to the Astara Stud when Ariadne, say, decides to retire to Bournemouth?'

'That's Ariadne's business!' he shouted back. 'And of no possible concern to you, Fran!'

And sometimes, the direct approach doesn't.

Meanwhile, we'd reached a commercially planted plantation of conifers. A wide track skirted the edge of it. Now and again a wide swathe of clear ground ran off at right-angles between the trees.

'Firebreaks,' said Jamie, pointing up at a wooden watch-tower.

I asked if the plantation was privately owned, but he said it belonged to the forestry commission. He turned his horse's head into one of the broad firebreak tracks and I followed. The trees rustled darkly to either side. It was a sinister spot. Jamie informed me there were deer in the woodland, but we'd be unlikely to see any at this time of day.

At that moment, a shot rang out, closely followed by another. Something winged across the front of me, narrowly missing Dolly's ears. There was a crack and splintering of wood. A white scar appeared on the nearest tree-trunk. The next second, Dolly had taken off like a bat out of hell.

'Hang on!' yelled Jamie.

There was nothing I could do about it but hang on and we thudded headlong down the track. Hauling on the reins had no effect. I prayed Dolly was sure-footed as the ground was uneven and rutted with tractor tracks. I became aware Jamie was galloping after me, before Dolly swerved without warning and changed direction.

We nearly parted company at that moment. I slipped sideways and just managed to haul myself back. I'd seen cossacks in a circus doing stunts like that, and never felt the slightest urge to join them. Dolly now bolted down a narrow path, probably made by deer, between trees.

There was just about room for her. I grabbed the pommel of the saddle and Dolly's mane and crouched flat to avoid being swept to the ground by overhanging branches. I sensed, rather than heard, that I'd lost Jamie. He wasn't behind me, at any rate. The track must come out somewhere and perhaps he was riding round in an attempt to head me off at the other end.

Dolly plunged on. The ground was soft and uneven, in parts boggy so that Dolly's hoofs squelched in mud and came free with loud, sucking noises. We came to a stream and she leapt it easily. By now I'd lost both stirrups and only a miracle kept me glued to her back. We hurtled across an open glade. Dolly took a new path, at a right-angle to the first. She seemed to know where she was going, but it was unlikely Jamie did and wherever he'd headed off to, he'd probably fail to connect up with me now Dolly had changed direction.

Without warning we shot out of the trees into another wide firebreak. There, bumping along towards us was an old pick-up truck. Dolly saw it, checked and wheeled round. I carried on, like the arrow from the bow in the poem, and fell to earth, literally, in a stretch of mud.

I lay there winded, a singing in my ears. I was vaguely aware of cold mud creeping over my outflung hands and dampness oozing through my clothing. Dimly, I heard a familiar voice calling, 'Fran! Are you all right?'

I opened my eyes. Nick Bryant was stooping over me.

Most of the breath had been knocked out of my body, but I managed to wheeze the unnecessary information that I'd fallen off.

'Take it easy, you may have broken something.' In concern, he began checking me over. 'Try and move your arms, one at a time, then your legs.'

I tried. Everything seemed to be in working order. He gave me a hand to sit up.

I rested my arms on my knees and concentrated on getting my breathing back in pattern. I was in a terrible mess, muddy from head to toe. Dolly had disappeared.

'I'll take you home,' Nick said. 'The mare will probably go back on her own.'

I told him Jamie was around somewhere. Nick expressed the opinion that Jamie could also find his own way home. I argued that I ought to try and find him. He wasn't likely to go back to the Astara without me. We were wrangling about this, when hoofbeats announced the arrival of Jamie himself.

He leapt from the saddle and pounded over the turf towards us.

'What the hell – what are you doing here, Bryant?'

'Taking a short cut – good thing I was here! Why didn't you take better care of her?'

I was still sitting in my patch of mud, getting my breath back. They stood either side of me, glowering at one another like a couple of dogs disputing ownership of a bone.

'Oy,' I called up to them. 'How about someone giving me a hand up?'

They hauled me upright between them.

'I'm taking her home in the pick-up,' Nick said, holding tightly to my right arm.

'I'll find the mare,' Jamie argued, gripping my left. 'She won't have gone far.'

'You can't expect Fran to ride back!' I was jerked to the right.

'I'll take care of her, all right?' A tug to the left.

'If you don't mind!' I protested.

They gave me surprised looks and both released me.

'I don't know where the horse is,' I told Jamie. 'But she went that-a-way.' I pointed. 'If you don't mind, I'll accept Nick's offer of a lift back.'

'Look,' Jamie urged. 'I don't want either of the old people seeing you in that state! Especially Ariadne. They mustn't know about your taking a fall.'

'So, I'll creep in the back door!'

Reluctantly, he let me clamber into the pick-up.

'He's a fool,' said Nick, as we bumped down the track with a grinding of gears. 'Taking a novice rider out on such a long hack across country.'

'It wasn't his fault. Someone fired a gun off and frightened Dolly, the mare. The shot only just missed me.'

'A gun?' He glanced at me, frowning. 'Might have been someone shooting pigeons or even a poacher after a deer. Venison fetches a good price nowadays. I'll phone the

forest warden when we get back. He can send a couple of
rangers out to check.'

I persuaded him to set me down in the lane leading to
the stud. I hobbled the remaining stretch home and slipped into the house through the kitchen door.

Ruby was there and let out a squawk. I explained Jamie
was following after, once he'd found the mare.

'You leave those muddy clothes with me,' she said.
'And go up and run yourself a good hot bath. Have a nice
long soak in it. Oh, and you won't let Mr Alastair or Mrs
Cameron know, it'd upset them to think you'd had any
accident.'

I soaked in the bath feeling a hundred years old. Any
plan I'd had of slipping out to find Ganesh was out of the
question now. I limped along to my room and collapsed
on the bed until dinner.

Ruby put her head round as I lay there, and informed
me Mr James was safely back with Dolly.

I was more than aware that the person who'd come back
safely, against all the odds, was myself. I wasn't meant to
return in one piece. Whoever fired off those shots wasn't
firing at pigeons or deer. He'd been firing at me. I
remembered Lundy's expression as I rode out of the yard.
But if it had been Lundy, had he been acting alone? Or
had the whole thing been set up with Jamie?

I hoped neither Alastair nor Ariadne had been a part of
it.

Chapter Sixteen

After dinner Alastair dug out some old family snapshot albums and insisted on showing them to me. They were interesting chiefly for the ones which showed Philip Monkton whom I hadn't had the opportunity to meet in the flesh. He appeared a heavily built, self-confident type of man, handsome in a florid way. In the couple of photographs in which he appeared with Terry, there was no appearance of closeness. The camera can lie, contrary to the saying. But attitudes don't. The pictures with father and daughter were obligatory family snaps. Looking closely at Philip, I decided he was a bully.

Meanwhile it started to rain heavily, beating against the windows.

'In for a nasty night,' said Alastair in the comfortable way of someone who hadn't to go out in the bad weather.

My mind was on Ganesh, sitting uncomfortably in the van, eating cold baked beans out of a tin, listening to the rain beat on the roof. I felt guilty. I had a warm bed upstairs. On the other hand, my bumps and bruises were coming out nicely and I was likely to be spending an equally uncomfortable night.

I limped to the window and peered out. It was tipping down.

'What's up?' Jamie asked, sounding suspicious. 'You've been fidgeting about for the last hour. What's out there?'

'Nothing,' I told him. 'I was just looking out at the weather.' Privately I muttered, 'I'm in agony!'

He scowled and glanced at Alastair, but he didn't ask again why I was so unsettled.

Poor old Ganesh. But it had been his idea to drive down here.

I awoke the next morning, hardly able to move a muscle. Every attempt was agony. Given free choice, I'd have remained where I was all day. But the choice wasn't mine. I got out of bed by sliding over the edge and finishing on my knees on the carpet. I hauled myself upright, yelping with pain, and I made my way down to the bathroom, hunched like Quasimodo. A hot bath helped a little and gave me the courage to tackle the stairs.

Making an entry into the breakfast room with the appearance of everything being all right, when everything hurt, took some doing. But Alastair didn't appear to notice anything amiss. Jamie wasn't there.

It had stopped raining. I managed to hide a toast and marmalade sandwich in my pocket and made my robotic way outside trying to look nonchalant. Gan probably had pneumonia by now. I'd find him coughing and expiring with just enough breath left to say 'I told you so!'

I took a deep breath. The air was filled with a wet-leaf smell. The overnight deluge had left deep puddles in the drive. The buddleia heads drooped and dripped moisture.

There was a rustle in the tangle of foliage. A voice whispered, 'Fran!'

I peered into the dripping jungle. 'Ganesh? Are you all right?'

He emerged, clearly anything but all right. He was in a dreadful mess, soaked, shivering and unshaven. But something more than physical discomfort troubled him as I could see from his drawn features and the look in his eyes.

I grabbed his hand. 'What happened, Ganesh?'

His fingers closed tightly on mine and then released them. 'Fran, we've got to get out of here. We've got to get back to London – we, I, have got to call the police!' He swallowed and looked nervously towards the house.

He was right to be cautious. 'Jamie snoops,' I told him. 'Back in the bushes, Gan!' I gave him a shove and we both retreated into the wet undergrowth. Water trickled down my neck and wet leaves slapped against my face. 'Just tell me,' I urged.

'The woods down there, where I parked the van.' He made an effort to pull himself together, pushing back his wet hair with both hands. 'I went into them to – well, the usual reason. Then I went wandering off further, just exploring.' His jaw wobbled. 'I found a grave, Fran.'

I couldn't say anything at first, only stare at him in growing horror and dismay. Somehow I managed to squeeze out, 'Are you sure about this, Ganesh? The terrain is pretty rough out there.'

'I tell you, it's a grave! The rain, it must have washed away the soil. It can't have been there long, you see. There – there was a hand sticking out among the leaves and brambles. I – I got a stick and just pushed aside a few more to uncover the face.' He paused and added in a choked voice, 'I'm so sorry, Fran. It's – it was someone we know.'

'Who?' I asked dully. But my guts, sickened with the knowledge of what he was going to say, heaved.

'It was Squib.' When I made no reply he added in a bewildered way, 'How's it possible, Fran? Down here? What was he doing—?'

'He had a plan!' I broke in miserably. 'Oh, Ganesh, this is my fault! I should have found out what was in his mind! But I didn't take him seriously. You know how he was—'

Ganesh grabbed my shoulders and shook me lightly. 'Yes, I know what Squib was like, but I don't know what you're talking about.'

'He knew about the Astara Stud. Terry had told him. He must have thought, somehow or other, he could get some money . . . He'd cleared out of the hostel and was on the run. He told me he was thick, poor sod, and he was thick! He hadn't worked out her killer could have come from here. If I'd only asked, I could have talked him out of it!'

'This isn't your fault!' Ganesh snapped.

I remembered the stub of chalk in Jamie's car. I'd thought it proved a visit to our house. But perhaps Squib had been in that car.

'The dog!' I exclaimed.

'No sign of it.'

'It wouldn't leave him and he wouldn't leave it. Squib thought the world of that dog.' So, somewhere in the woods would be a second, smaller grave. 'Take me there,' I said.

Ganesh shook his head. 'No, Fran,' he said gently.

'Squib was a friend!'

'Squib's dead. What's down there in the woods is a decomposing shell.' He paused. 'So, do we call the local cops?'

I struggled with my churning brain and shook my head. 'Not here. I don't want them swarming all over us here. I vote we go back to London and tell Janice. She'll be angry but she knows us. Here they don't know us, we're strangers. Gan, I suppose you couldn't tell how he died?'

That was asking a lot from a quick glimpse of a discoloured face and a hand.

Ganesh said fiercely, 'I didn't stay to find out! I couldn't *look* at it any longer, Fran!'

I gulped. 'Squib wouldn't have hurt *anyone*! It's foul – and fouler that you had to be the one to find him!'

'Someone had to find him. I wish it hadn't been me. Something, some animal, has been chewing at the fingers. The smell is indescribable, not foul exactly but sweet, like a mix of rotting fruit and disturbed stagnant water. It would have been bad enough even without knowing him. I threw up. If the police look around there, Fran, they'll find plenty of evidence to tell them I was there. The ground was soft. I must have left footprints. The van's tyre tracks. We have to go to the police before someone else stumbles over the body.'

I made a decision. The last thing I wanted was to be hauled away by the local police. They knew nothing about us, we were clearly out-of-towners and not the type of tourist a locality encourages. If, in addition, we told them the body was that of a friend of ours, they'd lock us up and toss away the key. I'd also be lying if I didn't admit to being afraid. It now seemed clear that what I'd suspected must be so, that someone at the Astara was involved in this whole blood-stained business.

I gripped Ganesh's hand. 'We'll go back to London right now. We'll tell Janice and she'll contact the locals here. I don't trust any coppers much but if I trust anyone, it's Janice.'

He mumbled, 'All right.'

He didn't need more problems, but I had to make a confession. 'I should tell you that someone took a potshot at me yesterday afternoon, while I was out riding, either hoping to hit me or spook the horse. But it couldn't have been Jamie who fired. He was with me. On the other hand, he was my guide and let me into the tree plantation. Or there's the groom, Lundy. He could have done it and would have done it, if Jamie ordered, I'm sure! I was set up. They set me up, dammit, between them!'

'What?' His confused look turned to surprise and then anger. 'I warned you, Fran!'

'All right, I know! I'll go indoors and—'

There was a screech of protesting metal followed by a grating sound, quite near at hand. Gan parted the undergrowth and we peered through the leaves. It was Jamie, over at the garage, pushing up the door.

'He's taking the car out,' I whispered. 'Can you see him? Is that the man you saw watching our house?'

'That's him!' Ganesh said firmly.

'Sure?'

'Absolutely positive.'

Jamie had gone into the garage and we could hear the engine being started up. The car slid out slowly backwards.

'Know where he's going?' Ganesh muttered.

'No idea.'

The car was coming towards us, still slowly. Jamie seemed to be looking about him. Looking for me, perhaps. He'd realised I wasn't in the house and he wanted to know where I was.

Just then something cold and wet fell off a branch and rolled down my neck. Stupidly I jumped. All the branches around me shook. Jamie saw it and slammed on the brake.

He was out of the car fast but I was quicker. I shot out of the shrubbery, hoping Ganesh was well hidden in the leaves behind me and hailed him brightly. 'Hullo, Jamie!'

'What were you doing in there?' he demanded. He tried to see past me but I moved to block him.

'Walking up and down trying to get some movement in my joints. I'm a wreck from that fall yesterday. There's not an inch of me which doesn't hurt.'

He wasted no sympathy on my ills. 'You've been creeping about in those shrubs. You're up to something! I damn well knew you were last night! What's in there?'

He shoved me aside roughly and pushed his way into the buddleias.

I held my breath. After a moment Jamie came out backwards, wet and furious.

'I want to know what you're doing, Fran!' He grabbed my arm. 'And if I have to shake it out of you, I will!'

I shrieked in agony as the sudden movement antagonised my aches and pains. The bushes further along rustled and Ganesh stepped out. I wondered briefly how he'd got down there without either Jamie or myself seeing him. Perhaps he had some mystic Eastern trick or two up his sleeve.

'Why don't you let go of her?' he asked unpleasantly.

Jamie released me and pushed me away. He stared disbelievingly at Ganesh and then burst out, 'I knew it! I knew you came out here to meet someone! You've been like a cat on hot bricks since yesterday.' He jabbed a finger at Ganesh and then whirled to face me. 'So, who the devil is that?'

'This is Ganesh Patel,' I said. 'He's a friend of mine and he's come to take me back to London.'

Jamie scowled at Ganesh. 'I've seen you somewhere before.'

This was bad. Gan had said that the man who had been watching the house the day Terry died, had noticed him. If Jamie now connected Gan up with that incident, he'd know Ganesh was the one who could finger him to the police. And he'd do something about it.

Very quickly I said, 'You'll be pleased I'm leaving, Jamie!'

That brought his attention back to me. 'Pleased! Yes, you could put it like that! You can't leave fast enough as far as I'm concerned. Is that your clapped-out old van parked down the road under the trees?' He turned to Ganesh.

'Yes,' said Gan shortly.

'If that gets all the way to London without breaking down, you'll be lucky!' Jamie said. 'You'll probably have to push it all the way!' He began to laugh.

I was afraid Gan was going to sock him so I jumped in with, 'I'm just going indoors to pack up my gear and say goodbye to everyone.'

Jamie had stopped laughing. He still wanted to have the last word. 'That's fine. I'm going down to Abbotsfield for half an hour. Try and be gone by the time I get back, right?'

I went indoors to pack my things and say goodbye to Alastair and Ariadne. I thanked them for everything. I really meant my thanks and they obviously realised it. They were both very nice and told me to come back again, although underneath it, I sensed they were relieved I was going. That, in turn, made me wonder if I'd been getting near the truth – and it was a truth they didn't want to hear.

'How will you travel?' Alastair asked.

I told them I had someone waiting outside for me. They immediately insisted I bring Ganesh indoors. They were clearly appalled when they saw the state of him. But Gan made a polite speech, apologising for his unkempt appearance, and they were very well bred about it.

Ruby wouldn't hear of us leaving before we'd had coffee and she'd cut some sandwiches for the journey.

This all took a little time and I kept expecting Jamie to return but he didn't. A niggle of worry formed at the back of my mind. What was he doing?

Time to go. Ruby and Alastair came out on to the drive to wave goodbye to us.

'I'll make your farewells to Jamie,' Alastair said. 'He'll be sorry to have missed you.'

He gripped my hand and addded quietly, 'And thank you, my dear, for caring. But to be honest with you, I'm beginning to have second thoughts about trying to do the work of the police for them. Sometimes it's better to let sleeping dogs lie.'

He sounded desperately sad. I guessed he was afraid my investigations might lead right back to the Astara and they'd had enough trouble. If someone here was a villain, they didn't want to know it.

I knew then we'd been right to keep stumm about Gan's

finding Squib's body. You had to take it a little at a time with someone of Alastair's age. I pressed his hand and thanked him again.

'They're nice people,' Ganesh said as we lurched down the drive. 'It's a pity you couldn't help them, Fran.'

'I've been trying to tell you that!' I knew I sounded exasperated. You can never tell men anything. They always have to work it out for themselves and then they pretend they thought of it first.

The van had reached the bottom of the drive. I looked at my watch. 'Where do you think Jamie is?'

'In the pub,' said Gan. He was probably right.

'Turn right!' He glanced at me surprised. He'd been about to turn left, taking the lane down to the main road.

'I just remembered,' I said. 'I need to call by a farm near here, say goodbye to the people there. Their name is Bryant.'

Nick was in the yard. The cows were bellowing in the shed behind him. There was an old chap in gumboots and a cloth cap squelching about in the mud in the background whom I supposed was Biles, the hired labourer.

Nick and Ganesh eyed one another like a pair of duellists, observing all the courtesies but waiting for a chance to jump in and gain advantage. Nick took us into the kitchen and offered us tea which we declined. We had a long drive ahead of us. Penny wasn't there, for which I was sorry.

'She's at the shop,' Nick told us. 'She'll be staying over in Winchester for the next couple of days. Her partner's sick again.'

Ganesh had been looking from me to Nick and back

again. Now he cheered up a bit because he knows all about running a shop. He and Nick had some conversation about that and afterwards, they seemed to get along better.

'If you find out anything,' Nick said. 'Give me a call, here, at the farm. Ma was fond of Theresa Monkton. She felt sorry for her. We all did, I guess. After you called the other morning, Fran, Ma talked about Theresa a lot. It's a really bad business.'

I had a similar request. 'If you find out anything, let me know, please.' I scribbled on a piece of paper. 'This is my address, my flat. I've no phone, but you can send me a letter.'

'He can phone the shop,' Ganesh said. 'Give him our number.'

So we did that and parted company. As I was getting into the car Nick put his hand on the door before I could close it and stooped to say, 'I hope you'll come down here again sometime.'

He sounded as though he meant it. I mumbled something because Ganesh was giving us funny looks again.

'You seem to have hit it off with him!' Ganesh said dourly as we drove off.

'They're nice people. He knew Terry and he's upset about her death. So is his mother. Don't fuss, Gan.'

Ganesh muttered, 'I've got more to worry about than him. I've got to explain to Morgan about finding Squib. I think we should have got in touch with the police here.'

'I don't. Believe me, Ganesh, I'm right on this one.'

'And what', he asked, 'if someone else finds Squib before we get to Morgan? Not only the body but my footprints and the marks left by the van, too? How do I talk my way out of that one?'

'Don't worry about things which haven't happened,' I advised. 'Just worry about the things which have.'

We sat silent for some miles after that, picking up the argument and rehashing it only when traffic on the motorway had slowed to a crawl. Ahead was London, the great magnet drawing it all inward. I could feel its power tugging me towards it.

We quit the motorway and negotiated the network of roads through suburbs which seemed never-ending, running into one another, linked by scraps of tired greenery, scrappy workshops and car-sale forecourts. At last respectability, or at least a façade of it, began to give way to a jumble of grimy streets. I was back where I belonged. I never thought I'd be so pleased to see grubby shops offering 'fire-damaged goods' or 'closing down sales', gutters filled with debris, vandalised telephone kiosks festooned with cards advertising the services of local prostitutes, spray-can graffiti from the hand of someone called Gaz. All the things which to me spelled home . . . with not a horse or a chicken or a cow in sight.

Home Sweet Home is what you want it to be.

Chapter Seventeen

'Just what did you think you were playing at? You can't just waltz off when you feel like it. How dare you tamper with other witnesses? Do you realise I could book you right here and now for obstructing the police and wasting my time?'

Janice had been rampaging around her office, hurling accusations and reproaches mixed with a variety of threats, until she appeared in danger of getting seriously overwrought.

You will have realised that our return hadn't been well received and when they heard about Ganesh's find in the woods, things got very nasty. They split us up, of course, as was their way. As Ganesh was marched off to give details of his discovery and for the Hampshire police to be alerted to go out and look for it, he managed to call to me.

'When I get out of here I'll have to go over and see my family. I'll get in touch later, Fran!'

'If he gets out of here!' said Janice unpleasantly. 'Nor am I overlooking your part in this latest development. When Mr Patel told you he'd found a body it was your duty to see the matter was reported at once to the local police. It wasn't just up to him. You knew. You share responsibility. After I've booked you for obstruction, I dare say the Hampshire force will do the same. You, Miss Varady, are in trouble!'

I wanted to reply, 'What's new?' But that wouldn't have been tactful. I realised at least a token apology was called for on my part. I'd had some stage training and if I couldn't put on a good show of abject regret, I had no talent at all. I hung my head, shuffled about on my chair and mumbled I was sorry for having caused any bother. As for reporting Squib's body, we had thought she ought to know about it first. We'd made an honest mistake. I wondered whether to squeeze out a few tears, but one can go over the top. She wasn't a fool.

I must have turned in quite a fair and well-judged performance because Janice calmed down considerably. She made a speech in which she said she realised that Ganesh and I had panicked. As for my going down to Abbotsfield, I probably thought I could help. But I was certainly intelligent enough to know that police investigations had to be conducted according to the rules. Apart from anything else, when a case got to court – if it did – defence lawyers would seize on any irregularity to get evidence thrown out. I didn't want that to happen, did I?

All of this was more or less a reprise of the kind of lecture my old headmistress used to deliver regularly to me. I'd long ago developed a technique for letting it flow over my head while keeping a reasonably alert expression on my face.

What I was really doing, as she droned on about responsibility and tax-payers' money (where did they get into it?), was studying her. I decided she was only about thirty-five. How did anyone get to be that institutionalised by the mid-thirties? She was dressed today as if she were sixty-five, in a grey flannel suit and a nylon crepe blouse with a tie-bow at the neck. Where on earth did she buy those clothes? The only place I'd ever seen them offered for sale was in newspaper ads aimed at the middle-aged, usually described as 'practical' and 'available direct from our warehouse'. She even had the round-toed shoes, low-heeled, with little tabs on the top, which are advertised with a promise that your feet will never hurt again. No store sells things like that now, surely? I felt a bit sorry for her. I realised that if she looked like a bimbo, she wouldn't be taken seriously as a police officer. But it seemed a shame that she had to make herself look like that. It was defensiveness, pure and simple. There had to be a compromise somewhere in between. I decided that if I ever got to know her better, and off-duty as it were, I'd have a quiet word with her about it.

'If you have anything else at all to tell me,' she was saying, 'let's hear it now. Be absolutely open, leave nothing out, and I might just overlook your behaviour. Don't hold out on me, Francesca. If you do, believe me, you're for the chop!'

Now, it seemed to me there was a touch of muddled thinking here, having her cake and eating it. I was being carpeted for interfering, but she wanted to know what I'd learned in the country. I gave her a stern look to let her know I'd rumbled her.

Then I settled down to tell her about the shot in the plantation, about Lundy and his habit of violence towards his wife, about the solicitor's visit to Ariadne and anything else I could.

'You can't just ignore Jamie Monkton!' I finished. 'He has a motive. He runs the stud and Lundy takes his orders from him. He took me out into that plantation and set me up. Get both his and Lundy's dabs off them. You must have prints from our house you haven't identified. Match up just one set with either Jamie or Lundy and it puts him in that house. Let whoever it is explain it away, if he can. Jamie says he never went there and I know he lies.'

'You don't know it,' she said coldly. 'I'll decide what's to be done about Mr James Monkton and, indeed, this other man, Lundy.' She turned her steely gaze on me. 'As for you, Francesca. Please go back to your flat and stay there. I want to be able to find you when I need you, OK?'

'OK!' I said meekly.

I took the bus home, as I laughingly thought of the place. It didn't appear any more welcoming than when I'd left it. Some new and more imaginative graffiti decorated the walls and a few more windows were boarded up. The lift was still broken and the electric light on the staircase was out. Perhaps there had been a general power failure.

It was getting dark by now and I'd have appreciated the electricity. Meagre light through broken windowpanes at each landing illuminated the lower three or four flights. The rest ran on into the gloom. The middle section had to be negotiated in the dark, until the light from the next landing cast grey comfort on my faltering footsteps. A chill wind was funnelled up the stairwell. I made as fast a progress as I could, promising myself a cup of tea when I got to the flat.

It wasn't possible to hurry too much. It was quite likely that someone had left an object on the staircase to trip up climbers. The kids here liked doing that sort of thing. So I made my way carefully up, keeping one hand on the greasy walls. Disgusting though it all was, each gloomy cold tread took me nearer my goal. Then, as I turned to face the last flight and began to climb up, out of the lighted lower portion into the murk, I became aware that I wasn't alone. Above me in the darkness, another human being was waiting in silence.

I stopped. I couldn't see a thing but I could hear the soft in- and out-take of breath. I was, presumably, about to be mugged.

I called up, 'I haven't got any money. If I had any, I wouldn't be living here!'

He moved. He was, possibly, just a jolly local rapist.

Or he was, and I didn't know why I hadn't thought of this at first, the person who had killed Terry, come to kill me.

Panic seized me. I whirled round and ran, heedless of breaking my neck as I plunged down the way I'd come up. Somehow, in my panic and my headlong flight, I became aware that someone called my name. It came from above, echoing down the stairwell.

'Fran! Wait! It's only me! It's Ganesh!'

I leaned panting against the wall, my heart leaping about in my chest like a yoyo. What on earth was he playing at? I crawled back up the stairs and found him at the top, on my landing. Or at least, a shadowy outline which turned out to be him. I did not feel kindly towards him.

'Are you mad?' I raged. 'I nearly had a heart-attack! I didn't know who was up there! The lights are out. Anyway, I thought you'd gone home.'

'I did but they all started on at me. I walked out. Besides, I was wondering about you. How did you get on?'

'Could have been worse. Let's go in and have a cup of tea. I'll tell you about it when we get into the flat.'

He moved to intercept me as I started off down the dark corridor towards my front door.

'You can't, Fran. You can't go to the flat.'

'Why ever not?' I'd had enough and the only thing I wanted was to get into my own place. 'Don't fool around out here, Gan. I'm desperate for a cuppa.' I gave him a shove, but he stood firm and gripped my arm.

'I've already been along there, Fran. While you've been away someone's broken in—'

I jerked my arm free and ran past him along the landing, fumbling for my key, although I no longer needed it.

My visitors had smashed in the front door completely so that it didn't lock any more. Even if it had locked, there was a hole in the middle of it.

I gave it a push. It swung inward. I put my hand round and fumbled for the light. It ought to be on a different circuit to the public staircase. It was. It came on, the yellow beam flooding out through the wrecked door and bathing Ganesh and me in its glare.

Ganesh took hold of my shoulders. 'Fran, don't go in. You don't want to go in there.' He sounded sympathetic but I didn't want sympathy. I wanted to know what had been going on.

'Yes, I do!' I said tightly. 'It's not much, but it's the only home I've got!'

'Fran—!' He tried to hold me back. I shrugged him off. He let me go.

It didn't take long to see what had happened in my absence. The block's kids, a small army of competent vandals, had broken in and had a field day. They'd rampaged through every room. Obscene graffiti covered the walls. All my furniture, including that got for me by Euan, was broken up. The armchair was ripped with a knife and all the stuffing pulled out. They'd tried to set fire to it but fortunately it hadn't burned, only smouldered. They'd stolen all my personal stuff. Nev's books had been left, but torn up and the pages scattered around the room. I think I minded more about Nev's books than losing my gear. Nev had really cared about his books and his giving them to me had meant a great deal to both of us.

All the mould I'd cleaned off with bleach had grown back again in the bathroom and the cistern had been pulled out of the wall and flooded the floor. The floorboards sagged in the middle and the water was probably leaking right through, down into the flat below which wasn't occupied.

On top of it all, as if anything more was needed, the place smelled foul, acrid from the singed chair stuffing, stale from the mould and damp, but mostly because one of the little charmers had crapped right in the middle of the sitting room floor.

'I tried to warn you,' Ganesh said. 'You can't stay here. You'll have to come back to our place. Mum will fix you up with a bed.'

'Thanks, but no,' I told him. 'I'd be answering their questions half the night and you know they wouldn't understand.'

'So where are you going to sleep?' He looked round in disgust. 'This is a pigsty – look at that filth! Come on, Fran. Even Morgan wouldn't expect you to stay here!'

I thought about it. 'I'll go back to the squat!'

He stared at me. 'You're crazy. It's boarded up.'

'So – unboard it. You're always opening crates of fruit. You ought to be able to prise a few boards off a window. We did it before, Squib and Nev and I, when we went back for our gear.'

He looked exasperated. 'But you can't stay there on your own! I'll stay with you. Always supposing we can get in and the place isn't already occupied by half a dozen winos.'

'No, you won't. You'll go home and make it up with your parents. That's what I want, Gan? OK? I'll be all right.'

I was glad to be going back to the squat. The flat had never been anything but a prison. The squat, with all its imperfections and despite the dreadful thing which had happened there, had been home. We'd been happy enough there. I knew the old house and it knew me. We'd keep each other company.

But by the time we got there it was dark and the street was deserted and sinister, like an old B-movie set. Every house had been emptied and only two street lights worked. The only sign of life came from the flat above the Patels' shop at the corner where they were obviously waiting up for Ganesh, probably with a deputation of aunts and uncles sitting around to lend weight. We stood outside and looked up at the windows.

'I didn't ask you how you got on with the police after they split us up,' I said. 'Sorry to be so self-centred. Did they give you a bad time?'

'Could've been worse.' He spoke absently. 'They phoned through to Hampshire who sent out a car right away to the woods. They must've found Squib. There was a lot of yakking on the phone between coppers which didn't include me. Then I was told I could go home but I have to report back in tomorrow first thing in the morning. I'll probably have to go back to Hampshire, under police escort. They'll want to talk to me down there.'

'Did you tell your family, I mean, about finding a body?'

'No – they've got enough troubles. Dad's had a letter,' Ganesh sighed. 'We've got to go, too. The shop's coming down. They've offered compensation. But where will we go?'

'I'm sorry,' I said again. 'I thought that would happen. I know your dad had plans about a different kind of shop for the new houses and flats that will come. But they were bound to want to clear the entire area.'

'When they rebuild, we won't be able to afford to rent, much less buy, around here.' Ganesh pushed his hands into his pockets. 'The family's very upset. It sounds selfish, but at least it takes the pressure off me. Really, they've got more to worry about than me.'

A sari-ed figure appeared at an upper window, outlined against the lamplight within. It looked out at us, and then shimmered away like a *peri* in an oriental fairy-tale. The curtain was drawn.

'Usha,' Gan said. 'Don't worry, even if she saw us, she won't give us away.'

We trailed down the dismal street to our old house. The council had repaired the breakage we'd made last time and nailed new boards over the windows and doors, stronger than before. Ganesh got a chisel from the toolbox in the van and we went round the back. The kitchen window was still the most promising. After Ganesh had levered at it for quite a while one of the wooden panels came loose. I swiveled it around and judged I could squeeze through.

'This', said Ganesh gloomily, 'is breaking and entering. We can get done for this. Do you realise that?'

'Entering what? Only a condemned house. Come on, Gan. There's nothing to pinch in there.'

There certainly wasn't. When we'd managed to scramble inside we found that the council had emptied it of any remaining furniture and only bare boards were left.

I tried the kitchen tap. The water was still running. But when I went upstairs to try the taps in the bathroom I found that the council had filled the loo with concrete as a deterrent to anyone else hoping to move into the place.

'You can't stay here,' Ganesh said. 'You couldn't even take a leak.'

'I'll go out in the garden, behind a bush. We've got enough bushes out there. It's like a jungle.'

'And where will you sleep? On the floorboards? It's going to be cold in here tonight. It's out of the question!'

'Look!' I said crossly. 'It's for one night and I'll manage. Tomorrow I'll go and see Euan at the council and ask them to clean up the flat for me and fix up another door. Or if they won't do that, they can move me into one of the other highly desirable residences they've got empty in that block.'

Ganesh looked miserable. 'You're crackers, Fran. How can I leave you here?'

I told him that he could quite easily, and if I was

crackers, then that was my problem. I said if he wanted to help he could lend me the sleeping bag from the van.

He went off to get it, muttering and mumbling.

I took a look round. To be quite honest, now it was really dark I was having second thoughts about staying here overnight, all alone. But I was too proud and obstinate to admit that to Ganesh when he'd get back. He'd given me a torch from the van. I flashed it around, telling myself that so long as I *was* alone, I was OK.

Ganesh had been gone some time, longer than just to fetch the sleeping bag. At last he reappeared and called to me to take the stuff he was going to push through the kitchen window. He'd been home and fetched a roll of plastic sheeting and an empty crate.

'For you to sit on.'

He'd also brought a Thermos of hot tea and a bag of peaches.

'Mum says', he panted as he climbed through the window after I'd collected all this stuff, 'why don't you come to our place? Honestly, Fran, they wouldn't mind. She's really worried about you down here.'

'Tell her thanks, but now I've got the sleeping bag and all the rest of it, I'll really be fine.'

'I've got this as well.' He was fumbling with the plastic sheeting. 'It's thin stuff but if we put it down on the floor boards under the sleeping bag, at least it will stop the damp rising. Otherwise you won't be able to get up tomorrow. Your joints will be set solid.'

They'd probably be set solid anyway. I was still suffering from my equestrian adventures.

He spread the plastic on the floor. I spread the sleeping bag on it and put the crate alongside like a bedside table, with the Thermos on the top. It didn't look so bad.

'Quite cosy,' I said.

'You're not just crazy,' he told me. 'You're weird.' He sat on the floor with his arms resting on his knees and frowned at me in the light from the torch. 'I'll come over in the morning before I go down to the station and turn myself in for interrogation by the Hampshire Constabulary. Sure you don't want me to stay here?'

'Sure, Gan. You should go home and sort things out. I'm really tired. I've got all I need and I'll sleep like a log.'

'Not a chance!' he said discouragingly.

'How are things at your place?' I asked.

'Bad, but I can handle that, don't worry about it. Worry about yourself.'

He didn't want to go but he went.

I didn't really want him to go, but the notice to quit must have come as a bombshell to his parents and they needed him there.

I settled down for the night. I drank the tea and ate a couple of peaches and told myself that morning would soon come and although I might be a bit stiff, I'd suffer nothing worse.

I couldn't get off to sleep. I ached. My mind ran on furiously. I began to imagine things. Right above me was what had been Terry's room. Every time I heard a creak, which happened every few minutes, I thought about her body dangling from the light fitting up there. I began to think about ghosts. I wondered if she'd turn up and accuse me of deserting the job, down there at the Astara. I felt I had deserted her. I hadn't established who had killed her, though I'd established a fair motive for Jamie and a lesser one for Lundy. The idea that Jamie and Lundy might've worked together was more and more feasible. Jamie would have been the planner and Lundy his executioner. I would go and see Janice in the morning and argue it through with her again. That had to be the way it had been. She had at least to talk to Jamie.

Not that it would do any good, not unless they did find any prints in the house and the more I thought about that, the more it seemed a long shot. Even the crassest amateur knows to wear gloves these days. As for Janice questioning Jamie, he'd be more than capable of fending off her queries. He'd be plausible. He'd sit there looking handsome and frank and turning on the charm. Janice, going through her divorce, was vulnerable. There'd she be in her crepe blouse and one of her dowdy suits, putty in Jamie's hands.

And why not? He wasn't a dropout who lived in a squat, but a respectable member of society with a clean record sheet and probably some influential friends.

'You're no good as a detective, Fran Varady,' I said to myself. 'You're full of big ideas but, when it comes down to it, you've accomplished zilch. A couple of fuzzy snapshots and an unprovable theory about a will.'

I'd just meddled, that's what I'd done. Made things worse. Meddlers make themselves unpopular. Jamie wouldn't just be satisfied with clearing his name with Janice. He'd want to drop me in it, Gan also, if he could. He'd counter my theory with another for Janice to consider. In his scenario, I'd be the villain.

At this gloomy point in my musings, exhaustion took over. Not even the hard floor could keep me awake. I drifted off into uneasy sleep.

I dreamed about Abbotsfield. I was standing just inside the churchyard, by the tomb on which I'd sat to eat my sandwich. The church was ahead of me and Terry was standing some distance off by her lopsided cross in a long white nightgown. Her long fair hair fluttered around her face.

She called to me and asked what I was doing there. I said I'd come to see her and began to walk towards her. She beckoned encouragingly. But when I got closer I saw that the grave stood open. I wasn't surprised. Obviously she'd climbed out. I saw now that her white gown was smeared with earth. I felt very cold but I knew she was colder.

She was smiling with her lips but not with her eyes, which were like the round glass eyes of the toy animals, quite expressionless and unblinking. She held out her hand for me to take, but I was afraid to take it, because I knew I could never free myself from her grip and she would drag me down with her into the open pit behind her.

I turned and ran blindly, until I found myself, with the strange logic of dreams, in Terry's room. All the plush toy animals which had been on top of her cupboard were there. They came to life and walked round, glaring at me with those accusing glass eyes, like Terry in the churchyard. I told them to leave me alone and they began to squeak at me, as soft toys do when you press their plush stomachs.

At that point I woke up. All the nightmare visions vanished, but not the cold, and not squeaks. I could still hear those.

It was pitch dark. Ganesh's plastic sheet hadn't kept out the damp. No wonder I'd dreamed as I had. I didn't know what time it was. Then I heard that shrill squeak again. Not floorboards or wainscoting, not this time. A different noise. Something outside in the garden? Something inside? A rat?

Oh God! I sat up in a panic, fumbling for the torch. Before I could find it, I heard a louder noise and I realised that what I could hear was someone manoeuvring the loosened board over the kitchen window. Someone was climbing in.

Chapter Eighteen

Even now, when I think of that moment, I get goose bumps. I can't tell you what it was like. That was something you'd have to experience although I hope you never do. Fear held me paralysed. My brain refused to send any messages to my limbs telling them to move. Even to breathe was an effort. My heart must have been beating, but to me it was as if it had stopped. Everything had stopped. The only thing which moved was out there and, very soon, would be coming this way.

There was a dull thud as whoever it was dropped to the floor inside the house. The sound broke the spell which held me frozen. I slid out of the sleeping bag and managed to find the torch, gripping it with clammy fingers and afraid it would slip from my grasp. At least I had the presence of mind not to switch it on yet. Its sudden beam would give me a powerful surprise weapon, throwing the intruder off track. Whoever it was couldn't know I was there. Like me, he was probably looking for a place to doss. The sudden beam of the torch would frighten him. For a moment I would be in charge. I had to stay in charge. With luck, we could come to some arrangement.

Even as I worked all this out, I knew I was grasping at straws. The surprise was on me and the advantage his. For all I knew he could be some psychopath or schizophrenic released into what's laughingly known as 'community care'. I could be shut in here with a madman.

Then I had a thought which was as bad or even more frightening. Perhaps he *did* know I was there. Perhaps he wasn't just some homeless wanderer of the streets or a junkie looking for a place to indulge his habit or a kid bent on sniffing glue. Perhaps he was looking for *me*. I remembered how scared I'd been on the staircase at the flats. Perhaps, whoever he was, he had been there too, waiting in the dark, and only the presence of Ganesh had thrown him off his stride.

I tried to tell myself that, just as back at the flats, it might turn out to be Ganesh again, come back to check on me.

But I knew with an awful sickening certitude, that it was Jamie Monkton – or Lundy – or both.

Of course Jamie wasn't going to leave me free to roam around poking and prying into Theresa's death. I'd left Abbotsfield suddenly and within hours, the police had been down at the dell, digging up Squib's remains. The two things couldn't be unconnected. He must have guessed that if I hadn't found Squib, then Ganesh had. He had seen Ganesh's van parked in the dell. He was going to do something about us both, something final to shut us up and he was beginning with me. He didn't know what else I'd found out. But he did know about this house.

If he'd been to the tower block and seen the smashed-up flat, he'd have worked out I'd come here. That I'd run like a hunted animal back to my den. He'd killed Terry and poor Squib, even Squib's dog, and he'd have not the slightest compunction about killing me. No one would ever know, because he'd be away by morning. Ganesh would find my body and it would be another unsolved crime.

I didn't have time to dwell on that now. Jamie – or his executioner – was moving down the hallway towards the front room where I had been sleeping. I started cautiously towards the door, hoping to get behind it as it opened. The idea was that I'd slip out behind him, make it to the kitchen and get out of the window before he could stop me. All very unlikely, but the only chance I'd got.

But the plastic sheeting Ganesh had put down was slippy under my feet in socks, and as I skidded and tried to keep my footing, the door opened.

At first I couldn't see him. I could hear his breathing, a laboured breath because he'd struggled through the forced window with difficulty. Then my eyes adjusted to the degree of moonlight which had entered with him through the kitchen window. I saw his silhouette. If I'd had any lingering hope that it would be Ganesh, it was dispelled. The silhouetted figure was too tall and bulky. Besides, after the mistake at the flats, he would have called out at once to let me know he was there. Both Jamie and Lundy were a lot bigger than Gan. The menacing figure in the doorway could be either.

I did the only thing I could think of. I switched on the torch and directed the beam straight at him, hoping to dazzle him so that I could run past.

But I didn't run. I just stood there transfixed. Because the face the torchlight picked up, making it shimmer and gleam yellow and unreal, wasn't that of Jamie Monkton or the unlovely Lundy. It was Nick Bryant's.

I asked stupidly, 'Nick? What are you doing here?'

His voice, in reply, sounded odd, as if some switch had been flicked, distorting it in pitch and tone. 'I thought I'd find you here.' No expression in the words, no satisfaction or enmity. Nothing at all. A crazy voice, belonging to someone with whom there could be no reasoning.

The paralysis of fear and horror threatened to return and I thrust it away. I didn't entirely understand all this, but I must not just fold in the face of it. He had moved into the room and I saw he was cradling something in his arms: a double-barrelled shotgun.

'What do you want?' Another silly question. My voice croaked it out, sounding in all probability as distorted as his.

All the time my brain was racing. Nick? *Nick*? It didn't seem possible. Had I got it all wrong? Nice was *nice*. He was a nice person. His mother was a nice person. And he *liked* me. Nick liked me. I knew he did. He wouldn't hurt me, would he?

Yes, he would. I knew it.

I must have moved because he swung up the shotgun and I found myself staring down the twin barrels.

'No!' he ordered. 'Just sit down, right there where you are.'

I sat down on the quilted sleeping bag, wrapped my arms round my knees and waited. He moved towards me and kicked the crate across the room. He sat on it, between me and the door, and rested the shotgun on his knees.

I was still holding the torch and he said, 'Put that down beside you and don't touch it again.'

I put it down. Its beam shone straight ahead along the floor and illuminated his feet. The rest of him was in dusk but the shotgun barrels gleamed.

I said, 'If you fire that, someone will hear.'

'Who? This street is nothing but empty houses. Nothing between here and that corner shop. Anyway, around here if anyone heard a gunshot they would pretend they hadn't. Or even if they rang the police, by the time the coppers got here, I'd be gone.'

There was a horrid logic about his argument. I hadn't an answer to that one. My father used to say that there was an answer to all our problems if we thought about things calmly. But I wasn't in a state to think calmly and I don't think it would have helped if I had been.

I said, 'You fired before at me. You fired in the plantation and made the horse bolt. Were you trying to hit me or just spook the mare?'

'Knew you couldn't ride,' he said. 'Thought you'd break your neck.' He moved slightly as he spoke and twitched as if that switch had been thrown again. When he next spoke, his voice sounded more reasonable. I realised he had hyped himself up to this. In his own way, he was as nervous as I was. He'd tried to kill in the plantation by stealth. This, face to face, was trickier.

'I'm sorry about this, Fran.' The gun barrels sank a little, no longer aimed at my chest but at my shins. He sounded as if he did regret it. But not enough to make him change his mind. 'You're a really nice girl. But you ask too many questions and you're too bright. I've just got to stop you.'

'I can't believe this,' I told him. 'How could you? How could you do what you did to Terry?'

'It was her fault!' The gun barrels quivered and pointed at my chest again. I should have kept my big mouth shut. I hoped his finger wasn't going to slip on the trigger.

'I loved her. I really did!' he said hoarsely.

That made me angry. I stopped being scared and snapped, 'You killed her! What kind of love is that?'

'I didn't mean to do it!' he shouted.

'Oh? You strung her up there from the light fitting by accident? And after trying to rape her, too, to go by the bruises!'

'Shut up!'

He was in a rage and a voice in my head told me I ought to shut up. The madder he got, the sooner he'd do something drastic. Another voice told me that he was going to do that, anyway. However, the longer I kept him talking and the calmer I kept us both, the longer I had to think of something, although I couldn't for the life of me imagine what. I made a superhuman effort. He was nervous, scared, dreading the moment when he was going to have to shoot me. He, too, might long to put it off for a minute or two. Just until he could get his nerves under control. Nervous people talk.

'Tell me about it,' I invited in a nice pleasant voice.

'You wouldn't understand.' He sounded sullen.

'Try me.'

He hesitated. 'She was so beautiful. You didn't see her when she was pretty. When she lived here, she'd changed. When I saw her here I could've cried, honestly. She looked so thin and dirty and as if no one cared. But I cared, even though she'd changed so much. If you'd known her a few years back, there was no one like her, she was perfect.'

Terry the pretty doll. Alastair, Ariadne and Nick had all wanted to preserve her like that, in Cellophane. No wonder she'd run away. I thought of Kelly in the stable-yard. She'd never stood a chance of capturing Nick's attention. Nick had eyes only for the pretty little girl with the fair hair like spaniel's ears. Galumphing Kelly with the ham-like thighs would've made a first-rate farmer's wife for Nick, capable and devoted. But we don't want what we can have – and we certainly never like what's good for us.

Nick had momentarily wandered away down memory lane. 'I'd watched her grow up. Every time she came home from school on holiday she was prettier. She'd chat to me too those days. She wasn't afraid. Things changed one evening. It was at a Young Farmers' Club Christmas dance. Her hair was pinned up on top of her head and she had a really nice dress. She looked – I can't describe it. Just beautiful, that's all.'

He spoke the words with an almost pathetic naïveté and I remembered the photograph I'd seen on Ariadne's mantelshelf, showing Terry in a ball gown, looking like a million dollars. I told him I'd seen the photo of her in her finery and I could imagine how she'd looked at the Young Farmers' bash. That pleased him and he smiled. But I spoiled it straight off, because I couldn't dismiss an incongruous image of all those red-faced, healthy country types, lumbering around the dance floor with the cream of the county crumpet in their arms.

'You're *laughing*!' Nick exclaimed and the shotgun barrels leapt again in a way I really didn't like.

'No, I'm not! Why on earth should I be laughing now, for goodness sake? In my situation?'

'OK,' he said grudgingly but he relaxed, I was pleased to see, and even turned the gun barrels away from my chest. 'I told her that night that I loved her. It was true. But the more I tried to tell her how I felt, the less I seemed able to make her understand. Sometimes she acted as if she was scared of me. But I only wanted to love her. She should have understood that.'

He looked up suddenly and I could see the craziness on his face. I had to keep him talking. It was the only thing I could do. Keep him talking until I thought of something.

'But I don't understand,' I said. 'What about Squib? And what about Jamie Monkton?'

Nick chuckled. It was a cold, mirthless sound and made my blood freeze. 'Jamie Monkton? He led me to her. I knew he was looking for her and all I had to do was watch him. He'd find her for me.' He leaned forward again, earnestness on his face and in his voice. 'I thought, I'll learn about it from Kelly. She's always dropping by the farm and chattering away. So I waited and one morning, bingo! I didn't need Kelly. I'd taken the old truck down to the garage in Abbotsfield. It was in the repair shop and I was in there talking to the mechanic about it, when I saw Jamie's car outside by the petrol pumps. He was standing by it, talking to the proprietor, Jepson. They were always pals, those two. Both driving around in flash cars. I could hear every word. He said he knew now where his cousin was living. He'd had a bit of luck. He'd been asking around in pubs and he met some rock guitarist or other—'

'Declan!' I muttered fiercely. By the worst mischance, Jamie, scouring the pubs, had come across Declan and

Declan, whom Terry had rather fancied, had betrayed her. Even Squib hadn't done that. I just hoped, if I survived this night, I'd run into Declan again. I had things I wanted very much to say to him.

'Jamie talked about the place and how the whole street, Jubilee Street, was due for demolition and most of it empty and boarded up. He'd been there but no one had been at home. He said he was going back the next day and was filling up the car with juice ready for the trip. He asked Jepson not to say anything to Alastair, if he came by. He wanted to get it all sorted out first.

'It was my chance. Ma was away from the farm, over at the shop in Winchester. I told Biles I was taking the next day off and gave him a tenner to stop him telling Ma. I went up to London, to Jubilee Street, broke into an empty house opposite and waited. I saw you all go out. The one with the dog first and then you and some other fellow. I hoped Theresa was on her own there. I saw Jamie arrive and go to the door. He knocked for some time and I was afraid he was out of luck again. Then an upstairs window was pushed up and Theresa put out her head. I'd found her.'

'Did she let Jamie in?' I wondered, if I was very quick, I could grab the shotgun. But he was too far away.

He nodded. 'Eventually she did, but he didn't stay long. He came out and she slammed the door on him. He went off down the road towards an old graveyard of some sort. He looked pretty wild. He'd asked her to go home, I guessed, and she'd refused. I waited a few minutes until he'd gone, then went across and knocked at the door. I thought she'd look out, as she'd done before. But she must have thought it was Jamie come back, because she opened the front door straight away, ready to yell at him again. And then she saw who it was, that it was me.'

The horror of that moment must have been complete. Terry had opened the door to the one person she feared more than any. The one she'd run away from and hidden from so successfully.

I'd remembered something and frowned. 'I found a piece of blue chalk in Jamie's car.'

Nick nodded. 'I put it there. But I didn't pick it up that day in London, I got it – later.'

'When you killed poor Squib,' I accused him. 'If you'd given him twenty quid, he'd have gone away happy. He was a simple soul.'

Nick began to look angry. 'I didn't know that, did I? He came to the farm. He said he was looking for the Astara Stud. I didn't know whether he'd really made a mistake, was looking for Jamie, or whether he was looking for me. I couldn't take the risk he'd mess things up. I was on my own at the farm when he came. I offered him a cup of tea. It was easy . . .'

How could he just say it like that? He might have been talking about someone else who had done this dreadful thing. He appeared to feel no guilt or responsibility.

'I got rid of the chalks,' he said, 'and all his gear. But I kept a small piece of blue chalk, hoping I'd get a chance to plant it on Jamie Monkton somehow. You see, I wanted the police to know he'd been to the house, just in case he continued to keep quiet about it. I wanted them to think that it was Jamie's finding her that had made her kill herself. It was already clear to me that old Alastair Monkton and Mrs Cameron knew nothing of Jamie's visit to Jubilee Street. It was as he'd told Jepson, he meant to drive up to the Astara one day in triumph with Theresa in his car, that was his idea. Then, when she was found dead, he panicked and decided to tell no one he'd been there. Jepson would've kept quiet. Like I said, he and Jamie Monkton were always as thick as thieves. But I wasn't lettting him get away with that!

'I went up to the Astara on the pretext of seeing Alastair. Only Lundy was in the yard. But Jamie's car was by the garage. I pushed the chalk under the front passenger seat. You found it, did you?' He scowled. 'You messed up all my plans, Fran. You shouldn't have done that.' He lifted the gun and the twin barrels swung to point their ugly mouths at my chest.

I knew I had to put on the best acting performance of my life. *For* my life. I had to act someone who was calm and in control when my every instinct was to start screaming. I started thinking, with a crazy vanity, what a mess that shotgun was going to make of me. He must have quite an armoury at home. In the plantation he'd shot at me with a rifle.

'Now, Nick,' I said, 'you really can't do this. You can't go round killing people. It's got to stop.'

'I'm only going to kill *you*,' he argued, 'and you'll be the last.' He added, rather to my surprise, 'I'm not going to shoot you. I'm going to make it look like an accident. Just like I tried to do before with Theresa, but this time I'll get it right. You're going to lie down again on that quilt. Only take that plastic wrap out from underneath it and drape it over the top. They'll think you did that for some reason and it got over your face and suffocated you.'

Oh, nice. This was the same person at whose kitchen table I'd sat, drinking coffee and talking to him and his mother. Telling them everything. I was angry with myself for being such a fool. I was angry with myself for telling Ganesh I'd be all right here, when obviously I wasn't and, if I'd thought it through properly, I'd have realised that.

But you never know what's going to happen, that's for sure. And right now I'd seen something he hadn't.

He was sitting with his back to the door. It had swung closed behind him but not clicked shut and now it was slowly and silently opening again.

Chapter Nineteen

I didn't know who it was out there in the hall. But unless they were lining up in turn to have a crack at killing me, it ought to mean help. The trouble was, I didn't know if whoever was out there, knew Nick had a gun.

Nick must have sensed something, either from my manner, or because a draught from the opened door brushed his neck. He swung round.

At the same moment the door opened wide and Ganesh stepped in.

I jumped up and yelled, 'He's got a gun!'

At the same time, I threw myself across the room at Nick and crashed into him, knocking him to one side.

There was a deafening explosion. Large chunks of ceiling fell down round our ears. Then Ganesh and Nick were wrestling for the gun which swerved terrifyingly back and forth between them as they lurched to and fro.

I was as sure as I'd ever been of anything that someone was going to get killed and it was more than likely to be me, because the ugly twin mouths of the barrels kept swinging round to point at me as I dodged around the room and the two men.

It's not my way to do nothing and, as usual, I acted on instinct. Lacking any weapon except the torch which was a small thing and useless, I grabbed the crate, swung it up and cracked it on the back of Nick's head. It might not have been the most sensible thing to do in the circumstances as I realised after I'd done it. He staggered forward and the gun went off again.

This time a whole section of the wall fell out. Plaster dust filled the air, getting into my eyes, nose and mouth. In the semi-darkness and dust, Ganesh yelled, 'What do you think you're doing, Fran?'

It was the most wonderful sound I'd ever heard because I thought he'd just had his head blown off.

Nick had regained his balance in the distraction and was trying to swing up the gunstock to use it as a club. Ganesh grabbed his arm and slammed him back against the wall, dislodging another lump of plaster.

I grasped the torch in both hands and held it out level, trained on them, because I couldn't see what was going on.

To my surprise, somehow Ganesh had got hold of the shotgun and had it pressed lengthways across Nick's throat. Nick's eyes bulged and he was uttering a strangled gargle.

Ganesh said very nastily, 'Right, my son! That's both barrels fired. Now it's just you and me!'

I have to say that – with all due respect to Ganesh – Nick was an awful lot bigger and even if he was pinned against the wall at the moment, I wouldn't have bet he couldn't get free. But just then, a massive great chunk of ornamental cornice fell out of the corner of the ceiling above them. It landed right on top of Nick's head and he went down like a skittle.

There was a silence. More plaster dust had filled the air and my nostrils, and I coughed. Gan stepped back, holding the shotgun.

'You all right?'

'Yes!' I croaked. 'Why did you come back?'

'I couldn't sleep, worried about you.' He pushed the still form of Nick with his foot. 'I started to climb through the window and I heard his voice. So I kept it as quiet as I could.'

'He was going to kill me. He killed Terry and Squib. He's nuts.'

'I gathered that.'

I said in a very small voice, 'Thank you, Ganesh.'

'Don't mention it. I'll sit here with him and you go up to my place and call the police.' He sat down on the crate. 'And don't mention the shotgun to my family because they'll go crazy.'

As it turned out, Ganesh was wasting his breath with his request. By the time I reached the shop, the entire Patel clan was going crazy. They'd heard the shots, of course. Mr Patel was standing in the doorway with a wicked-looking cleaver. Mrs Patel was already phoning the police and all the aunts and uncles were milling about. It was obvious the action wasn't over by any means.

They came very quickly, the boys in blue. In the quiet of the night, the shots had been heard, not just up at the shop, but in the surrounding streets from which the inhabitants hadn't yet been cleared. Everyone was phoning the police. Nick had certainly been wrong about that.

The police surrounded the area in double-quick time

and brought up an armed response unit, all kitted out in body armour.

I tried to tell them what had happened, that they didn't need all that weaponry, it was all over, but I couldn't get anyone to listen to me. The one in charge just kept bawling through a loud-hailer.

'Now, everyone keep back! You, too, love! There's an armed man holed up in that building down there!'

'No, there isn't!' I argued, and Ganesh's parents and all the aunts and uncles argued, too. 'The gun's been fired. It's a double-barrelled shotgun, both barrels are empty, and anyway, the gunman is unconscious.'

'No, he isn't. He's moving around in there and he's probably got another weapon or ammunition.'

'No, he hasn't! You don't understand. That's not the gunman, it's only Ganesh . . . '

I tried to get it across to them but they just wouldn't listen. I asked, I begged, them to fetch Inspector Morgan, to wake her up if she was at home asleep, and tell her it was me, Fran Varady, and Ganesh Patel.

Useless. They pushed us all back behind a barrier, me, the Patels, and all the people who'd come running from houses in the street behind to see what was going on. You never saw such a motley crowd in all your life, every kind of clothing from nightwear to daywear, Doc Martens, fluffy slippers, saris, the lot. One old lady in a dressing gown but with a felt hat stuck on her head, kept asking, 'Is it a bomb?'

'Tell them to go away,' whispered a voice by my ear and a familiar smell made itself known. Edna had been tempted out from her graveyard by curiosity and stood beside me. She was nursing the kittens which, safe in their tomb hideaway, must have escaped the charity cat-nappers.

'I don't like them,' she persisted. 'Tell them to go away.'

I explained, with feeling, that no one listened to me. I suggested she take both herself and the kits back to the graveyard, out of harm's way. She wasn't listening to me, either.

'What are they doing?' she began to sound frightened. The kittens mewled in her embrace, squirming as she clasped them tighter.

Frankly, I hadn't time to worry about her. The police had fixed up temporary lights, and marksmen were swarming down the side alley of the squat, and taking up positions in the garden behind, training their weapons on the kitchen window. Nick *was* being over-optimistic when he'd said no one would do anything if they heard the shots and he'd get away. It was like Custer's Last Stand down there.

The man with the loud-hailer was roaring, 'Come out with your hands up!'

Mr Patel and the uncles were shouting at them. Mrs Patel and the aunts were wailing. Usha was threatening to call a solicitor. (I suppose she and Jay knew one. I certainly didn't.) I was jumping up and down, yelling they should get hold of Inspector Janice. To put the finishing touch, Edna began to scream in a thin, high sound like some kind of radio signal. It went on and on, as if she didn't need to draw breath.

None of our efforts was achieving anything. I had to do something. At this rate, they would almost certainly shoot Ganesh in error. I couldn't get down the street now because they'd blocked it off. But I knew this area better than they did. I headed for Edna's graveyard.

Beside it stood the first house of the terrace. I scrambled

over the wall and dropped down into the garden. I landed on a stack of abandoned dustbins. There was a hideous clamour, but nobody heard it, or paid it any attention, in the general uproar.

I started across the adjacent gardens, one at a time, hauling myself over walls, getting my feet caught in old fruit netting and beanpole frames. It was like tackling one of those obstacle courses the Army sets up. I ricked my ankle and scraped my hands and just kept going, because I was getting nearer and nearer the back garden of the squat and the scene of the action.

I fell over the last wall and landed amongst the bushes just at the moment Ganesh threw the gun out of the kitchen window. Then he climbed out. All the coppers jumped him.

They had him pinned to the ground and I was convinced he'd suffocate under all that lot. They kept shouting things like, 'All right, sunshine, don't offer any resistance!' while I was still yelling that the man they wanted was inside the house under a lump of ceiling, unconscious. Although, for all I knew, he was coming round by now and would make his escape while all the attention was fixed on poor old Ganesh.

I tried to pull them off him, howling, 'You've got the wrong man, you idiots!' till I was hoarse. So they arrested me too and marched us both off to the station.

It was bedlam down there. They took our fingerprints. This gave me a definite feeling of *déjà vu*. I told them, they needn't bother to take mine, they already had mine, in connection with the murder enquiry at that house.

That really put the cat among the pigeons. They got so

excited I thought they'd have a collective fit. I think they thought they'd got a gang of urban terrorists.

Eventually, Inspector Janice turned up in jeans and a baggy sweater, with matching bags under her eyes, and rescued us.

I was really pleased to see her.

I jumped up, shouting, 'Did they find him? Did they find Nick Bryant? They didn't let him get away, did they?'

'No, Fran, they didn't let him get away,' she said soothingly. 'They searched the place and he was just coming round. He didn't give any trouble.'

I collapsed back on my chair. 'Thank God for that! So it's all over.'

'Now, I wouldn't want you to run away with that idea,' she said coolly. 'You've got an awful lot of explaining to do – to *me*!'

Chapter Twenty

'He's been telling us everything,' Janice said.

It was two days since 'The Siege of Jubilee Street' as the newspapers were calling it. Janice had calmed down considerably and even Parry had smiled at me as I'd arrived today and said, 'Hullo, it's Annie Oakley!' I was still so relieved, just to be alive, that I let him get away with that.

Ganesh and I were sitting in Morgan's office. We'd been offered tea straight away this time and some rather boring biscuits.

They were all being particularly nice to Ganesh because of the mistake they'd made. They had been dropping hints about a bravery award and all the swelling and bruises were clearing up.

Another bonus was that he could do no wrong in his family's eyes now. He was a hero. For the time being, anyway.

'I still can't believe it,' I told the inspector. 'I was so convinced Jamie or Lundy killed her and either of them could have come after me. I shone the torch at the intruder, fully expecting, in fact, prepared, to see either of them. I had hazy plans how I'd deal with the situation.

When I saw Nick, I just froze like an idiot. I couldn't believe my eyes. I thought I must still be dreaming. Most ridiculous of all, I still believed he liked me, as if that meant he wouldn't harm me! Huh! He loved Terry and he murdered her! What kind of a nutter is he anyway? He seemed so normal, too, down there on his farm. Sort of reassuring.'

'I told you you didn't know anything about the country,' said Ganesh, radiating smugness and glee. If we hadn't been in Janice's office, I'd have thrown something at him. He had been saying 'I told you so' in a dozen or more different ways, ever since the police had picked up Nick and released us.

All I could do for the moment was challenge him with, 'You met Nick yourself. If he struck you as a killer, you kept very quiet about it! You thought the same as me. He was fine.'

'I didn't think anything. I didn't make any judgement. You did. You decided he was Mr Nice Guy. And he wasn't.'

The tone of proceedings was becoming acrimonious and Janice hastened to break it up.

'Bryant isn't Mr Nice Guy but he isn't a regular villain, either. It's rather sad. He keeps insisting he loved Theresa. But it wasn't really love so much as obsession. He was truly obsessed with her.'

'You mean,' I said, 'he's a headcase.'

'Strong emotions', said Janice, sounding like an Agony Aunt, 'make people behave in unlooked-for ways.' She looked knowing and a bit glazed about the eyes at the same time. I supposed she knew what she was talking about, being a policewoman. But I also suspected she read those paperback romances in her spare time. 'He insists', she went on, 'that he didn't intend to kill her. But they argued and he had a sort of black-out. He doesn't remember what he did, but when he came out of it, she was lying on the floor. He thought she was dead. He decided, in a panic, to make it look like suicide. He rigged up the – well, you know what. His head was in a whirl, in a crazy state.'

'The man's a maniac,' I said firmly. 'He just went around killing people who got in his way. He killed poor Squib. I suppose no one thinks Squib matters, but I do. I suppose you didn't see any sign of Squib's dog?' I added without much hope.

Janice denied indignantly that they were not treating Squib's death as equally important and added that they'd found a dead dog in bushes near the body. She said she was sorry. She looked sorry as she said it and I suspected that she was more upset by the death of the dog than by Squib's death.

But she insisted again that I mustn't think they were giving Squib's murder anything less than full attention. 'It was a cold-blooded business,' she said. 'Bryant had no excuse of passion that time and he'd have killed you in the same calculated way.'

'Thank you,' I told her. 'I know.'

'Once he killed the girl,' Ganesh said unexpectedly, 'he was on the slippery slope. Couldn't stop. Had to keep on killing.'

'It all might have been avoided,' Janice mused, 'if only Theresa could have confided in someone, asked for some help in dealing with the problem of Bryant's obsession. Something might have been done about it to stop it right there, at the beginning. But I suppose she felt her grandfather and great-aunt were too elderly and frail to be bothered with it. And she didn't like or trust her cousin, Jamie Monkton. So she kept it to herself. She was already unhappy at home for other reasons, mostly connected with that will, as you rightly surmised, Francesca. Ariadne Cameron had named Theresa as sole beneficiary and expected her to behave as someone who was going to inherit a fortune and a thriving business. Alastair Monkton had the sentimental view that old gentlemen have of their grandchildren. He didn't want to hear about anything nasty. Jamie Monkton was stalking round the place, glowering because he'd been cut out of the will, despite the fact that he was doing all the work and had virtually saved the stud from bankruptcy. She hardly needed Bryant, half crazy with jealousy, lurking about the lanes waiting for her. She'd run away before and she did it again. Lord knows, who could blame her?' Janice concluded in heartfelt tones.

Neither of us could quarrel with that. I wasn't surprised she'd left. It only surprised me she'd gone back a couple of times before making the final break.

There was a long silence. Ganesh stared out of the window. I sat looking at the floor. Janice Morgan looked at me.

'We do realise, Francesca,' she said, 'that we would never have got to Bryant if it hadn't been for you. But you took a terrible risk, and you nearly came to grief.'

She was looking quite human and I decided she wasn't such a bad sort. But she had that pussy-cat bow blouse on again. When she'd turned up in the early hours to rescue Gan and me, she'd worn jeans and looked normal. Now she looked like an early version of the Iron Lady again.

I felt I ought to put her right on one thing. 'OK,' I said. 'But, as you said, you wouldn't have got him if I hadn't gone down there and found him . . . and got him worried enough to follow me to London. So the risk was worth it, I reckon.'

'I don't!' said Ganesh. 'I think it was daft. I always thought it was daft, from the beginning. I kept telling you so.'

'Listen to Mr Patel another time, will you?' Janice asked me.

Ganesh beamed at her.

But I'd got used to making my own decisions and I think she knew that.

Ganesh and I went back to the Astara to see Alastair and Ariadne.

It was strange returning there. The whole place looked so familiar this time, unlike when I'd first arrived there, out of the blue. I realise now I must have seemed to them rather like one of those evacuee kids from the East End who were pitched out into the villages during the Second World War. They'd welcomed me in much as they'd have done to the wartime children.

But familiarity didn't completely wipe away the awkwardness. I spotted Kelly in the yard. She gave me a despairing look and disappeared into the stables. Her world had ended with Nick's arrest. She probably still loved him and was indulging in some dream of his coming out of jail ready to recognise her devotion and let her help him rebuild his life. She was wasting her time.

Jamie wasn't there. He'd gone to Germany, it seemed, to see some horses bred at the stud, compete in some competition or other. I couldn't help wondering whether he, now, would be Ariadne's heir. It seemed to me she hadn't much choice. But it wasn't one of the things we discussed.

They told us that Penny Bryant was selling the farm. I felt sorry for Penny. I wished I could go and see her but obviously it was better I didn't. Both Alastair and Ariadne expressed concern at the danger I'd been in. Alastair said he felt responsible, since he'd come to see me in London and set me on the murderer's trail, as he put it.

I assured him he wasn't responsible, which was what he wanted to hear. He made an excuse to get me alone and handed over an envelope.

'As agreed,' he said.

I didn't want to take it, but beggars can't be choosers. I needed the money and I considered that I'd earned it.

Before we drove home we did make one more visit, Ganesh and I. We went down to the churchyard where Terry was buried. I felt I had to go. I wanted to tell her it was all right now. But perhaps she knew.

It was very pretty down there, the trees and nicely cut grass. A brand new white headstone had replaced the lopsided wooden cross and fresh flowers had been put in a marble vase. It felt calm and I thought she was at peace and probably glad it had all been sorted out. I didn't feel I owed her anything any more. In a way, I felt I knew her better now and liked her better . . . and if she still cared anything about me wherever she was now, she felt the same way about me. We were friends now, at last.

Ganesh has this idea about reincarnation and says Terry is somewhere else in the world in another body, probably a baby which has just been born somewhere. But I'm not keen on that idea. I like to know who I am.

I'm me, Fran Varady.

Oh, and I ran into Declan and did he hear from *me*!

Alastair says he thinks he knows of a flat I can rent. It's a basement flat in a house belonging to a retired lady librarian he knows in NW1. That sounds very upmarket to me. I'd like to talk to someone about books. As soon as I get any money to spare, I'm going to replace all Nev's which he gave me and got torn up by those wretched kids.

Ganesh is indulging in a monumental sulk because I'm talking of moving away.

'You won't like it, up north,' he said, as if I was headed for Hadrian's Wall, not NW1. 'They won't be friendly, like we are, round here.'

'Who is?' I retorted. 'Edna in the churchyard? Or the kids who did over my flat?'

'You know what I mean,' he said. 'At least everyone round here is skint. It sort of binds people together, having nothing.'

'Rubbish!' I told him firmly. 'It just makes them all better at nicking what anyone else does have.'

'You'll see,' he said smugly. And just to finish it off he added, 'And you won't be able to walk down to the river and look across at the Crystal City, as we do now.'

I told him, I wasn't leaving him behind, only getting a better address than the derelict flat Euan had found for me to replace the other one. Euan-speak described it as 'short-term accommodation' but it was just like the last. In the adjacent tower block, in fact. I'd had it with Euan's bright ideas. The pipes in the new place had started rattling all night long and I knew – I just *knew* – there were mice. They'd eaten a hole in my packet of corn-flakes.

'So, it has to be better. Either of us would only have to get on a bus if we wanted to visit.'

'Better?' he snarled at me. 'What's better about it? I've been up there, you know, and seen them all poncing around. Have you seen the prices they charge for greens and fruit up there? Four times what Dad and I charge here.'

I pointed out that their shop was under the axe and why didn't they all think of moving too, to a classier area where people would have more money. 'You'd double your takings and your dad could do his speciality foods, the way he's always talked of doing.'

Ganesh said sourly, 'You may be getting somewhere at a cheap rent. We wouldn't.'

I gave up arguing with him about it because when he gets in a mood like that, the only thing to do is leave him until he comes round. He does eventually but he likes to take his time.

All in all, there's going to have to be something pretty horrendously wrong with lady librarian's flat to stop me taking it. Besides, I've got this idea. I didn't do so badly as a detective and I might start up in business. Nothing big, just small personal inquiries, because I haven't the organisation. I've only got Ganesh and his van (when he gets over his mood).

When he does – get over it – I'll tell him about my idea.

A selection of bestsellers from Headline

ASKING FOR TROUBLE	Ann Granger	£5.99	☐
FAITHFUL UNTO DEATH	Caroline Graham	£5.99	☐
THE WICKED WINTER	Kate Sedley	£5.99	☐
HOTEL PARADISE	Martha Grimes	£5.99	☐
MURDER IN THE MOTORSTABLE	Amy Myers	£5.99	☐
WEIGHED IN THE BALANCE	Anne Perry	£5.99	☐
THE DEVIL'S HUNT	P C Doherty	£5.99	☐
EVERY DEADLY SIN	D M Greenwood	£4.99	☐
SKINNER'S ORDEAL	Quintin Jardine	£5.99	☐
HONKY TONK KAT	Karen Kijewski	£5.99	☐
THE QUICK AND THE DEAD	Alison Joseph	£5.99	☐
THE RELIC MURDERS	Michael Clynes	£5.99	☐

All Headline books are available at your local bookshop or newsagent, or can be ordered direct from the publisher. Just tick the titles you want and fill in the form below. Prices and availability subject to change without notice.

Headline Book Publishing, Cash Sales Department, Bookpoint, 39 Milton Park, Abingdon, OXON, OX14 4TD, UK. If you have a credit card you may order by telephone – 01235 400400.

Please enclose a cheque or postal order made payable to Bookpoint Ltd to the value of the cover price and allow the following for postage and packing:

UK & BFPO: £1.00 for the first book, 50p for the second book and 30p for each additional book ordered up to a maximum charge of £3.00.
OVERSEAS & EIRE: £2.00 for the first book, £1.00 for the second book and 50p for each additional book.

Name ....

Address ....

....

....

If you would prefer to pay by credit card, please complete:
Please debit my Visa/Access/Diner's Card/American Express (delete as applicable) card no:

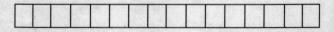

Signature .... Expiry Date ....